DESIRÉE M. NICCOLI

HAVEN COVE, BOOK 2

SONG OF LORELEI

SONG OF LORELEI

DESIRÉE M. NICCOLI

CITY OWL
PRESS

SONG OF LORELEI
Haven Cove, Book 2

CITY OWL PRESS
www.cityowlpress.com

Cover Design by MiblArt. All stock photos licensed appropriately.

Edited by Tee Tate.

For information on subsidiary rights, please contact the publisher at info@cityowlpress.com.

Print Edition ISBN: 978-1-64898-281-1

Digital Edition ISBN: 978-1-64898-282-8

Printed in the United States of America

PRAISE FOR THE WORKS OF DESIRÉE M. NICCOLI

"There's something really special about an author who can make you believe in a romance that seems impossible. Desirée M. Niccoli is one of those authors. Not only did I buy her love story about a handsome sea captain and a flesh-eating mermaid, I bought it hook, line and sinker. *Song of Lorelei* made me want to believe in the impossible. I relished each moment and can't wait to read more by this author." — *Rosanna Leo, author of Darke Passion*

"Niccoli creates a perfect blend of gothic atmosphere and tender romance. From the indulgent small town autumn vibes to the creeping coastal mystery, this book doesn't hold back on the romance while keeping you on your toes with its man-eating mermaid." — *Kate Prior, author of Love, Laugh, Lich*

"Niccoli might be a siren herself with the way she lures readers into a beautiful tale full of passion and terror." — *Charish Reid, author of I'll Come Back for You*

"*Song of Lorelei* dives deep into the soul of both Lorelei and the fearsome mermaid community she comes from, to reveal a deeply human story of love and the monster within." — *Agatha Andrews, She Wore Black Podcast*

"Creepy, sexy, and oh so full of atmosphere — I sunk my teeth in and couldn't put it down." — *Nisha J. Tuli, author of Wicked is the Reaper*

"In this not to be missed sequel, Niccoli serves up adventure, steamy romance, and a suspenseful plot with a side of clever, wry humor. *Song of Lorelei* is an irresistible mermaid tale with heart and humanity." — *Paulette Kennedy, author of Parting the Veil and The Witch of Tin Mountain*

*To embracing yourself
and wielding your voice.*

AUTHOR'S NOTE

You should always feel confident and safe when reading a book. As such, I've included a list of content information available on my website at: dmniccoli.com/books/song-of-lorelei/

If you have any concerns about the contents of this book, please be sure to check that page first. Thank you and enjoy!

CHAPTER
ONE

KILLIAN

SCIENCE QUANTIFIED THE MYSTICAL, BOILED IT DOWN TO logic, data, and biological processes. But there was a kind of magic to new discoveries, and the discovery that murderous sirens lurked in ocean's deep captivated the world and brought the New England fishing industry where they'd been found to its knees.

Myth had become universal truth, and modern fishermen wanted no part of it.

The sirens should have scared away *Dawn Chaser*'s crew, but stubbornness outweighed fear, and they did not flee the Gulf of Maine like most of their offshore competition.

Idle chatter and laughter rang out across the decks as the crew prepared the nets, and Captain Killian Quinn listened to them from the pilothouse, their muffled voices drifting to where he stood at the helm. He couldn't make out the words, but their cheer was unmistakable, and the corners of his mouth lifted.

This could have been just another day at sea.

Strong morale was good for crew retention, and these days, that's what kept him in business. But more than that, his crew was like a family to him, more so than his own flesh and blood, and he liked hearing them in high spirits.

A sharp ping from the boat's navigation system jolted Killian from his thoughts. Glancing down at the charts, the sectioned off area he programmed into the computer flashed up at him, and the small smile he wore died.

He slammed the throttle forward.

Dawn Chaser's engines rumbled loudly as it crossed into siren territory. The louder the better to repel any uninvited visitors.

Killian waved over the helmsman. "Take over for me and maintain speed." Crossing the pilothouse to look out the back window, he lifted his personal radio to his mouth. "Noise cancellation headsets on now."

A hush fell over the crew, prey animals alerted to lurking danger.

Every man reached for the black headsets hooked to their utility belts, and fitted them over their ears, their movements almost in complete unison with one another. Given the threat they faced, deadly siren song, it was an ironic display of puppetry, and Killian the puppeteer. But instead of supernatural manipulation, they were compelled by trust.

He hoped that trust was not misplaced.

The crew yanked off the tarps covering crates of canned meat, their tribute to the seafolk. They shuffled about the task in silence, casting wary glances over the side for movement in the waves below—the telltale flash of bright, colorful scales just beneath the dark surface.

How oblivious he and his crew had once been to the vicious sirens of the deep—as dangerous as they were beautiful with their wicked claws, razor-sharp teeth, and dark hunger for human flesh. Though the sailors of old must have gotten drunk on grog during their long, cold months at sea, the superstitious tales they told about seafolk were true.

Killian clenched his jaw. He wasn't one for grog, but he could use a shot of whiskey right about now.

It had almost been a year since news broke across the world about the sirens' existence. Many fishermen and sailors reconsidered their professions, but not even a school of bloodthirsty merfolk stopped Killian's crew from coming to the pier before sunrise each day. A seafaring life was all they'd ever known. They didn't want or know how to do anything else. For them, that was reason enough to stay on.

Not that there were a lot of job alternatives in rural, coastal Maine. The logging industry wasn't what it used to be, and while increased tourism was a boon for commercial real estate development, construction jobs were hard to come by with the influx of ex-fishermen looking for new careers. But with their competition thinning out, the pay Killian could now offer was quite compelling.

While money couldn't buy bravery, it certainly helped.

The noise cancellation headsets Killian gave to his crew had a built-in radio communication system that allowed them to talk with one another without succumbing to the sirens' seductive crooning. They were designed by an acoustics physicist hired by Dr. Lila Branson, the marine biologist credited with discovering the siren species, and Killian's good friend. She had one in captivity and brought in a physicist to study the frequency of her call. With three loved ones in the fishing industry—a husband, a father, and a close friend—Lila had spared no expense pushing the project along.

After donning his own headset, more for show than safety, Killian jogged down the pilot house steps and joined his crew. He didn't need to wear it, but he couldn't explain to them how he was immune to most siren song.

He wore the ear-coverings slightly off-kilter, allowing in outside sound. He would adjust them soon, but he needed to hear those roaring engines just a bit longer for his own peace of mind. If they ran strong, the hearing-sensitive sirens would not come anywhere near his boat.

One by one, his crew members nodded to him as he passed. Even as the sun pierced through the clouds overhead, hot and bright, their sun-tanned faces paled. They squinted at him through the light, waiting. This part of their offshore runs never got any easier. The anticipation. The fear that *this time* something might go wrong. But they always toughed it out for the bountiful promise of a good haul. When they fished just beyond siren territory, skirting its edges, they never went home empty-handed.

Killian took stock of his crew.

Despite the summer's heat, they shivered in their boots. No, not shivered. *Quaked.* Only Walter "Walt" Walsh, a former fishing captain, and Will Branson, Killian's lead deckhand and best friend, stood steady. Walt held a wide stance, dark brown thumbs casually hooked through his front belt loops, and Will crossed his arms, heavily freckled, "tan" for his ruddy white skin, both men a picture of cool and collected, but their lips were pinched tight. They understood better than anyone else on the crew exactly what they faced out here on the open water.

Killian unclipped a knife from his pocket and unfolded the blade. He crouched before the crates of canned pork and slashed open the tethers holding them in place, hoping the quick motion hid his trembling hands. With a barked command from Branson, the crew sprung to life, hefting crates away from the stack. Killian's own fear wasn't forgotten but working with his hands helped. Idleness only allowed fear to dig its ugly claws in deeper.

All around him his crew wedged crowbars beneath the lids, the wood creaking as it splintered and was pried apart. Waves splashed against the hull, and the boat's engine continued to roar. There was also a weird ringing in his ears, but likely had to do with the headset sitting half on, half off.

And yet, despite all the noise, his crew's silence was the loudest of all.

He adjusted his headset, fitting it snugly over his ears. The engines, the waves, the ringing, everything disappeared, save for the low staticky hum of an open radio channel. The crew tore off the rest of the lids and prepped the crates for dumping overboard.

While everyone threw themselves into work, the youngest crew member, Ian, stared blankly ahead at the water, frozen to the spot. The sandy-haired kid didn't even blink when another crew member bumped into him. Or squint at the sun, for that matter, even though he'd taken off his sunglasses, the skin directly around his eyes shone a lily white where the rest of his face was deeply tanned.

The glare off the water should've been blinding. Kid was probably damaging his eyes staring like that.

Killian clasped the young man's shoulder and found it damp to the touch. "You okay?" His voice crackled across the comms.

Ian blinked twice and looked up at him. The hairs at the back of the young man's neck rose above prickled gooseflesh, and although his eyes were glassy and unfocused, he nodded. The movement was slight, barely a dip of the chin.

Killian squeezed his shoulder. "It'll be all right." The kid didn't usually get this worked up, but some days the fear of what lurked below just gripped tighter. "Why don't you give Walt a hand with that crate? Helps to stay busy."

"Okay," Ian mumbled.

Killian left him to grab a broom. With his crew handling all the heavy lifting, the least he could do was sweep up wood shards and tether cuttings. Just because he was captain didn't mean he was above the work.

As he went to open the deck box, a round, black object, with its center cut out like a donut, caught his eye against the steel deck. He crouched down and picked it up, squishing it between his fingers. Wrinkled foam. Like the cushioning in their headsets, which not only provided comfort, it also created the sound-blocking seal.

One side was slightly tacky, like glue, and there were puncture marks all throughout like someone's dog had used it for a chew toy.

"Ian! Where d'you think you're going, son?" Walt called out, his voice loud and clear over the radio. Killian glanced over to where the young man had last stood but the spot was empty. "Ian?" Walt repeated, his voice dropping low in volume. The seasoned fisherman took a hesitant step forward, his brow furrowed, a strong gust of wind whipping back his mane of tight, curly white hair.

The kid didn't respond.

Killian rocked back on his heels for momentum and leapt to his feet. He followed Walt's gaze to the pilot house steps, where Ian steadily climbed up. There was no hard rule saying he couldn't be there, but there wasn't a reason for him or other members of the crew to be. Their place, their work was on deck.

Although Ian was no model for good posture, his shoulders were slumped more than usual, the movement of his lanky limbs slowed as if filled with wet sand. When the kid paused on the steps to tilt his head and shake, Killian half expected seawater to trickle out.

And that's when he saw it.

Shit.

Ian's noise cancellation headset sat off kilter on top of his head... because he was missing the ear-padding on one side.

He dashed after the kid.

How had he not seen it before? He should have been paying better attention. While the tech was effective, it wasn't foolproof. Unless the earpieces sat snuggly over top the ears, creating a seal that blocked out sound, the headsets lost all their protective qualities.

Ian continued to the door. "It's so loud," he whined, reaching for the handle.

The memory of a mermaid named Undine thrashing on deck, clawed hands covering her ears from the sound of the boat's engines, spurred Killian up the stairs. When they caught Undine in their nets, she hummed until Branson shut off the engine, and she almost successfully compelled Lila to set her free.

"McAdams! Don't let him shut the engines off!" Killian shouted to his helmsman.

"Wha—oh, shit. Ian, what the hell are you doing?"

The comms crackled with the sounds of a scuffle.

As Killian bounded up the steps, two at a time, he felt the vibrations from another set of feet pounding up the stairs behind him.

"Right behind you, Cap," Branson's voice assured.

A loud *thunk*, followed by a sharp cry over the radio, chilled Killian's blood. He lurched forward, bracing himself against the pilot house door. Not because they sped up, but because the boat had abruptly stopped, its engine cut.

"Open those crates and then get yourselves below deck," he ordered the others, wrenching the door open.

Inside, McAdams lay unconscious on the floor.

Armed with a paper weight, Ian stood guard over the navigation console, trembling. Killian stopped short and raised his hands. Ian may not have been a sturdy kid, but he was scrappy.

"Whoa, easy there, Ian. You can put that down. I'm not going to hurt you."

"Captain, we gotta keep these engines off," Ian pleaded. "They're too loud."

"Okay, no problem. I just need you to look at me, listen to the sound of my voice, and set the weight down. Can you do that for me, Ian?"

The kid's eyes remained glassy, but he lowered his arm.

Killian licked his lips nervously. He needed to get to the console asap, but he didn't want to hurt the kid to get to it, if he didn't have to. "That's it. Good. Now can you take a step toward me?" He gestured the kid forward.

Ian planted his feet and shook his head.

Somewhere behind Killian, Branson grumbled under his breath and brushed past him. Ian swung the paperweight at the lead deckhand's head as he approached, but Branson blocked his wrist and socked the kid right in the face. The paperweight clattered to the floor, and Ian followed, knocked out cold. Stepping over him, Branson reached for the controls, blood trickling from his busted knuckles.

"Did he—?" Branson swore, slamming his palm on top of the console. "He broke the key in the ignition."

Cries of panic erupted over the comms. "Cap! They're swimming for the boat!"

"Get below now," Killian barked, dashing outside. He silently cursed the siren's supernatural swim speeds.

In just a matter of seconds, they were scaling the side of his boat.

"Hurry, man! Hurry!" a crew member yelled.

The whole lot of them were bottlenecked at the stairs. Walt took up the back of the line with a crowbar in his hands, his face a mask of fierce resignation. He would defend the crew until his last breath, if need be, but the old man wouldn't stand a chance. None of them would.

Pulling a gun from his hip holster, which he'd bought for emergencies exactly like this, Killian fired a warning shot into the air.

The sirens hunkered down and shrieked. If it weren't for the headset he wore, his own ears would be ringing right now.

Please let that be enough to scare them away.

The sirens shook their heads, flinging water from strands of sea-soaked hair. When the shaking stopped, seven pairs of eyes locked on the last of his crew, funneling through the door.

They kept climbing.

Oh, hell no.

Killian fired another shot and trained his gun on the nearest one—a dark-haired creature with amber eyes and silvery scales streaked with orange.

Pressing her ear to her shoulder, she glared at him and hissed. But her gaze didn't stray to the rest of the crew. Message received...he hoped. While he wouldn't hesitate to shoot, doing so probably wouldn't bode well for future fishing expeditions. And what would Lorelei think? All her peacemaking efforts swallowed whole.

He swiped his brow with the back of his arm to keep the sweat from burning his eyes.

One by one, seven sirens slinked over the side, one scaled leg after the other. Their claws clicked against the metal as they walked on all fours across the deck toward the abandoned crates. They tore into the canned pork, ripping apart the aluminum tins and cramming the meat into their mouths, canning juices running down their chins.

Bile rose at the back of Killian's throat. He looked away before he spewed his lunch all over the deck.

At least it wasn't his crew they feasted on.

A door slammed shut beneath Killian, the vibration from the door's swing coursing through his boots. Every siren on board jumped, hackles raised. He prayed they didn't rush the door and try to batter their way in, but they returned to their meal with little more than a few dirty looks cast in his direction.

"We're all in," Walt radioed. "Get yourself back into the pilot house and bar the door."

Killian exhaled. "We're good. They're just chowing down on deck. I'm gonna stick around and make sure they leave."

The radio fell silent, long enough that Killian didn't think he would respond, but the old fisherman replied in a soft voice, "Be careful, son."

He would wait until they had their fill before attempting to shoo them away. Best not get between them and one of their favorite meals. He wasn't about to present himself as dessert.

The sirens wore arm and neck pieces fashioned from metal taken from past offerings of canned meat, unaware how ridiculous wearing the canned pork brand appeared to their two-legged prey. If he wasn't so freaked out about having people-eating sirens crawling around on his boat, he would have laughed.

When they were all safely back on shore, he would have to tell Lorelei, and maybe then he could laugh with his feet planted on solid ground, and the only siren in sight more likely to kiss him than eat him.

The sirens just kept eating and eating, their bellies bulging from their gorging.

What about the rest of the pod? Shouldn't they be leaving enough for them? And where was Undine? He didn't think the leader of the sirens would approve of this. As he understood it, their regular potted meat tribute was meant to be shared, and it was supposed to keep the sirens away from his boat, not hosting a family dinner on deck.

Leave. Just take it all and go.

Why draw it out? It didn't make any sense. Sirens disliked being above water.

Maybe this was a rogue group, or maybe Undine sanctioned this breach of their agreement to demonstrate her power, to show the humans who really held all the cards out in the open ocean.

A dull ache formed behind Killian's eyes.

He waited until the seven sirens onboard slowed their eating. They sat back, lounging on deck, and patted their rounded bellies, making themselves at home. His temper flared. Switching off his mouthpiece, so he didn't blow out the eardrums of his crew, he yelled, "All right, you've had enough. Get the fuck off my boat!"

They looked up in unison. He made a shooing motion to emphasize his point.

The amber-eyed one cocked her head to the side and smirked.

The nerve...he shot the crate next to the siren, sending splintered wood flying. They all jumped back, covering their ears and snarling.

"GET. OFF. MY. BOAT," he repeated, pointing out at the water. If this provoked an attack, he had another magazine in his pocket. He didn't want to have to use it, but he would.

Beneath his boots, the whole boat vibrated, the engines roaring to life. Branson must have found a way to pry the broken key out and used the spare. The sirens shrieked and hurtled themselves over the side. He watched their brightly colored bodies streak away before they dove down into the deep.

Why did the engines send them away and not the gunshots? Was it one loud noise too many? Or was it the continuous drone that bothered them? He sat heavily on the steps, *Dawn Chaser* chugging along at full speed. He didn't get it, but whatever it was, he was grateful they were gone.

He switched his mouthpiece back on. "They're gone. You can come out now."

One by one his crew filed out onto the deck. He didn't have to say anything. They just began hurling the remaining crates of canned pork over the side and cleaned up wood shards, empty cans, and splattered meat. In all their years together at sea, *Dawn Chaser*'s fishing crew had never seen anything that would make any of them even think the word "siren" or "mermaid." But his dealings with Undine last year opened a door he could not close. And despite his best efforts to keep the siren's hunger for human flesh in check, it only seemed to embolden them further.

Killian swiped a hand over his face. He failed his crew today and could lose them. Not that he'd blame them. Vicious mermaid attacks weren't what they signed up for.

The sirens must have planned this. That they happened to be singing while Ian was wearing a faulty headset couldn't be a coincidence. It made him suspect that they might always sing when his boat entered their waters, lying in wait for the moment he and his crew showed weakness, hoping for exactly what happened here today.

But then why hadn't he heard their song when his own headset was askew? There was that weird ringing, but it hadn't felt compulsory. Maybe it had something to do with the fact that he was attuned to only one siren's song—the love of his life, his wife-to-be.

Lorelei.

He'd pulled her from these very waters almost a year ago, when the ship she was on sank, its entire crew devoured by her murderous kin. But as a Midwest transplant, who at the time had never been to sea, Lorelei hadn't known what she was. The maritime tragedy awakened that dormant part of her, and with her transformation, came cravings for human flesh.

If it weren't for Lila's help, Lorelei might've been lost to him, irrevocably called to the deep, and unable to resist the carnivorous drive that turned loved ones into prey. She could have been one of the sirens scaling the side of his boat today.

Arms draped across his knees, he stared out over the water, wondering if they were still nearby, lurking, following, waiting for another mistake. This wasn't the first time he'd had an unfriendly siren on his boat, but every day for almost a year, he'd hoped and prayed it would be the last.

A series of events led Killian, Lorelei, and a small knit group of their closest friends and family to live capture a mermaid—Undine—the siren's leader. And they made a deal. Potted meat in exchange for safe passage. A "cure" in exchange for a siren to study.

Because the siren hunger for human flesh wasn't innate. It was viral.

Every time, fisherman.

Undine's last words haunted him. She'd said it with a wink that was a disturbing mix of flirtation and warning. No skipped meals. No tribute could mean retaliation. He'd been diligent, but maybe she *was* behind this, but whatever the case might be, he would be a fool if he thought this incident was just a fluke, and the last of their troubles with the sirens.

The prey animal that he was felt it down to the marrow with chilling certainty.

Dawn Chaser was marked. And so was he.

CHAPTER
TWO

LORELEI

Participating in the research of a fellow siren never stopped feeling strange.

Taking Nireed by the hand, Lorelei helped her out of her aquarium and onto the metal-grated platform connected at the top. Nireed leaned heavily into her, legs wobbling as they adjusted to holding weight on solid ground.

Water seeped through Lorelei's blazer where they touched, but she didn't mind.

A damp shoulder was nothing compared to what had become Nireed's life—strange surroundings and daily scientific poking and prodding. The ocean-raised siren was a literal fish out of water, and although Lorelei taught her how to walk months before, the activity still gave her trouble. Nireed spent most of her days swimming inside the aquarium, through one million gallons of piped-in seawater, her legs fused together, and feet stretched out into flowy fins.

She only ever walked long enough to reach a medical chair.

Glancing over the railing, Nireed sucked in a long, rasping breath, the sound tearing in her throat like paper. Lorelei touched her own throat briefly, remembering how scratchy and dry it could get during winter. Nireed's affliction was like that, but worse, because for her entire life she filtered oxygen from the water through her gills. Before coming to shore, her throat and lungs rarely felt the passage of air.

How merfolk had both respiratory systems was an evolutionary mystery. Maybe the answer could be found in the study of lungfish...but that was Lila's domain.

The siren lifted her elbow and expelled a wracking cough that shook her whole body. Lorelei placed a hand on her shoulder to steady her. The last thing she needed was for Nireed to topple over the railing and plummet to the floor thirty-five feet below.

Rooting through a hole in her blazer pocket, Lorelei grasped the lozenge that had fallen into the lining with her fingertips. She unwrapped the hard tack and handed it to Nireed. After popping it into her mouth, Nireed touched her chin with her fingertips and lowered her hand toward Lorelei.

"You're welcome," Lorelei replied.

Straightening, Nireed braced her weight against the handrail. But her legs still trembled, and she grasped Lorelei's hand again. The handrail groaned, and Lorelei winced, the siren's grip crushing both bone and metal.

"I hate this floating feeling." Nireed gulped, glancing down through the metal grating. She squeezed her eyes shut. The hard tack clicked against the siren's teeth as it rolled around her mouth.

Lorelei worried her lower lip.

Nireed was paler than usual. And for a creature that rarely saw the sun, living deep beneath the waves, she had been pale to begin with. When they first met, her skin was nearly translucent, every purple vein charting a course beneath her skin like branching coral, but iridescent in its pearl-like shimmer. But standing here, thirty-five feet above the ground, there was no trace of her skin's healthy luster. While she was opaquer now from a year of living in photic waters, i.e., a tank on land, she also looked grey. Sick.

With a growing knot in her stomach, Lorelei suspected the siren's life in captivity played a part in this, not just her fear of heights.

Nireed searched for the stairs with her foot. "Just as bad as the first time."

Falling was a new, terrifying concept to a siren used to living in constant suspension. "I know," Lorelei murmured, coaxing her down onto the first step. "You've been very brave."

The siren kept her eyes closed the whole way down and did not open them until her toes touched the observation room's sterile, white-tiled floors. Nireed hated that the steps had open backs, and Lorelei didn't blame her, she herself having an irrational fear of them. Some illogical part of her brain was sure she'd fall through, a holdover from childhood, despite knowing she was much too big to fit through even if she tried. Sometimes walking up and down them made her woozy.

Lorelei passed Nireed a terrycloth robe.

Nakedness didn't bother the siren, but she put it on anyway, not because she cared about observing "two-legger" clothing decorum, but because she saw the robe as a gift.

Without toweling herself off, Nireed wrapped the robe around her body and tied it in a bow like Lorelei taught her. Being dry was another foreign and disturbing concept to the siren. As she crossed the room to sit in one of the office chairs for their daily language lessons, she dripped water onto the floor, leaving behind a trail of puddles. Lorelei skirted around them so she didn't slip. She would mop it up after Nireed returned to the tank.

Lorelei sat across from her and rubbed her eyes, aching from months of little sleep. The lab's harsh overhead florescent light hurt, but they also kept her awake while the world outside was still bathed in the dark hours of early morning, well before any members of the research team were due to arrive.

Except for Lila, Lorelei stayed out of the scientific team's way as much as possible. While she had her own keycard into the Mermaid Lab at Haven Cove Marine Research Center, Lila's team didn't like that Lorelei could come and go as she pleased, a non-scientist employee. Director of the research center's new affiliated museum gave Lorelei some weight to throw around, but it wasn't an appropriate credential to earn her a seat at the lab's highly competitive table.

And yet, Lorelei was the only one Nireed would talk to—so the scientists needed her—and it bothered them that they didn't know why.

Sitting next to Nireed, Lorelei pressed a closed fist to her chest, saying 'hello.' The sirens spoke with their hands beneath the waves.

Sound travelled far in water—the sharp clicks and whistles of dolphins, the deep lowing of whales, and far less pleasant, the constant onslaught of noise pollution—but the sirens preferred silence. In a loud ocean, it was stealthier, yes, but also a reprieve.

Silence was a gift. A choice.

With research, Lorelei recognized many of the hand signs they used. Not all were the same as the ones used in American Sign Language, but they bore a lot of similarities. Having a base to work from, and the ability to practice with how-to videos and diagrams at home, made learning the sirens' language easier.

Nireed repeated the gesture, and then extended her hand, palm facing down, and walked two fingers across the top with the other. "Hello Shorewalker," she said. It was the siren word for someone like Lorelei, a siren raised on land, not in the sea.

While the pod of sirens Nireed belonged to did have a sung language, a pidgin of English and whatever their own spoken language had been before, it was rarely used, save to lure, seduce, and devour sailors. Or to communicate with one another on the surface when the sun was bright and blinding. Most of her ocean-born kin did not often venture up from the dark deep, staying far away from noisy engine-powered boats and ships.

But Lorelei wanted to learn it anyway.

It was difficult.

Nireed said their sung language was easier to teach below the waves than above them. She also pointed out that, because Lorelei was a shorewalker, she'd never learned to "sing" properly and much of their lessons focused on reproducing the right basic sounds. The language made Lorelei use parts of her mouth and throat in ways she never had before. It felt unnatural to her, but theoretically made more sense underwater while filtering in oxygen through her gills rather than her lungs.

Teaching their respective languages felt like trial by fire most days, but they managed, making lots of progress over the last year.

For Nireed's English lessons, they used a grade school primer for guidance. Most of the pictures in the book were of things Nireed had never seen and had no equivalent words for like A for Apple, B for Bumble Bee, or C for Cat, but Lorelei replaced all the examples with oceanic ones. Their lessons also involved drawing, charades, and show-and-tell. Nireed was a fast learner, much faster than Lorelei. But she probably had to be, surrounded by folk her kind once considered prey, who spoke strange words and stuck her with needles.

Lorelei signed her way through the week's vocabulary list. Whenever she made a mistake, Nireed stilled her hands and adjusted their positioning and movement. Observing them once, Lila commented that being moved around like that would drive her nuts, but Lorelei preferred the tactile method. It helped with muscle memory. And these days, her brain needed every bit of extra help it could get.

Nireed nodded along with each correct sign, a grin creeping up the sides of her mouth to reveal a wicked set of fangs. "Yer much better."

"*You're* much better," Lorelei corrected gently. "It's more of an 'oar' sound." Nireed repeated the phrase for the sake of practice. Lorelei smiled. "So are you. You're a faster learner than I."

Nireed nodded, never hesitant to own her merits.

The siren could now speak conversational English and perform rudimentary reading and writing tasks. But it was more a testament to Nireed's capabilities as a student, than Lorelei's as a teacher. The siren's mind was a sponge. She picked up so much between their lessons, just by listening to the scientists talk around her. Lorelei would envy her if it weren't for the circumstances.

Lorelei's earliest lessons with Nireed had a dual purpose—not just the basic ability to communicate, but also to get Nireed to the point where she could give informed consent to being a research subject. If she declined, Lila, her team, and the whole research institution had to let her go. Despite the questionable manner they'd gotten her back to shore with them, their pursuit of informed consent wasn't disingenuous.

They couldn't have predicted Nireed's opinion on the matter. It had been *quite* strong.

Lorelei drifted into the memory, recalling that day.

ONE OF LILA'S NEW TEAM MEMBERS HAD BROUGHT A SET OF documents for Nireed to sign and explained the concept of informed consent. Lorelei had been present for communication help, while Lila was there to observe as research lead and to be another friendly, familiar face in the room.

"Good morning, Nireed." Lila inclined her head to the siren with respect but maintained a healthy amount of personal space. Whenever possible, Nireed preferred not to be touched. "We have a guest today. The one we talked about?"

Nireed repeated the greeting and said, "I remember."

Normally when Lorelei saw the marine biologist at work, she wore blouses and dress slacks in vibrant jewel tones that complimented her rich brown skin and exuberant personality, but inside the mermaid lab, Lila wore a white lab coat over her clothes—that was standard lab protocol—and yet, it wasn't the only sharp contrast Lorelei noticed. Her friend was more formal, more reserved the moment she donned it, but she'd been especially stiff through introductions that day.

An older gentleman plodded into the room after her, a dour expression on his face. In appearance, and appearance alone, he could have been a carbon copy of Doc from *Back to the Future*, but with grey hair instead of white, and a pair of wireframe spectacles perched on the end of his nose.

"This is Dr.—"

Lorelei didn't catch the man's name—Jerry, maybe? But given what followed, she didn't feel bad about missing it either.

Without any warning, he grabbed the siren's hand and shook it once, squeezing hard. Unnecessarily hard.

Hissing, Nireed ripped back her hand, and pushed the chair she sat in behind Lorelei. The siren wasn't fearful. Anger burned bright in her eyes, and yet, she remained seated. It was a miracle she hadn't slashed Lila's colleague to pieces right then and there.

"Did we not just discuss no touching?" Lila snapped, knifing through the air with her hand.

"She's been amongst humans for three months now," he scoffed, and with one finger, pushed his glasses up the bridge of his greasy nose. "She ought to get used to it. You're not doing her any favors by babying her, Dr. Branson."

"That's her call." Lila's voice dropped low, losing none of its severity. "Not yours, or mine, and for someone the board appointed to handle consent issues in this study, you've a concerning lack of it."

The man grumbled nonsense, before flipping through the stack of papers attached to his clipboard, and saying, "Mea culpa. Shall we proceed?"

Despite the bumpy beginning, the siren listened carefully to the scientist's slowly spoken words, frowning more and more. It was a tedious process. Even though Nireed was a quick learner, she was new to English, and there were a lot of unfamiliar words to go over with her.

They'd started first thing in the morning, but it was nearly five o'clock by the time they'd finished.

Dr. Something-or-Whatever sighed heavily, drumming his fingernails against the underside of his clipboard in an impatient tattoo. Peering over his glasses at the mermaid, he arched one scraggly caterpillar of an eyebrow, and in a snide tone said, "Do you understand what we mean by 'informed consent?' now? And that we need you to be able to give it before we begin testing?"

For someone whose job it was to establish research compliance and subject consent, he really was rather a dick about it, as if the whole process was a complete waste of his time, and that attitude wasn't lost in translation, even though much of the paperwork had been.

Nireed shot out of her chair, slapping the clipboard out of his hand. It launched across the room, and Lila yelped, barely ducking in time, as the clipboard grazed her halo of springy, corkscrew curls. It smacked the wall behind her before clattering to the floor.

A furious storm brewed in Nireed's eyes, and her lips curled back in a snarl, pointed teeth flashing in the florescent light. And while Lorelei sympathized with her, half wanting to eat the man herself, letting the siren devour someone didn't bode well for anyone. So, she stepped in between them, her hands outstretched, and fingers splayed. She motioned downward, parallel to the ground, with the flat palms of her hands, trying to get Nireed to calm down.

The cocky attitude disappeared.

Fear radiated off the scientist behind her in a fog so thick, Lorelei gagged on it, but her stomach grumbled, too, and saliva filled her mouth. That was bad. She'd even eaten canned pork with her breakfast that morning, but it wasn't really helping.

If she started hunting, too, Dr. Dickhead was as good as dead, and Lila not far behind.

That could not happen.

Nireed's nostrils flared, eyes locking onto the frightened scientist with laser precision. In response, Lorelei widened her stance, the hair on the back of her neck bristling. If only the reaction was purely protective, but the way her gums and nail beds ached, on the verge of unsheathing the sharp teeth and claws beneath, it was also an instinctual reaction to a challenger over prey.

"Shit."

In her periphery, Lorelei saw Lila snatch a can of potted meat from the lab's supply cabinet. They kept it well stocked with the canned meat. Cracking open the can, Lila waved it about as if to get its scent in the air, reminiscent of Dr. Grant distracting a Tyrannosaurus Rex with a flare in *Jurassic Park*.

Lorelei sniffed the air—make that Ian Malcolm. The overpowering scent of fear seared her olfactory senses. Not even a whiff of canned meat. And if Lorelei couldn't smell it, Nireed couldn't either. Lorelei pinched her nose and shook her head. Lila swore again and slid the can across the floor.

It hit Nireed's bare foot.

The siren jumped, claws out and ready to eviscerate whatever touched her. If it weren't for the gravity of the situation, Lorelei might have laughed at how cat-like it was.

Recognizing the blue and yellow can for what it was, Nireed crouched down and gobbled its contents. "No sudden movements," Lila said in a low, firm tone. "Just back away slowly."

"Should I call security?" the other scientist asked.

"No. We'll be fine. Just do what I say, for once."

Shoes scuffed against the tiled floor, followed by the lab door opening and clicking shut. Lorelei glanced over her shoulder. Dr. What's-His-Face hadn't gone far. He reappeared behind the shatterproof glass window, separating this part of the lab from the observation room. Through an intercom system, he could listen in and speak to them.

Lorelei sniffed again—just canned pork and Lila's perfume. She sighed. That had been close. But the relief she felt wasn't only for her colleague's safety. It was her unburdening conscience. "We can have you out of here by the end of the day."

"Uh…" Lila scrunched up her face. "What?"

Nireed rose to her feet, glaring at them in turn. "No."

Lorelei furrowed her brow. "No?"

All that stood between the siren and freedom was a series of doors, two sets of security guards, a sidewalk, and the rocky shore. If she wanted to leave immediately, Lila could probably get her out of the building. Haven Cove Marine Research Center staff didn't question the lead researcher too much.

The siren jabbed one clawed finger in Lorelei's direction. "You wasted our time. Start the testing NOW." She slapped the back of one hand against her palm. "We need the cure. You promised!"

The scientist behind the glass insisted that Nireed's verbal consent wasn't enough. It needed to be documented in writing. Nireed hissed at him. "You will not work unless I write on a piece of dead tree?"

"Uh, yeaaah."

Lorelei could wring his neck.

While Dr. Asshole didn't follow with a "duh," she heard it plainly in his tone. Safe behind a wall of shatterproof glass, he could afford to have an attitude again, but the research team owed Nireed more patience and understanding. Not only was there a lingual, social, and cultural barrier to bridge—they weren't even the same species.

"Those are the dumbest words I have ever heard, Two-Legger."

Lorelei hid a smirk behind her hand and glanced over her shoulder to witness the scientist's reaction.

His cheeks reddened. "Just do it," he muttered under his breath.

"My word is not good?" Nireed growled, kicking out her foot. It didn't connect with anyone or anything. Rather, the frustration behind the gesture struck Lorelei as the equivalent of a stamped foot. Only, considering that Nireed normally had fins, that movement must have translated into something like an irritated flick of the tail.

It took some coaxing, but in the spirit of "not wasting anymore time," Nireed scrawled her name where needed, grumbling the entire time.

As much as Lorelei disliked making Nireed follow human bureaucracy and scientific protocol she didn't agree with or understand, they couldn't hand wave it, especially with the whole world watching their work. But most of all, for Lorelei, the need for Nireed to give informed consent went deeper to a selfish, guilt-ridden place, a place that kept her awake at night.

She took Nireed from the ocean and brought her to this nightmare on shore. *She* was responsible for any mistreatment or discomfort the siren suffered.

Not Lila. Not Killian, or Walt, or Will, or Jackie. Not even Dr. Asshole.

SOMETIMES THE MEMORY OF NIREED'S AGGRESSIVE CONSENT to be studied made Lorelei feel better. Today it didn't. Guilt gnawed and dug its claws in deep.

"Shorewalker?" Nireed poked Lorelei's shoulder, startling her from the memory. "You are lost," she said, her brow pinched.

Was the siren concerned for her?

Lorelei rubbed her eyes, trying to bring herself back to the present. She really needed to brew herself a cup of coffee. Or three. The tea she had on her drive to work just wasn't cutting it. "Sorry. I was just remembering something. How's your neck?" Lorelei pressed her thumb to her index and middle fingers near the base of her head, like the motion used to give injections. The sirens didn't have a sign for "shots," so Lorelei learned the one used in American Sign Language and showed it to Nireed. She had deemed it apt, and they'd used it ever since.

Nireed rotated her neck gingerly. "Not good, but not bad like before."

Because the merfolk sickness was a brain virus, a mutated marine morbillivirus with aggressive rabies-like symptoms, treatment had to be delivered via intracerebroventricular injection to bypass the blood brain barrier. Unpleasant, but necessary, and Nireed took it with a lot of grace.

What Nireed and the other sirens called "the cure" was really a new, rarely funded experimental treatment. It wasn't even a vaccine, but something the marine epidemiologists called a "virophage." Basically, an injected virus that attacks another virus already living in the body. It didn't kill the virus, but in theory, it weakened it to the point of being ineffective. And with the mermaid morbillivirus being generational, mutated, and less severe as it passed down the family line, a biological pivot to keep the host body alive longer, time had already done some of that work for them.

Lorelei begged Lila to test the different virophages on her, as well, to give Nireed a break, but the marine biologist refused—claiming Killian would kill her if she experimented on his fiancée.

That didn't sit well.

Who would hold them all accountable if Nireed suffered adverse effects from the experimental treatment? While Lorelei knew Lila and her team did what they could to make Nireed comfortable in an intrusive research process, and that they would fight for her life if the tests ever went horribly awry, her good health fell second to the research.

Nireed wasn't expendable, but they took risks with her.

Bile rose at the back of Lorelei's throat for her own part to play in Nireed's captivity. She swallowed, trying to ignore the knots pressing against the walls of her stomach. "I'm really sorry about that. Lila thinks they're getting close. The one they tried before did some damage to the virus. We're hoping the next will critically weaken it, and this will all be over soon."

Nireed shrugged. "It will, or it won't be. I'm doing this for my people, no matter what."

"We didn't give you a choice."

Undine, the leader of the sirens, had offered Nireed up as collateral —her life to study in exchange for a possible "cure"—but it was Lorelei herself and the rest of the live capture team who accepted.

For one hazy moment, on that mermaid-finding expedition late last year, it had felt justified that the siren paid for her people's crimes. The sirens had mercilessly devoured *The Osprey* crew, of which Lorelei had been a student member.

But remembering Undine describe the sickness that made them mad for human flesh and then watching Nireed shiver and cower on deck when she was left behind, Lorelei's anger had ebbed. She knew firsthand how powerful that hunger could be. Even with her human-raised sensibilities, she wasn't stronger than the sickness.

If she hadn't revealed herself to Lila, asked for help, and found an alternative meat source to stave it off, Lorelei knew the madness would have consumed her. Of that she had no doubt. She had almost killed someone.

So no, Lorelei did not think Nireed deserved to live in a literal giant fishbowl for what could be the rest of her life. If anyone deserved it, it was Lorelei for putting Nireed there, paying for her own anonymity as a siren with another's freedom.

"You never had the chance to refuse." Her conscience demanded that she lay this brutal truth bare between them. Not doing so would be harboring a lie, and she couldn't lie to Nireed or herself—not about this. It would infect her soul and fester from the inside out like a necrotic disease. It had already been eating away at her for so long.

Nireed shrugged, looking out the window at the sea.

The sun had begun to rise over the horizon, casting the grey morning sky with a red glow.

Red sky at morning, sailors take warning.

Nireed put on a good show of resilience, but Lorelei felt the siren's longing roll off in waves. She didn't know what to say to reassure her. They were getting closer to a treatment, yes, but who knew how much longer it would take? For humans, this sort of thing usually took years, a decade even, if at all. There was no foreseeable future in which Nireed would return to the sea. And she would not hurt Nireed with false hope.

"Two-Leggers care too much about themselves and not enough about their people. I saw it as my duty. And Undine did ask. She did not have to."

Lorelei straightened. "She did? I'd always thought she'd issued an order..."

"Does it matter? It had to be done."

Lorelei swallowed, daring to ask the question that burned a hole in her mind. "Do you hate us for bringing you here?" She had to know, even if she didn't like the answer.

"For us," Nireed began, crossing her hands at the wrist, fingertips skyward. She made a beckoning motion toward her chest like fins through the water—it was the hand sign the seafolk used to signify themselves. "There is no worse end than living on shore. Or so I thought. Now, I know a worse one." Nireed gestured flippantly toward the tank. "Living in there and still seeing the sea everyday through two walls of glass. I should hate you for the life I have now."

Guilt twisted like a knife in Lorelei's gut. Any hope of coming to terms with bringing Nireed to shore vanished. Nireed suffered—a worse fate than the seafolk could have imagined—and this was all Lorelei's fault. She blinked back the tears that stung her eyes. There was no way she was going to cry in front of the siren. "Why don't you?"

The siren glanced back at her and shrugged. "Maybe it is because you are kin. Or it is my chosen duty to my people. Or because I eat well and can swim without fear of sharks."

Comfortable captivity was still captivity.

"But I think it is this. I am never alone. Too many," Nireed signed 'injection,' "for that. And still I feel alone. But talking with you is the best part of the day, because I forget that feeling for a little while."

Shame washed over Lorelei anew. She dried her eyes before any tears slipped down her cheeks and swallowed the lump in her throat. "Then we will continue to have these talks for as long as you are here. I can at least do that much."

"Good." Touching her drying hair, the siren grimaced. "It is time for me to go back."

If the circumstances had been different, they might have become friends.

CHAPTER
THREE

LORELEI

INDIGO WAVES ROLLED INTO SHORE, AND LORELEI SAT AT the kitchen table, staring out the open window at the horizon, a glass of homemade iced tea pressed between her hands. Cool condensation licked her fingers, the taste of lemon and fresh mint lingering on her tongue. A strong sea breeze carrying in the scents of salt, pine, and kelp, caught the loose strands of her hair and tickled her cheeks.

She sung a little under her breath, repeating just the chorus of a sailor's song to herself. Greta, her adoptive mother, had taught her a variation of the traditional one she learned while sailing on *The Osprey*. Singing always soothed Lorelei when her mind was troubled.

Upon one summer's morning, I carelessly did stray,
Down by the Coves of Haven, where I met a sailor gay,
Conversing with a young lass, who seem'd to be in pain,
Saying, Sailor, when you go, I fear you will ne'er return again.
My heart is pierced by Cupid, I disdain all glittering gold,
There is nothing can console me but my jolly sailor bold.

By all accounts, it was the perfect summer evening in coastal Maine, but its tranquility did not quite reach her. The skies were clear, but a thick fog encased Lorelei's thoughts, which these days, were predominated by her job and Nireed's well-being.

Her leather work bag sat in a heap by the door where it had slid from her shoulder, ignored. There was more to get done this evening, but so little room to breathe, and it was all she could do to stay afloat with the museum grand opening looming.

There was the...and she had to do the...

Lorelei cupped her forehead.

What did she have to do again? There was just so much, enough to drown in, but she couldn't recall a single thing. No matter. She'd study her notes later. She kept detailed to-do lists for moments of forgetfulness like this. But for now, she would try to enjoy her break and allow herself some time to reset from the office.

An itch prickled along Lorelei's neck.

She rubbed the spot—three lines of rough, raised skin grazing against her palms—but it would not go away. And she had just applied medicated lotion maybe a half hour ago. Sighing, Lorelei squeezed more from the tube, expensive stuff her dermatologist prescribed her, and massaged it into the creases where her gills would be.

It wasn't just her neck that was irritated. All over her skin was dry, and in some spots cracking, like on her hands and feet. If had been winter, and not the end of August, Lorelei might have chalked it up to the season. But it just seemed like her body couldn't hold onto moisture anymore.

Ever since sirens had become a world-wide sensation almost a year ago, Lorelei had stepped neither foot nor fin into the ocean. Someone could see her. Identify her. And she had already come far too close—not just once, but twice—to that happening last year to take the risk. First, when Killian's ex-girlfriend Carrie Prior trespassed onto his property and posted video footage of her swimming in siren form online. And second, when Lorelei saved a drowning boy, and his Go-Pro recorded the rescue. Only a combination of distance, dark turbulent waters, the help of her newfound Maine family, and a reporter friend's subterfuge, had kept her secret safe.

Well, that, and Nireed's sacrifice.

She would not take that risk again and make their efforts in vain.

Sitting back in her chair, Lorelei stared at the waves rolling into shore. She imagined herself gliding through the chill water, guided out into the open ocean by the currents. Even in the summer, ocean temps in Maine rarely climbed above 50 degrees. Its touch would be numbing to a human but brisk and enlivening against her own skin.

She missed the ocean so much her bones ached. She'd grown up away from it, but now that she'd had a taste of its freedoms and mysteries and dangers, she was hooked. She needed it like humans need sunshine in the dead of winter, possibly even more.

But she wanted her privacy and freedom above all.

She shuddered to consider how terrible the separation must feel for Nireed.

A door slammed shut outside, followed by a short beep.

Her heart raced a little. Lorelei hadn't even heard anyone come up the driveway. It sounded like the locking mechanism for Killian's truck, but what if it wasn't? While Carrie hadn't trespassed on Killian's property since they threatened to get a restraining order against her, that wasn't a guarantee she never would again, right? Lorelei wrung her hands, her joints aching, but otherwise remained frozen to the spot.

A Carrie confrontation was the last thing she needed today.

But Killian shuffled in through the doorway moments later with his sea bag slung over one shoulder and a paper pharmacy bag in his other hand.

Lorelei sighed with relief.

She didn't know why the thought of Carrie coming onto their property made her anxious. She could bite that woman's face off if she wanted to. Lorelei swallowed the saliva pooling in her mouth. Maybe that was why. Self-control wasn't exactly her strong suit when she was tired and cornered.

If Carrie did come snooping around again, Lorelei probably would bite her face off.

"Hey, beautiful." Killian smiled, setting down his cream canvas seabag. The corded muscles in his forearm flexed under the weight. He wore a black tee that hugged his biceps and pulled taut across his chest, tapering down to hug his waist. If any stretch of the fabric moved an inch, sun-bronzed skin would give way to white, but God, tan lines, and all, she loved looking at him. "How are you?"

Sliding from her seat, Lorelei padded barefoot across the cool hardwood floor. She wrapped her arms around his middle and sunk her head into his chest, firm beneath her forehead. Despite the summer temps, she basked in the comfort of his touch and his heady male heat. "Better now that you are here."

The pharmacy bag bumped against her elbow as Killian slung an arm across her shoulders and cupped the back of her head, his fingers threading through the loosened, frazzled plaits of her fishtail braid. He laid his cheek on top, where a few strands of her hair were sure to get caught in the dark scruff that lined his jaw, but she loved being enveloped by him. He was a steadying force. "Work still kicking your butt?"

Lorelei grumbled nonsensical words. She didn't have the energy to talk about her day. Work already took up enough space in her life and made her head want to explode. Killian squeezed her tight. "Made a detour after stopping by the pharmacy to pick up your medication and got you something." He bumped the bag against her arm. "Take a look."

Lorelei withdrew from his arms and opened it.

Inside, next to her scripts, was a red silk bag. The gold logo on the front denoted he'd paid The Pearl a visit, a fancy spa in town that drew the more well-to-do tourist crowds. She plucked loose the drawstring bow. A white orb marbled with blues and greens sat at the bottom.

Her lips quirked upwards. "Is this a bath bomb?"

"Yeah, the shopkeeper said it's infused with sea salt and kelp extract or something." He scratched the back of his neck. "I don't remember exactly, but I thought it might help. It's not the ocean, I know. Nothing can replace that, but maybe it'll help?"

Hugging the bag to her chest, she stood up on her toes to give him a kiss. "That was really sweet of you. I can't wait to try it."

Twin rosy dots flushed his tanned cheeks. Even after almost a year of dating and an engagement, Killian still became bashful when she paid him compliments. "I can draw a bath for you after dinner."

She glanced at her work bag, shoulders slumping.

Killian said her name firmly, his embarrassment forgotten. "You can work while I get dinner ready, but after that you need to take some time for yourself. You're burning the candle at both ends. You've got to slow down."

"I don't want to fall behind…"

He placed his hands on her shoulders. "You're in charge. You make the schedule, and the deadlines. If you need more time to get stuff done, take more time."

She chewed at her lower lip again, even though it was cracked and sore. If only it were that simple. "The exhibits are ready. It's the rest of it—the marketing, ticketing, event planning, staffing, and half a million other things—that I've got to get ready in time for the opening."

While Killian gently brushed her collarbones with his thumbs, the look he gave her was stern. When it came to self-care, Lorelei had a bad habit of letting it fall to the wayside. If it weren't for him, she would have burnt out long ago.

"You're just one person, Lorelei. You can't sustain this. Could you maybe talk to your boss about hiring more staff? And not interns or other entry level folks. Someone mid-or top-level who can help you do the heavy lifting. If I didn't have Branson helping me run *Dawn Chaser*, I would be drowning in work."

Lorelei swiped a hand over her face. "I know. It's just I'd have to go through the whole process of hiring and training someone and that takes time. Time, I don't have. But maybe I should make time and a new hire will make up for what I lose. The grand opening date isn't exactly flexible, but you're right. This is becoming too much for me to handle on my own."

"So, you'll take a break this evening?"

Lorelei nodded, a smile cracking across her face. A real break. She hadn't had one of those in…she couldn't remember when.

Killian grinned. "That's my girl."

She soaked in that smile, a beacon of light that always kept her from crashing upon the rocky shores of life. Reaching up, Lorelei brushed through his crop of dark brown hair threaded with grey and trailed her fingers down his cheek. "How about you—how was your trip?"

Killian didn't stop smiling, but his eyes dimmed a bit, the dimple beside his left one twitching. He didn't answer right away, and that hesitation was worrisome.

"Killian, what happened?"

"I don't want to worry you."

"You can tell me. I'm not fragile."

"Far from it, I know. But you're overwhelmed and stressed out enough as it is."

She crossed her arms. "When it comes to my kin, I need to know."

Killian sighed. "We had a bit of a situation," he began reluctantly. "A group of sirens came onboard the boat—there were seven of them. They didn't hurt anyone directly, and everyone's mostly okay, but they did compel Ian to knock out McAdams and shut off our engines."

Anger flared through her. *What the hell, Undine?* That wasn't part of their deal. "What did they want?"

"I don't know. They just ate as much of the potted meat as they could. No intent to share with the rest of the merfolk. I can't be sure, but it seemed like they might be a rogue group. Undine wasn't there."

"What did they look like? I can ask Nireed tomorrow about them. She might be able to provide some insight into who they are, and what they want."

Killian described their coloring. When he mentioned silvery scales slashed with orange, Lorelei straightened. That sounded like Nireed's coloring. A relative perhaps, which could point to motive—revenge for Nireed's captivity.

Or maybe they were trying to get her back.

Swishing her hand through the water, the bath bomb fizzled and swirled across the surface. Notes of sea salt and kelp rose with the steam, but it had the clean, fresh overtone of a bathing product rather than nature. The reminder was both ecstasy and torture. It gave Lorelei the barest taste of what she could not have, but it did nothing to quell the longing in her heart, nor negate the magnetic pull on her bones.

She rubbed her aching joints.

It was the kind of ache that comes with changing seasonings and fluctuating atmospheric pressure, only it never went away. The ocean always beckoned. And resisting its call hurt.

Lorelei glanced out the window at the sky streaked in orange and purple. The sun would be setting soon. As the tub filled with hot water and sea-nostalgic scents, Killian busied himself with lighting candles and poured Lorelei a glass of red wine, smokey and bourbon barrel aged. She accepted it from his outstretched hand, sipping it before setting it down on her bath caddy alongside her body scrubs and shampoo.

Rising from her perch on the bathtub's edge, Lorelei hummed a tune. Nothing noteworthy, just something low and wistful to fill the silence as she unbuttoned her blouse. Killian stepped forward, his eyes dark and glittering, but also with the unfocused quality of dream walking or trance.

The hum died in Lorelei's throat. "Sorry. I didn't mean to do that."

Killian blinked once, then twice. "It's all right."

Lorelei shook her head. For a siren, she sang terribly, and while it still drew him near, it was never this compulsory. It was her hummed tunes that affected him the most, and she needed to remember that. "But you don't have a choice."

He leaned against the wall with his arms folded and a smile cresting his lips. "I like listening though. And the power you have over me," he trailed, gaze dipping to the swell of breasts beneath black lace. "It's intoxicating. I like being pulled toward you."

Her pulse quickened. "You do?"

"I really do." He pushed off from the wall, a hulking mass before her. This large man who enjoyed relinquishing control. He slid her hairband from the end of her braid and onto his wrist. "I'd like you to use it on me some time," Killian remarked, unraveling the plaits of her braid. "When you're in the mood. But for right now, let me take care of you."

Lorelei tilted her head up, peeling her silken blouse from damp skin. "I could use a little pampering."

He chucked her under the chin. "You're overdue. Now let's get you out of these pants." Kneeling, Killian unzipped her grey dress slacks and tugged them over her hips. The first time they'd ever done this, he'd looked away—she the sole survivor of a maritime tragedy, and he her handsome rescuer. She trailed her hand up the side of his arm and across his shoulder to cup his cheek, the gold engagement ring on her finger glinting in the candlelight. He pressed a kiss between her breasts.

Once divested of all her clothes, Lorelei dipped a toe in the water to test the temperature, then eased herself in, moaning as she submerged. It was heavenly. She rubbed her hands up and down her arms, and then across her neck, the motion chasing away the pesky itch that had become a constant. Under the bath's watery caress, Lorelei's skin tingled from waist to foot, the once familiar sensation now uncomfortable. It had been far too long. "I'm going to shift."

Killian brushed hair away from her face. She leaned back and closed her eyes, letting the transformation overtake her. The tingling intensified as her skin knitted itself together and her scales emerged. Ah. That was better.

A choked cry escaped Killian's lips.

Lorelei's eyes shot wide open, her attention on the anguished expression he now wore. He pressed his lips into a thin, grim line. "What is it? What's wrong?" He'd never reacted negatively to her transformation before…

Covering his mouth with his hand, he nodded to her tail. Were… were those tears in his eyes? Cold dread washed over Lorelei. It must be bad to garner a reaction like that from him, the most loving and accepting person in her life.

CHAPTER
FOUR

KILLIAN

"Does it hurt?" Killian asked, watching Lorelei visibly swallow. God, it was bad. If he had known, if he had suspected...

Several scales pulled loose as she brushed her hands along the sides of her tail. "No," she whispered, and tears slipped down her cheeks. One after the other each watery drop fell into the bath, rippling the surface. Her once vibrant scales had faded and so had the dull yellows, greens, and blues in her fins. Patches of scales were gone, and the skin beneath was blistered and red. A milky puss leaked out from her gills. "The water actually feels quite nice."

Guilt yanked him up by the heartstrings. He took her dry skin condition at face-value and hadn't stopped to question that it might be a symptom of a much larger problem. "You've been away from the ocean too long," he said hoarsely. "You have to go back. At least just for a little bit. You can just swim around the cove, and I can stand watch to make sure no one comes along to see."

Hope shimmered in Lorelei's eyes before her expression hardened. Not in anger at him but in stubborn resolve—he'd come to know the difference. "I can't. It's too risky," she bit out. "What if Carrie comes back? She's not exactly the type of person you can just shoo away real quick. Or what about the tourists who drove up the driveway last week, because they thought it was an access road to a public beach?"

Killian swiped his palm over his face. That had only happened once this summer. Lorelei was being too paranoid, too stubborn, but he squashed his rising irritation right along with the urge to sling her over his shoulder and dump her in the ocean. She also had the most to lose. "Not even to even to dip your feet in?"

Uncertainty cracked her resolve. She glanced out the window, rubbing her arms. A frown tugged at the corners of her mouth. "I've been away from it for so long. I don't know if I'll be able to control myself."

To think he, a mere man, was striving to tempt a seductress of the sea with his words. "What if I take you out? Somewhere far from shore, where people can't see you?"

A sad smile arrested her lips as her eyes locked onto his, but there was a firm tone to her voice that brooked no argument. It grated against his nerves. "I would love that, but I don't have time to go on a boat trip like that. I have so much work I have to do."

Why couldn't she just agree to take care of herself? And look for solutions, not problems? Killian didn't bother suggesting she bring her work along for the ride. He could bring that up another time. This evening was about her self-care, not picking apart her words and logic until an argument broke out.

Locating his e-book reader, Killian bought the book Lorelei had been dying to read but never had the time to. Smoothing back her wet hair, Killian bent to kiss her forehead and slipped the e-reader into her hands. "Let's focus on what we can control then—a nice relaxing bath."

Lorelei smiled up at him, tears glistening at the corners of her eyes. She cupped his cheek with one clawed hand. The nail beds were red, almost raw, and her nails were chipped. He placed his hand over hers and leaned into her touch, blinking back the pricking tears that threatened to fall from his own eyes.

Glancing at the book on screen, Lorelei's smile broadened. "Thank you so much, Killian. You always know just what I need. I don't know what I would do without you."

This outpouring of gratitude over so small a gesture pierced his heart. This evening, just a brief snapshot of happiness, would only carry her so far. It was little more than a band-aid over a festering wound. She needed so much more.

Killian wanted to give her the ocean, but all she would accept was a measly e-book and an overpriced bath bomb.

He rose to leave, but she grabbed his wrist and begged him to stay with her. He wouldn't deny her anything, much less his company. They didn't really spend much quality time together anymore. Work always conspired to keep them apart.

As Lorelei read, he settled onto the bathroom floor beside her and leaned against the wall. Lorelei laid within, and he sat without, separated only by a short wall of porcelain. He draped his arm over the edge, dipping his fingers into the water, and watched her sink down into the tub with a grin on her face. She laughed and gasped at regular intervals, her fins swishing above the surface, grazing against tile, as she lost herself in the story.

Killian browsed fencing company websites on his phone, occasionally brushing Lorelei's healthier scales with his fingertips. If the fear of trespassers was all that kept Lorelei from swimming in their little private cove, Killian would happily shell out for a privacy fence along the perimeter of his remote property, and for a security gate at the bottom of his driveway. He didn't care if it made him look like one of those rich, uppity Maine transplants who built their summer mansions along the coast.

LORELEI STAYED IN THE BATH LONG AFTER THE WATER HAD cooled. But when she pulled the drain stopper and shifted back into human form, they retreated to the bedroom so Killian could apply medicated lotion to her skin. It looked better after the bath but was still dry in areas.

The sun had set, and a chill, summer night's breeze blew through the open window, rustling the gauzy curtains that draped either side. Cloud cover hid the stars and moon overhead, so Killian lit several candles around the room while Lorelei got situated and found a music streaming playlist on his phone that played spa music. Whatever that was. But the soft and soothing instrumentals lulled Lorelei into a puddle face-down on their bed.

Stripping down to his boxers, Killian climbed on top and straddled the backs of her thighs. He rubbed his hands together to warm them and squeezed a generous amount of lotion into his palm.

Starting at her neck, Killian massaged lotion into her skin, and worked his way down her back, kneading the tension from her muscles. Eyes drifting closed, Lorelei buried her face into a pillow, her muffled moans a song of pleasure. After paying an excessive amount of time on the globes of her ass, he gently maneuvered Lorelei's arms above her head and rubbed the lotion all along their length, paying particular attention to her hands and elbows.

Lorelei transformed again, right on top of their bed. That sometimes happened when she was relaxed or aroused.

Her emerging scales tickled Killian's inner thighs. He might have thrilled at the sensation were it not for the shimmery silver-blue scales flaking off and sticking to his skin. He shifted his weight off her. "Are you going to stay away from the ocean forever?" He hadn't meant it to, but his tone had a testy edge.

Twisting her head to the side, Lorelei cracked open one eye to see what had irked him. "I don't know," she muttered under her breath.

Killian frowned. He'd asked in frustration, but that she seriously considered never returning... He'd have to talk to Lila about this. Perhaps stage an intervention. If Lorelei continued down this path, she might not survive. Resisting the ocean's call could kill her.

Peering down at her battered, ailing tail, he corrected himself.

It *was* killing her.

CHAPTER
FIVE

LORELEI

THE FOG ENSHROUDING LORELEI'S MIND LIFTED.

Not quite clear skies, but it dissipated enough after an evening of relaxation and a good night's sleep that she didn't need two cups of coffee to propel herself out of bed the next morning. But as soon as she sat down at her desk at the research center, and turned on her monitor, the fog rolled back in thick. Yesterday evening, she'd been given a glimpse of the sun. Having to continue without it settled heavy in her chest.

For several long minutes, she stared numbly at the screen and the pile of work in front of her, unable to string two coherent thoughts together. She breathed in deep and counted to ten before exhaling, but the tightness in her chest didn't go away.

Start with something easy. Clear out your email inbox.

She had so much work to do, but there was no shame in starting off the day with light-lift tasks. Some days just required starting off simple to get the ball rolling. Her momentum would pick up…

Rubbing circles into her temples, in a failed attempt to ease the headache forming there, she leaned forward in her chair and squinted, really trying to focus on distinguishing junk emails from the important stuff. That shouldn't be too hard, right? But as Lorelei reread the same subject line over and over, the words blurred into digital mush. Nothing held meaning.

Nausea followed in the wake of her sharpening headache. Lorelei sat back and closed her eyes, hoping to quell the riotous pitch of her hastily eaten breakfast. Looking away from her screen helped. When she thought she had her stomach under control, Lorelei peeked open one eye and all the nausea came rushing back.

Fuck. She couldn't afford to waste a day, but she wasn't going to get anywhere with her mountainous to-do list feeling like this. Pushing back from her desk, Lorelei buried her face into her hands. Who the hell did she think she was to take this job? It sounded great on paper, but, in practice, it was sucking the life out of her. She wasn't cut out for this.

Switching off her monitor, Lorelei rose from her desk and walked down the hall to Lila's office. Through the glass door, she saw Lila typing away at her computer, tongue tucked between her lip and the corner of her mouth. Her long brown legs stretched out in front of her beneath a mauve pencil-skirt, crossed casually at the ankles. Busy, but relaxed.

Open file folders full of papers were scattered across her glass top desk, stuck with hundreds of multicolored sticky tabs. To those who didn't know her, it looked untidy, but there was complete order in the chaos. Everything had its place, and Lila never lost track of a single item, her mind a sponge for details both great and small.

Amongst the clutter sat frames filled with pictures of family, potted plants, and two tiny metal sculptures that always sat side-by-side, as if one might protect the other: one of Yemaya, the Goddess of the Oceans and Mother of the Orishas, and the other, a North Atlantic right whale, one of the world's most endangered large whale species. There was a stack of books, too, piled on the corner of the desk, and although the spines faced Lila, Lorelei knew from her time working alongside the marine biologist that they all featured Black marine scientists: Ernest Everett Just, Roger Arliner Young, Joan Murrell Owens, as well as contemporaries and colleagues. Their stories, their work always within reach. Lorelei rapped on the door twice before entering.

"Hey, what's up?" Lila looked up from her screen. Beneath her makeup, there was a faint outline of bags under her eyes, but her smile was bright, and aside from a little tiredness, Lila seemed to be in a pleasant mood.

Lorelei slumped in one of the two chairs situated in front of Lila's desk. These days, as lead researcher in the mermaid lab, the marine biologist regularly took meetings in her office. "I'm sorry to take up your time like this." Pain hammered against Lorelei's skull. How had it gotten worse? She bent forward and buried her face in her hands, surprised by the tears rolling down her cheeks. But now that they'd started, she couldn't get them to stop. Was this what the breaking point felt like? "I need help."

Wheels rolled against tile as Lila scooched her chair back. The clack of her heels retreated across the room, and Lorelei heard Lila draw the blinds to her office. Then she returned and sat in the chair beside her, placing an arm around her shoulders. Lorelei snatched a tissue from her desk and leaned into the embrace. Her chest felt even tighter than it had in her own office.

"I know what I have to do," Lorelei began, letting out a shuddering breath. She used the tissue to dry her eyes, but the tears just kept coming. This whole past year. It was too much. And was finally catching up with her.

Lila hugged her tighter. "Just let it out, Lorelei. And then we can talk."

A choked sob escaped her lips.

It was permission she didn't know she needed. She rested her head on top of Lila's shoulder and pressed the ragged tissue into the corners of her eyes, trying to keep her tears from staining Lila's blouse. It was a good, ugly cry. One that shakes the whole body from the shoulders down. Everything that she bottled inside—every little thing compounding over the last year, the guilt, the self-doubt, and self-loathing—came flooding out. Her problems weren't yet solved, but this was catharsis.

Sniffing, Lorelei straightened once her body rung out every raw emotion. She laughed a little at herself. "Wow, I needed that."

Lila handed her a new tissue. "What is it—mermaid troubles? Work stress? Wedding planning woes? Is Killian being a butthead? Cause if he is…"

Far from it. Killian pampered her. Took care of dinner, most of the other household chores, and virtually all the wedding planning. Lorelei just said "yes" or "no" to things. If anyone was a butthead, it was her for overworking and not chipping in enough at home. "No, no, no. Just the first two. But mostly work today. I need to talk to Phil about hiring another person. But I'm worried that the hiring process is going to eat into time I don't have." Phil Simmons, the Director of the Haven Cove Marine Research Center, was both their bosses.

"It always does, but it doesn't have to be as much as you fear. In the past, I've handled all the nitty-gritties of hiring myself with HR oversight, like what I did when I hired you, but now I let HR and Phil take care of it. I just give them a rundown of the type of personnel I need—what qualifications, experience, etc. They draft the job description and run it by me, but they handle all the job listings, recruiting, and scheduling of interviews. I just come in for the final rounds to decide. They can do that for you, too."

Lorelei exhaled. "Really? That would be fantastic."

Withdrawing her arm, Lila slid a pen and notepad off her desk. She flipped to a crisp new sheet. "Really. Here, I'll help you brainstorm."

Lorelei glanced at Lila's work computer, biting her lower lip. "Don't you have your own work? I don't want to set you behind."

Lila blew air between her lips. "Pssht. I have minions. I'm fine."

Recalling the bags under Lila's eyes, Lorelei crossed her arms and searched the marine biologist's face for signs of a fib, but the shine in her eyes was just as bright and cheery as her smile. As if reading her mind, Lila added, "I have this whole decompressing ritual when I go home—exercise, a shower, some meditation, a glass of wine…dessert. I just stay up too late binging Nat Geo or the latest TV drama. I do love me some juicy political angst. You should try it, just, you know, go to bed on time."

They spent the next half hour sketching out the role for an Assistant Museum Director. After referencing several sources online, Lorelei also emailed her former boss in Marquette, Michigan, asking if she could pick her brain sometime soon on museum operations.

When Lorelei rose from her seat, Lila offered her a bit of parting advice. "Just start thinking about the first couple projects you want your new team member to knock out for you. Makes onboarding a lot easier and helpful."

"Thanks Lila. You're a lifesaver, as always. Do you want to go out for drinks with me after work? My treat."

"Hell yes."

Lorelei left Lila's office with a little spark to her step.

RUNNING INTO CARRIE PRIOR IN THE WOMEN'S BATHROOM was the last thing Lorelei expected on this bad morning turned to workday hell. All she wanted was to splash cool water on her face, and touch up her makeup, so she didn't look like a sad, blotchy raccoon when she put in a hiring request with her boss. But no. Killian's ex just had to be there to witness the aftermath of her meltdown. The woman's penchant for showing up at the worst possible moment bordered on supernatural.

Lorelei found Killian's ex at a sink washing her hands when she pushed open the bathroom door with her elbow. Carrie didn't even turn her head, but whatever she saw out of the corner of her eye made her jump back. No sound but a breathless wheeze escaped her lips as she opened her mouth in pure terror. Her drained complexion could have rivaled printer paper.

When Lorelei took a step forward, Carrie moved back and held out her trembling wet hands as if to ward her off. But all she accomplished was drip water onto the floor. Lorelei glanced at her own reflection in the mirror. She looked bad. But not the type of bad that fills the room with fear so thick and cloying, it stuck in the air like someone had gone heavy on the air freshener. Mixed with unpleasant bathroom odors, and amplifying them, Carrie's fear burned her throat, a noxious combination leaving a foul taste on her tongue that she didn't want to think too much about.

Turning her head into her elbow, Lorelei coughed. "God, it stinks in here."

Recognition settled over Carrie's features and bright pink color returned to her cheeks. She swiped a paper towel from the dispenser with a ferocious yank. "Jesus, Lori. You scared the shit out of me!"

"Smells like it," Lorelei grumbled under her breath. She stepped up to the open sink furthest from Carrie and set her makeup bag on a clean paper towel on top of the counter.

"What did you say?"

Lorelei ran the cold water and splashed her face several times. It wouldn't do much to reduce the puffiness around her eyes, but it did make her feel better. At least, as good as she could feel with Carrie hovering nearby. Patting her face dry with a towelette, Lorelei ignored the question by asking one of her own. "What are you doing here?"

Carrie tapped the visitor's pass clipped to her lapel with one perfectly manicured nail. "I'm here for an open house tour. And then I have lunch with my cousin at noon."

Lorelei arched an eyebrow. "With...Lila?" The marine biologist didn't like her husband's cousin any more than Lorelei did, but she tried to be civil for the sake of family. Maybe this was one of those obligatory family meetups. But it was odd Lila hadn't warned her Carrie would be at the research center today, given the trouble they had with her in the past.

Carrie tossed her used towel into the trash and stepped in front of the mirror, turning ivory porcelain cheeks this way, to check her perfect makeup and primp her perfect light brown locks, curled gently at the ends. It was wholly unnecessary and a not-so-sly, unspoken jab at Lorelei's frazzled appearance.

While Lorelei was no slouch, Carrie came to the research center dressed to impress with her navy-blue blazer, light wash jeans, and beige, peep-toe, ankle boots. Save for a concave dip in her calf muscle, where Lorelei may have accidentally, on purpose, taken a chunk out of her leg, Carrie filled out every single curve in her tight, tailored jeans.

Carrie had the look of someone on top of their game.

Glancing down at her left hand, she spun her engagement ring around with her thumb. She tried really, really, hard not to think about the fact that this was a woman Killian once loved. Neither Carrie nor Killian had ever given her any reason to be jealous of their history, but exhaustion wore her emotional resilience thin, and Lorelei fumbled.

Self-doubt was a cruel, wicked beast.

A smug little smile curled up the corners of Carrie's mouth. "No. With the director."

"Phil's your cousin? And Will's?" Lorelei kept her tone light, as she rifled through her makeup bag for her CC cream, but on the inside, she was reeling at the revelation. Could this town be any smaller?

"Different side of the family, and second cousin technically, but who really keeps track? Anyway, I have a tour to catch." With one last fluff, Carrie pivoted on her heels and strode toward the door. Lorelei thought she was in the clear, but Carrie paused halfway out the door and glanced over her shoulder. "Oh, and Lori? You're going to need a hell of a lot more than CC cream."

Lorelei scowled. But once Carrie was gone, she begrudgingly rooted around her makeup bag for concealer.

CHAPTER

SIX

LORELEI

Liquid mask of professionalism in place, Lorelei found the research center director in his east-facing office after lunch. She'd shot off an email ahead of time, asking if they could meet to discuss hiring an Assistant Director for the museum, and he quickly accepted.

Phil Simmons had been talking on the phone at his desk when she arrived, which made her hesitate and consider rescheduling with his secretary, but he waved her in, mouthing, "I only need a minute," before carrying on.

In one breath, it sounded like he was talking to a board member about a budgetary item, but in the next, a relative, when he asked, 'will I see you at the family reunion?' Was Phil related to someone on the board? Not unheard of or even unusual, especially in a small town, but she hadn't thought of the research center as being family-run. They certainly didn't advertise themselves that way.

Stop eavesdropping, Lorelei. It's rude.

The whole back wall of Phil's office was just one large window overlooking the rich blue water of the harbor beyond. One could watch the sunrise here, and every lobster and fishing boat in Haven Cove as they chased the horizon. Lorelei looked away. She didn't need to see the ocean to feel it's call, this magnetic pull that burrowed into the marrow of her bones, but seeing it made that feeling worse.

She distracted herself by taking in the layout of the office.

Bookshelves lined the left wall, rows of hardbound scientific journals with gold-embossed lettering occupying every shelf alongside sea creature knickknacks and family pictures. Not a speck of dust could be seen on any one of his books, but none of the spines were cracked.

A large tank rested against the right wall, filled with colorful fish, none of which lived remotely close to Maine. They were likely bought at a local pet supply store. An intern stood on a step stool to sprinkle fish food in through the top. The fish within swarmed, gobbling up every flake in an insatiable frenzy, but soon, they would go back to swimming in a leisurely circle around their tank. Round and around. Day after day for the rest of their short lives.

Did they know they were not free?

Lorelei tore her eyes away from the tank. She didn't have space in her brain to contemplate that. It hit too close to a sore spot.

When Phil hung up the phone, she greeted him amicably and placed the job role notes she drafted with Lila on his desk.

Sliding it closer, he murmured, "Let's see what we have here." He spared the page only a brief glance before leaning back in his cushy black leather office chair, hands steepled. There was more written on the page than his ten-second perusal could have adequately covered, but he wouldn't have so readily agreed to meet if he wasn't seriously considering her hiring request, right?

Her boss was in his late-forties, distinguishable by his shock of straight, straw-colored hair, watery blue eyes, and a thick layer of facial scruff that was quickly approaching beard territory. If he shared any genetic makeup with Carrie besides paler features, she couldn't tell. Their noses and cheekbones were distinctly theirs.

However, he seemed to share Carrie's flare for tailored fashion— from his crisp, creaseless shirts and rolled up sleeves down to his bespoke leather shoes from the Netherlands. On casual dress days he swapped out his solid ties and socks for ones with loud colors and silly patterns. Last week he wore a red tie with llamas on them and matching socks.

"It's funny that you wanted to talk about hiring someone today." Director Simmons had a slow, contemplative way of speaking, and a deceptively down-to-earth manner that made him easy to talk and listen to, but Lorelei couldn't be sure it was genuine. Sometimes he was *too* affable with employees, and she couldn't help but wonder if he ever used what he learned against them, whenever it suited. "It was something I wanted to discuss, as well. Aside from needing people to run the ticket counter and gift shop and take guests on tours, we need to hire someone to help you out. I've noticed the long hours you've been logging between your museum position and the lab. I talked to Dr. Branson about you dropping the lab work, but she said your help has been invaluable, and that they can't part with you. I guess that mermaid's taken a shine to you, and that's just something I've got to accept for now. I was thinking we hire someone who could handle promotions and customer service. Slap the title Assistant Museum Director on it. What do you think?"

That was exactly what she had said when she first entered his office, and while she didn't like how he casually claimed her and Lila's ideas, the fact that he seemed to be onboard with fulfilling her hiring ask eased some of the tension from her shoulders. She did not have the energy right now to fight over who got what credit for ideas. "That would be a great help."

The director studied her expression and leaned forward. "If there's something else bothering you, or something's unclear, you need to speak up. I can't help you if you don't."

That he noticed made Lorelei feel slightly better about his leadership. Sighing, she opened up a little about her struggles and doubts but framed it more as an honest plea for professional advice, not a sign that she was the wrong person for the job. "I've skipped a lot of rungs on the ladder. Last year, I was designing exhibits. This year, I'm trying to launch and run a new museum. I just want to make sure I'm meeting expectations."

Phil listened thoughtfully, those steepled fingers pressed to his lips.

When she finished, he said, "Run the museum how you want to run it. Don't think about what others in your position are doing. This isn't the Met. Will our museum be popular to tourists because of the mermaid research we're doing here? Yes. But you don't have to worry about curation too much. Dr. Branson's got that covered. She'll funnel whatever research we want to see reflected in the museum to you, and she's got people on her team that know how to handle artifacts and specimens and whatever. And I'm here to help you with the business side of things. I have to oversee it anyway. You're not going this alone, Ms. Roth. You've got the entire research center behind you. How about we schedule a planning meeting for next week to hammer out some of the specifics? And work out a bit of delegation?"

Lorelei's smile became a genuine one. Maybe her suspicion that he was a too-good-to-be-true boss was unfair and unfounded. "That would be great. Would you mind sending a note to Becki in HR that I will be coming by to see her about hiring staff for the museum? That way she knows you approved it."

Phil nodded, turning his computer screen toward himself. He began to type. "I've copied you on this so you can schedule a time to meet."

"Thank you so much."

The idea stealing had rubbed her wrong, but he didn't hesitate to offer advice and help, which she'd desperately needed.

As Lorelei left the director's office, her phone vibrated in her pocket from an incoming call. Checking the screen, she saw that it was her former boss and mentor, Susan Lennard, Director of the Marquette Maritime Museum in Michigan. Her heart leapt. If anyone could completely soothe her self-doubts, and turn this workday around, it was Susan. Lorelei was a frazzled, overstressed undergrad intern when they first began working together.

Their conversation lasted for hours, but Lorelei could justify every minute of it—her notebook filled with pages upon pages of notes. By the time 5:00 p.m. rolled around, and Lila swung by Lorelei's office to go get drinks together at an outdoor bar, her mental fog had cleared, and the sun peaked out from behind the clouds.

CHAPTER

SEVEN

KILLIAN

"I saw Carrie at the shooting range this morning." Branson leaned on one arm against the squat rack with a hand on his hip. The gym bustled all around them, busy with the evening crowd.

Taking a deep breath, Killian lowered into his last rep and held the squat for five long seconds. Carrie-anything was the last thing he wanted to be thinking about with two hundred and fifty pounds of weight digging into his shoulders. Exhaling, he rose, pushing past the burn, and offloaded the barbell with more clammer than he meant to. The woman at the lat pulldown machine beside them jumped.

"Sorry." He breathed heavily, taking a long slug of water.

The fellow gym-goer had earbuds in, but she acknowledged his apology with a nod.

Wiping the sweat off his forehead with the sleeve of his shirt, Killian shot Branson a dirty look and grumbled, "Why are you bringing this up?"

"Because it's concerning as hell."

Killian raised an eyebrow at him as they switched places. Branson settled his shoulders beneath the bar and pushed up, walking out to the middle of the rack before dipping down. "Why? This is Maine. We all shot BB guns as kids. Our dads took us hunting. Carrie knows her way around a gun."

Branson didn't answer right away. He finished the set first. When he put the barbell back, far more gently than Killian had, he answered breathlessly, "This wasn't a BB gun or hunting rifle she was shooting. She had a pistol. Why the hell would she need that?"

Carrie may have grown up here, but she was still a woman living alone in the northern wilds of Maine. It didn't strike Killian as odd that she might want it to protect herself. When he said as much to Branson, he shook his head. "She's been acting weird. Keeping to herself, unusually quiet on social media. Marci and Walt stopped by her house last month to bring a care package and her house was a wreck. They said she hadn't showered in days. Lila went over for a little girl time—was trying to be supportive, you know? Got the place cleaned up a bit, but Carrie was just out of it."

Killian scratched his head. "I'm sorry she's going through something. Is she... not adjusting well to being back?" He almost wasn't sure he wanted to ask. But he saw first-hand what depression could do to a person—first with his dad after his mom's death, and now with Lorelei —and he wouldn't wish that on anybody. Just because Carrie stomped all over his personal boundaries last year, didn't mean he wanted her to suffer. He wanted her to be happy. Just happy far away from him and the life he was building with Lorelei.

"No. It's not that." Branson edged closer and lowered his voice. "I think it has to do with the biting mishap. Lila said her dining room table was covered in articles and books about mermaids. I think that incident really shook her up, and she's fixating. Lila's been gently prodding her to see her therapist again, so I guess we'll see where that goes."

Recalling something Lorelei had texted on her lunch break, he said, "Maybe she did go. Lorelei mentioned she came by the research center earlier today. Walked around like she owned the place."

Branson reached past him to snag a cleaning wipe. As he wiped down the barbell, Killian slid off the plates, one by one. "Yeah, that sounds more like her. Maybe she's on an upswing, and I'm overthinking the gun thing."

"No, I see what you were saying. It's a valid concern. I'm glad you guys have been keeping an eye on her. Sounds like it's helping."

Branson nodded, meandering over to the leg press to work on his calves. He adjusted the footplate, but didn't sit down, distracted by something on his phone.

Seeing his own phone light up on top of where it rested on his gym bag, Killian hung back to look at the new text messages he got from Lorelei.

Something had changed over the course of the day.

Her regular updates kept him apprised of the emotional rollercoaster ride she was on at work, and more than once he almost called to beg her to take the rest of the day off and come home, particularly after the sharp dips in the early morning.

But after a long phone call with a former mentor, she seemed uplifted. Energized. All boosted by her girl's night with Lila this evening. She'd just needed some guidance. Tools to navigate unfamiliar waters.

Maybe she'd reconsider her ocean abstinence next.

He wouldn't push it though. Not today. She'd already put in enough emotional labor and deserved to enjoy her evening off to the fullest. Besides, he'd soon have some leverage to encourage her to swim again. Over his lunch break, he did more research on reputable fencing companies and scheduled a time for one to come out and survey their property.

If all went well, they could have a privacy fence up before the end of summer.

Killian studied the new messages Lorelei sent—a series of selfies of her with Lila at the bar, and one they must have gotten the bartender to take for them. It made his heart swell to see a genuine, easy-going smile on her face. There was a light in her eyes that had been absent for quite a long time. And the way the summer sunlight caught her auburn hair, and the sparkle of the ring he put on her finger, clasped around a dewy cocktail glass, did things below his waistline that made him grateful for the compression boxers he wore beneath his gym shorts.

He tapped out the word *'beautiful'* on his phone and sent it, followed by *'I can't believe I get to marry you.'*

A minute passed before three dots appeared on screen.

The next selfie was of just her. A sly, teasing grin crested her mouth, the collar of her blouse, two shades darker than the rosy color of her nipples, was pulled back to reveal the fine cut of her collarbone and sun-freckled skin. His ring on her finger still gleamed in the light. *'Say that to me again when we get home, future husband. And maybe help me unwind?'*

Fucking hell. He was going to have to cut this gym session short.

Clearing his throat, Killian picked up his gym bag. "I'm out," he told Branson.

"Okay, see you later, man." He clapped him on the back but didn't look up from his phone. Whatever it was put a goofy smile on his face.

Within the safety of his truck, Killian typed back, *'Dammit woman. You got me hard as a rock at the gym.'*

As soon as he got home, he made a b-line for the shower.

If it hadn't been months since he and Lorelei had last talked like this, stress being a supremely vicious libido killer, he wouldn't have dropped out midway through his workout routine to run home to jack off.

His erection hadn't gone down even a little on the drive home.

Stripping off his sweaty gym clothes, he turned on the hot water. As steam filled the bathroom, Killian gave himself a slow, tentative jerk, and checked whether Lorelei responded.

There was one message sent ten minutes ago. *Poor thing. Let me know when you're alone. I'll send you something ;)*

I'm alone.

Her response was immediate. *One minute.*

While waiting for her reply, Killian stepped into the shower, careful to keep his phone from getting wet. He laid it down on one of the outside corners and squeezed a generous amount of body wash into the palm of his hand.

His phone vibrated against the porcelain as he slathered soap all over his dick. With the hand not covered in soap, he swiped up on his phone screen to see the new picture she'd sent. A choked groan rumbled from the back of his throat. He leaned forward and pressed his forehead to the cold tile.

His soon-to-be wife was hot.

There were better, more poetic ways to describe Lorelei, but his downstairs brain was firing on all cylinders, and his upstairs brain couldn't give him more than a three-lettered word and caveman grunts.

She'd snuck away to the bathroom and unbuttoned her blouse to show him the lacy bra underneath, bursting bright with the color of ripe cranberries. Her grey slacks were unbuttoned, too, and half unzipped with one thumb hooked into the waistband of her black panties, teasing the soft, intimate stretch of skin below her navel.

The photo was accompanied with the text, *Any requests?*

Every inch of his skin tingled with anticipation.

'So beautiful. Let me see those lovely tits.'

She teased her cleavage with her ring finger in the next photo. *'They are right here.'* He growled. If she were somewhere in this house, he'd march his buck-naked ass right out of this shower, bend her over his knee, and spank her bottom pink for that wise remark. And oh, how it riled him up, seeing that band of gold featured in each shot. Lorelei must have known it, too.

Pull down the lace for me.

Though his flesh throbbed, he kept his strokes long and languid. Waiting for more was torturous, but he knew Lorelei would give it to him. Although they were in the middle of breaking a sexual drought right now, they'd learned a lot about each other's bodies in the months preceding. Hers burned hottest when he whispered filthy things in her ear.

For him, it was when she showed the parts of her that weren't human. But this ring flashing was coming in at a very, very close second.

His phone vibrated with another photo.

Lace shoved down, Lorelei cupped the underside of her breast and pushed up, one stiff, rosy peak pinched between finger and thumb. He imagined her claws were out, too, and her head tipped back mid-moan, wicked sharp teeth on display.

Lightning raced up the base of his spine.

Widening his stance, he fucked into his hand, slippery flesh gliding through palm, imagining he was pistoning into this dangerous sea goddess instead. He'd only taken her in full siren form once, and while he'd been quite nervous about it at the time, he longed to do it again.

Scales slid back at her front to reveal a pearly, petaled seam, smooth like the inside of a seashell and beaded with dewy pleasure. The feel of her was a little different. Inside, she was softer, plusher. Her swollen inner flesh ensconced him, creating a watertight seal that greedily milked every drop of his pleasure.

When he didn't respond right away, she messaged, *you like that don't you?*

Groaning, he typed out a simple *'yes,'* because 'I want to fuck your tail so bad and come to the sound of your siren song' was too wordy, and he wasn't about to drop his dick to type it.

What do I get in return?

Ah. Fair was fair. He slowed his rhythm but didn't stop.

Setting a timer on his camera, Killian propped his phone against a cluster of haircare bottles, so that the picture Lorelei got was of him braced against the shower wall, hot water streaming down his back, with soap-slicked shaft in hand. He may also have flexed his muscles taut. He worked too hard in the gym not to.

Fuck, Killian. I'm coming home now. Not getting myself off in a public bathroom.

You know where to find me.

It wouldn't take her long to get home. Although he could probably rub one out quick, he wanted to savor the pent-up energy between them. He washed the rest of himself and thoroughly rinsed off the obscene amount of soap on his dick, occasionally stroking it to keep himself keyed up.

He knew she was home when he heard the front door open and close. It was followed by hurried footsteps up the stairs and the sound of drawers opening and closing in their bedroom. His dick throbbed, precum beading at the tip. What the hell was she doing? It was taking forever, whatever it was, and his patience had worn out. He needed her bouncing up and down on his dick yesterday.

Yanking open the shower curtain, Killian stormed out of the bathroom and into their bedroom, not giving a shit that he left a trail of puddles. Lorelei yelped with surprise at the sight of him—a storm god swept in on a gale of male heat and virility, dripping water all over the floor. He caught her in her bra and panties, standing in front of the mirror, making utterly pointless adjustments. She was beautiful. And he was going to have her.

Without breaking his stride, Killian whisked Lorelei over his shoulder, and swiped the bottle of lube set out on the dresser. She squealed with surprise and delight as he carried her straight back into the shower with him. He set her down underneath the hot spray and fiercely ravaged her mouth, her tongue sweet from whatever fruity drinks she'd imbibed at the bar.

As her bra and panties got drenched, he roved his hands over every dip and swell of her body, pressing her mound against his aching flesh, shooting off red flares behind his eyes. Nothing but the feel of her sweet cunt could quell the tempest swirling within him. When he pushed up on her breasts, and squeezed them together, water pooled in the crease. He dipped down, laving that spot with his tongue, drinking, while fisting her panties so that they wedged in her pink seam and rubbed her clit.

Gasping, Lorelei jerked forward and grabbed his shoulders. He continued to tug at her panties, eliciting spasms and moans in equal measure. Rising, rising, rising, until she crashed with a sharp cry of pleasure.

He didn't know where the caveman strength came from, but he ripped off her panties, the sound of tearing fabric second only to Lorelei's aftershock moans, which he drank up with an open-mouthed kiss.

Her lacy bra went next, hitting the tub with a wet smack.

Breaking away from his voracious kiss, Lorelei's chest heaved. He took one rose pink nipple into his mouth and sucked, harder and harder, listening to her tell him how she finger-fucked herself the whole car ride home. An exploratory caress along her slippery, swollen entrance confirmed this, but he still applied a generous amount of lube to himself.

Hitching her leg over his hip, he dipped down, ignoring the burning muscles in his legs from squats at the gym, and slotted himself where they both needed him, groaning as he rocked himself to the root. Once fully seated, he hiked up her other leg, laid her back against the shower wall and thrust, peeling another sharp cry of pleasure from the both of them. She was so hot and swollen and her inner walls kept clenching all around him.

Her head lolled along the tiles, lips parted, eyes hooded. A drop of water clung desperately to her lower lip, wavering back and forth, as he bounced her. A thoroughly fucked expression—mindless to all but their acute shared pleasure.

Killian kissed away the drop. "I'm getting close," he said against her lips. Down fall of all the edging and months of abstinence.

"I'm going to need more after."

He rolled his hips. "You want more of this?"

She nipped at his lower lip with her teeth, then clamped her inner walls down around his dick. "Yes."

He came with a curse.

Water sluiced over flushed skin, and tensed muscle, and for a time, they did little more than clutch each other, chests heaving from their exertions. Once they caught their breath, lust's haze clearing, cheery, sated smiles erupted between them.

They'd so desperately needed this. He loved Lorelei, and nothing would ever change that, but he missed this sexual part of their relationship more than he could say.

Pressing their foreheads together, they shared a little laugh.

CHAPTER
EIGHT

LORELEI

EARLY THE NEXT MORNING, LORELEI SAT ACROSS FROM
Nireed in the mermaid observation room, ready to pick up where they
last left off on language lessons. "I'm sorry for not stopping by yesterday
morning. I just had a lot of personal stuff to deal with."

Nireed took a long sniff. "You were mating."

Lorelei choked on her coffee. "What?" she sputtered.

"I can smell your Two-Legger mate." Nireed waved a hand up and
down Lorelei's person.

Cheeks burning, Lorelei set down her coffee cup, so she didn't spill
it. "We weren't… I mean we did have…" Dammit. How did she explain
birth control to a mermaid?

Nireed shrugged. "I'm not mad."

Lorelei cleared her throat. "Anyway, moving on. Before we get started
with lessons, there was something I wanted to ask you." She told Nireed
about the merfolk that stormed Killian's boat, and how they gobbled up
most of the canned meat that was meant for the whole community. "I
thought some might be kin of yours, coming to look for you. Is there
some kind of message I can pass along to ease their worry?"

An emotion that looked strangely like guilt flashed across the siren's face. "Yes, Shorewalker. This sounds like my older sister, Aersila. She has challenged Undine many times. Undine sending me to shore would make her very angry. I did not say good-bye, so Aersila would not know it was my choice, too."

Was it really Nireed's choice? A gullible younger sister could easily be swayed by an authority figure, perhaps touting a romanticized picture of adventure, and the alluring promise of returning home a heroine of her people. But Nireed didn't really strike Lorelei as gullible, or like she went into this research situation with her eyes closed. Not after their last conversation. She had just seemed so young and vulnerable when they first met, but now Lorelei rather thought the siren wise beyond her years. And not someone to be trifled with.

"Teach your Two-Legger mate these signs. They should make Aersila stop." Nireed finger spelled E-M-E-R-A and opened her palm to make a waving motion with her hand like a fish's tail. Then she alternated clasping her hands one way and then another, finishing with her palms flat and separating them in a downwards motion.

Lorelei repeated the signs until she got each right. "What does it mean?"

"My family's name sign. And the sign for peace."

Touching her chin with her fingertips, Lorelei lowered her hand toward Nireed. More than usual, her knuckles were swollen and red. As Lorelei reached into her purse for lotion, Nireed pointed to the dry, cracking skin on her hands. "Shorewalker, when did you last swim?" Her tone was stern and...

Mothering?

Lorelei looked up in surprise. "I don't know. Sometime last year before we brought you to shore."

Nireed gaped. But the siren's reaction lasted for only a moment before it sharpened into anger. "Why?" she hissed, slapping the tabletop beside them. Lorelei jumped in her seat and watched as Nireed signed along with her next words. "What I would give to...Why would you do this?" The siren threw up her hands in frustration and gestured emphatically to the ocean just a wall and rocky shore away.

Lorelei stammered, "Well, I..." She wrung her hands, unsure how to tell the siren how wrong and selfish and dangerous it would be for her to do so.

Narrowing her eyes, Nireed leaned forward, so close their noses almost touched. Lorelei froze. This had never happened before, but some siren instinct told her it wasn't a threat, but rather a demand that she listen, and listen closely, because what was said next was important. The passing of old wisdom or a harsh truth.

"You are killing yourself with guilt." Nireed enunciated slowly and clearly. Each word smacked Lorelei's face with the gust of warm breath —fishy and steeped in ocean brine and just a hint of medicinal from the cough drops she'd eaten earlier. To a human, it would be repulsive, but, to Lorelei, it reminded her of home.

She squeezed her eyes shut, unable to take the siren's piercing gaze any longer.

Grasping her roughly by the chin, Nireed growled. "Look at me, Shorewalker." Lorelei's eyes snapped open, tears escaping down her cheeks. "You are no good to me dead."

"It's unpleasant, but it's not killing me..."

Letting her go, Nireed made the sign for lungs. "They will go next. And you will choke on air. There are stories about this, passed down to us by our foremothers, of those that go to shore and don't come back."

Lorelei sat back in her chair, touching her fingers to her throat. Memory of Nireed's rasping coughs echoed. Was the next step respiratory failure? "Are we killing you?"

Folding her arms across her chest, Nireed sat back, as well, with a stubborn expression. "Not yet."

"Will you tell me if it gets bad?"

"Yes. It is best for all that I live."

Examining Nireed's pale grey complexion, Lorelei decided that waiting until Nireed got bad was far too late. She picked up her phone and texted Lila that she needed help organizing a field trip.

CHAPTER
NINE

KILLIAN

REMOVING THE TARP FROM HIS GRILL, KILLIAN WHEELED IT out into the yard. The family group chat was blowing up with plans for a spontaneous cookout at his place—a cover for the last-minute mermaid swim at his private beach. He didn't mind one bit. While he was nervous about having a strange siren near his home and the people he loved, it was great news for Lorelei. The wretched state of her tail must have been a wake-up call. And one she sorely needed.

Retrieving a plastic fold out picnic table from the barn, Killian marveled at how quickly Walsh, Marci, Lila, and Branson all jumped in on the plan—to give Lorelei some peace of mind as her eyes and ears on land. It wasn't that it surprised him, but rather how fate deemed him lucky enough to have them.

Marci and Walsh arrived first with enough homemade mac n' cheese and potato salad to feed an army. He brushed off his hands and ushered them inside. "You didn't have to bring anything."

"Nonsense." Marci slid off her wicker sandals by the doorway and padded across the room to the kitchen, long dress swishing about brown ankles in alternate vertical lines of gold, orange, red, and blue. She must have just had her twists redone, because the last time he'd seen her, she was wearing her hair proudly in its natural halo. Marci placed a large cellophane-wrapped glass bowl on the counter, followed by Walsh with the baking dish. "What kind of guests would we be if we showed up empty-handed to a cook-out?"

Killian rubbed the back of his neck. "True, but a last minute one?"

Rifling through the utensil drawer for serving spoons, Marci glanced over her shoulder at him with an arched brow. "Manners are manners."

"Don't worry, son." Walsh clapped Killian on the shoulder. "She was already working on it this morning before we got Lila's text. I think she was planning on sending some over for all you kids. It's just what moms do."

"All right, all right. Thank you. Can I get you something to drink? A beer? Lemonade? Iced tea?"

"Lemonade. Gotta have my wits about me."

Wasn't that the truth? While Killian trusted Lorelei's judgement, and the hunger-curbing powers of canned pork, none of them could predict what Nireed would do once she got one whiff of that potent cocktail of real human flesh and salty sea air. An even darker, wheedling thought ate at the back of his mind. Lorelei hadn't felt the ocean's touch in almost a year. At least, Nireed had seawater piped into her tank. What if it wasn't Nireed they had to worry about? But Lorelei?

Killian broke out his noise cancellation headset just in-case and texted Branson to bring more from the boat. Compulsion they had a solution for already. But the rest...He really didn't want to know what he would do if Lorelei attacked their family.

Branson arrived next. He exited his truck a ball of nervous energy, his hands shaking as he withdrew a box filled with headsets from the backseat.

Killian took the box from him and set it on the picnic table. "You okay?"

Branson swiped his hands through his shoulder-length hair, down from its usual ponytail, before stuffing them into his front pockets. Killian hadn't seen his friend quite this worked up before. "I'm worried man. I know Lila's been working with Nireed all this time, and it's been mostly fine, and it's probably going to be all right now, too. But sometimes I have to protect her from that big, beautiful scientist brain of hers, you know? She sees something that fascinates her, and she just has to touch it. She forgets that it can bite her. Or... eat her. Those wheels are turning in full force now. She wants to see what reintroducing Nireed to the 'wild' is going to be like, and all this 'behavioral' stuff with Lorelei...and I just..." He was talking a mile a minute, but he paused, pulling his hands from his pockets. He clenched them like he wanted shake sense into the situation. Or Lila. "That's my wife, Killian. My mother-in-law, my father-in-law." He gestured to Killian next. "My best friend. What if something happens?"

Killian slumped against the side of Branson's truck and crossed his arms in front of his chest. He glanced at the cottage where Marci and Walsh were still inside, prepping ribs and chicken to go on the grill. "I know," he answered quietly. His gaze fell to his steel-toed boots. "I was just thinking that, too."

Their phones dinged at the same time.

Killian pulled out his and read out loud the text Lorelei sent to the group chat. "We've gorged ourselves on more canned meat than I care to admit and have spent the last ten minutes huffing vinegar. Can't smell a thing. We're on our way over."

Silence hung in the air between them.

"Should I tell her to abort?" His thumb hovered over the screen.

Branson pinched the bridge of his nose. "No. Let them come. They've prepared. And I..." His shoulders slumped. He motioned for Killian to follow him around to the back of his truck. "I might have brought a contingency plan. Don't be pissed."

Mind racing, Killian followed. Branson dropped the tailgate and hopped up, pulling a blue tarp off a long, narrow black box. Cold dread snaked its way down Killian's spine, and he clenched his fists. Branson opened the case. "It's a tranquilizer gun," he explained, pulling out one of the darts. "Nothing strong. Just enough to daze them... if they lose control."

Killian folded his arms on top the side of the truck bed and buried his face in the open space. He exhaled. "Jesus, Will. I thought you were about to show me a fucking sniper rifle."

There was a long pause. "What kind of monster do you think I am?"

Killian looked up. His best friend looked startled. "What else was I supposed to think? How long have you had that thing?"

Branson lifted it out of its case. "Since a bunch of people-eating mermaids climbed onto our boat."

Killian rubbed a hand over his scruff. He had to hand it to him. A tranquilizer gun was far more humane than the pistol he carried on offshore runs. Why hadn't he thought of that? He was about to tell Branson he was a genius, when the man opened his trap again.

"Do I have your blessing to shoot your fiancée if she tries to eat me?"

"Give me that." He swiped the gun out of Branson's hands. "If anyone's shooting Lorelei with a tranquilizer, it's me." He held out his hand for the darts.

Branson handed them over but said in a dead serious tone. "You say that now. But when you have that thing in your hands, and you're staring down the barrel at your future wife, you might feel very differently about that. And that's okay. It shouldn't be easy. I just want you to know that I'm there for you if you need me, okay?"

Killian nodded curtly. He loaded the gun, and when his friend wasn't looking, hid it behind the grill.

HE'D JUST GOT THE GRILL GOING WHEN LORELEI AND LILA arrived, helping Nireed out of the car. The siren clutched her stomach, looking rather green about the gills. Her nauseous fish out-of-water look was punctuated by all her head tilting and swiveling.

The motions reminded Killian of a cat—scoping out its surroundings, always on alert. She'd been dressed in a navy-blue sweatsuit with the Haven Cove Marine Research Center's logo printed in white on the chest and pants pocket. On her feet were Lorelei's gym shoes.

Wobbly-legged like a newborn deer, Nireed needed Lorelei and Lila's help walking up the driveway and into the yard. They each took her by an elbow. Seeing the siren like that, queasy from the car ride and still learning how to walk, it was hard to think of her as threatening.

The mermaid brightened at the sight of the ocean.

A tear rolled down her cheek as she signed, "Thank you, Shorewalker." Lorelei had showed it to him, absolutely thrilled to have her own name sign. Above the waves and below them, name signs were a gift from the Deaf community, and apparently, the mermaid one, too. They had to be given.

While Lila reintroduced Nireed to the family, Lorelei bumped Killian's hip with her own. A nervous smile tugged at her lips. "It's too soon to say for sure, but I think things are looking up." She sounded so hopeful.

He caught himself glancing at the spot where he stashed the tranquilizer gun. He hated hiding it from her. And the thought that he might have to use it on her... that killed him. But he had to protect her from herself. And he had to protect the others.

He could tell her that. But he didn't want to ruin this moment for her or make her feel like he didn't trust her. It would all be fine. It was just a precaution. These were extenuating circumstances. Nothing bad was going to happen, and she would never have to know.

Jesus. If they ever had to go to couples therapy...

"Hey." She touched his arm, pulling him out of his head. "I lost you there for a second."

He looked at her. Those beautiful green eyes, too bright to be human, reminded him of sea glass and home. Her mismatched eyebrows furrowed with worry, the arched one on the right emphasizing her unasked question. Killian swiped a little bit of potted meat from the corner of her mouth with his thumb.

She blushed. The question forgotten. "We had a little snack before our drive over."

He chuckled, brushing his hand off on his jeans. "You ready?"

"I'm kind of scared. It's been so long... I don't know what to expect."

He rubbed her shoulders, squashing down every urge to tell her the truth. "You won't be alone. You'll have Nireed in the water with you, and us right here on land."

CHAPTER
TEN

LORELEI

THE FAMILY TURNED AWAY WHILE LORELEI AND NIREED
stripped down at the water's edge. Every nerve-ending in Lorelei's body
was alight, an electric current surging through her. The ocean pulled and
pulled and pulled. And now she could finally say, 'yes.' At long last.

"You shake, Shorewalker."

A stupid smile plastered itself on her face as she shucked off the last
of her clothes and buried her toes in the wet sand. The tide rolled over
her feet, and sweet Jesus, it felt like heaven. She barely suppressed a
groan. "This might be so stupid and selfish, Nireed, but I am so damn
happy right now. I denied myself this for so long. And it's not just that. I
never really considered the possibility that I might swim with another
mermaid as a... friend." She almost hadn't said it, but the word hung in
her mouth, too heavy to swallow. She let the truth spill to be scrutinized
and rejected. She didn't deserve it, but she was beginning to think of
Nireed as a friend.

Nireed struggled with the elastic hems of her pants legs, but she
collapsed into the sand, and managed to tug her feet free. "You have not
felt ocean's true touch for just as long as I." She huffed, tossing the

sweatpants comically far, far away from her. At least, as far as physics would allow. She stayed there for a moment, staring out over the water, with her arms draped over her legs. Lorelei recognized the look. A moment of contemplation.

When it passed, Nireed looked up at Lorelei and held out her hand. Lorelei pulled her up.

Brushing sand off her backside, Nireed said, "You were punishing yourself."

Lorelei bit her lower lip and nodded. "I suppose I was."

"Do not return to shore with your guilt. We are friends, Lorelei." Nireed bowed her head and placed a closed fist to her chest, directly over her heart. This meant more than just forgiveness. It was respect and genuine caring.

Tears misting her eyes, Lorelei repeated the gesture. Then Nireed took her hand, and they entered the waves together.

SALT SHOULD HAVE BURNED THE OPEN WOUNDS ON Lorelei's tail, and the dry, split skin of her knuckles, but it was a soothing balm. The ocean welcomed its daughter back into its gentle, healing embrace. Already, new scales peeked through, filling in the patches of exposed flesh, and pushing out old, washed-out scales. While her gums and nail beds were sore from disuse when tooth and claw pushed through, the discomfort was brief and quickly forgotten. The ache in her bones eased, and she felt stronger. More alive.

Nireed swam circles around Lorelei, twisting and twirling, waiting for her transformation to complete. Her eyes flashed yellow as a grin spread across her face from ear to ear. Where Lorelei once would have seen sharp teeth and a wicked mouth designed to rip and tear, she now saw joy.

Lorelei tested out her fins, rotating them from side to side. They weren't new, but they felt new. She felt new. With a sharp snap, Lorelei shot through the water. Banking hard to the right, she spiraled down to the sea floor. As she ran her fingers through the sand, her eyes stung.

She couldn't believe she was back. When she woke up this morning, this wasn't even a possibility. Not one she would have allowed herself.

A half laugh, half sob escaped her lips, bubbling up in front of her. She would never stay away so long again. Clawed fingers clasped her shoulder. Lorelei looked up. The siren's brown hair billowed around her in a dark halo, and the grey pallor that had set in from months in captivity was gone, her healthy, pearlescent sheen restored.

Lorelei showed Nireed all her favorite spots along the cove. They even swam out to the sea cave Lorelei found last year, still unoccupied by other creatures. And a rarity according to Lila. The Gulf of Maine didn't really have those. Wrong type of rock. Sea caves were formed from limestone, and the gulf was filled with granite, shale, and schist.

Nireed's marveling accentuated that fact; she explored every bit of it and signed to Lorelei that her pod had never seen such a thing as this.

Lorelei used her hands to reply. "What is your home like?"

The siren smiled wistfully. Her hands swished gracefully in the water, a language in motion as beautiful as dance. "After Two-Legger friend finds cure, I will take you."

Overwhelmed by the promise, Lorelei placed her hand over her heart and inclined her head, but she didn't accept the offer outright. To enter deep into merfolk territory with only one ally, would be risky. And not just that. Lorelei wasn't sure she wanted to enter the home of those who ate her crewmates last year. While they had done it under the compulsion of a hunger they could not control—a hunger that ruled them—she wasn't quite at peace yet with what happened. Especially not with the one-year anniversary looming on the horizon.

In just one short month, it would be a year since *The Osprey* sank and mermaids devoured its crew. It was too much, too soon. Lorelei wasn't even sure how she'd handle that date on land.

Something sour and dank clouded the water, thick as an oil spill, making it almost impossible to breathe. Clasping her throat, just beneath her gills, Lorelei gagged, her bioluminescence sparkling frantically.

Nireed darted over. Wrapping an arm around her shoulders, she leaned in and blew bubbles against her gills, a soothing, slightly tickling gesture. While the unpleasant scent didn't go away, Lorelei could breathe a little bit better.

The siren coaxed her out of the cave, where the water was immediately less pungent.

"You're okay, Shorewalker. Just sad."

Oh.

Grief had a scent.

"I show you how to sing, and then we go back to shore." Nireed took Lorelei's hands and placed them on her throat, then placed her own on Lorelei's.

Song rumbled from within, an eerie, haunting melody that vibrated against Lorelei's fingers and down the lengths of her arms. She felt it so keenly, reverberating throughout her body, that matching her own voice to it was easy. Sound erupted from her throat clearer, crisper than ever before. Less dissonant, more fluid and relaxed.

Nireed nodded her approval.

They swam back to Killian's private cove, and as they neared shore, they heard raised voices above the surface. Lorelei grasped Nireed by the elbow and ducked behind a cluster of rocks. Motioning to Nireed to stay hidden, she peeked her head above the surface and looked around.

Killian and the others were clustered together outside the cottage, arguing with someone by the parked cars. When that person got in Lila's face, and started pointing, Lorelei's hackles raised. Nireed hissed quietly beside her. She couldn't see what was going on, but evidently the water was a conduit for their moods.

From their hiding spot, they were about a hundred yards from the beach, so even with her siren eyes, Lorelei had to squint to make out the intruder's facial features. It was a woman. Straight, light brown hair, boutique clothes... She dug her claws into the rock, scraping deep crevices into the surface.

"Follow me," Lorelei commanded.

Nireed didn't even blink.

They slipped quietly out of the water and into the woods.

CHAPTER
ELEVEN

KILLIAN

AFTER PUTTING THE RIBS ON THE GRILL, KILLIAN SAT DOWN with the rest of the group at the picnic table. Lila tucked into a bowl of potato salad, too hungry to wait for the rest of the food. Walsh pulled a handkerchief from his pants pocket and mopped his forehead. The others sipped cool drinks. While the sea breeze took the edge off the August heat, coastal Maine temperatures still reached into the high 80s.

"So how did you two do it?" Walsh asked. "Get Nireed out without anybody putting up a fuss."

Lila stabbed a potato chunk with her fork. "It was simple really. Just had to play it cool and act with authority. I sent the folks from my lab home a little early, got Nireed clothes from the gift shop, and just walked her out the front door. No one batted an eye. I did leave a note though for any folks who might come by and find the tank empty. I wrote that she needed a mental health break from all the tests and confined quarters, and that I took her out for a bit of fresh air."

Walsh's brow was pinched with worry. "You gonna get in trouble for doing that?"

She gestured to her phone on the table with her fork. It laid face up, so Killian could see all the new notifications popping up—one after another, after another. There wasn't enough space between them to let the screen go dark, but she'd silenced her phone, so it wasn't constantly dinging. "Judging by the millions of phone calls and texts I've been getting? Big trouble." She paused and looked out to the ocean. "But it's worth it. Nireed needed this. They both did. So, believe me when I say I will sleep like a baby tonight."

Marci rubbed Lila's back, speaking slowly and gently. "Could you lose your job over this?"

She shook her head. "I don't think so. Nireed's not an animal. For Christ's sake, she signed consent papers, so I am standing on the ethical high ground in this scenario." Lila sighed. She stabbed through another potato, striking the bottom of her bowl with a *cling*. "But after seeing how they're reacting to today's little field trip, that was probably more to humor me. I have a terrible feeling this will be the first and last time we get away with this."

Killian leaned forward. "Do you think they'll ever let her leave? When the study is done, and you've found a virophage that works?"

Shoulders slumping, Lila stirred her potato salad around. She suddenly looked so very tired, like the question had sapped all the energy out of her. "You see the thing about biology—and about a new species especially—is the specimen is studied for its entire lifecycle. If I can't convince my bosses to be decent human beings, and follow ethical code, they'll keep her until she dies, Killian."

He swore.

"That's fucked up, babe," Branson chimed in.

"Well, we can't let that happen. What do we do?"

"We've got plan A and plan B. Plan A is I gather evidence of mistreatment and breach of ethical code and file a case against them. However, even with the signed consent papers, our legal system doesn't include mermaids. The research center might be able to sweep it all under the rug."

"What's Plan B?"

"Plan B is we plan a jailbreak."

Branson folded his hands on top of the picnic table. "What if we just don't send Nireed back to the research center tonight?"

Walsh shook his head. "Lila still needs Nireed to develop the virophage, remember? There's a whole community of merfolk out there who need that treatment. And a whole lot of people who might get eaten if we don't get it to them."

"Oh right. How close is your team to one?"

Lila sucked her teeth. "It's hard to say. Usually virophages take years to develop, but this is a viral disease very much like marine morbillivirus and rabies, minus the fatal-to-its-host bit, so that gave our epidemiologists a head start. The last serum damaged the virus, so that's promising. But even when we develop an effective virophage, there's another question we got to answer. How long after Nireed stops having cravings do we still keep her at the research center for observation?"

Pushing away her bowl with a sigh, Lila leaned into her mother and placed her head on her shoulder. Marci wrapped her arms around her and rested her cheek on top of her tight curls. "I wish I had a good answer," Lila continued, "but I think it's going to depend on how much her mental and physical health can take."

Marci hugged her daughter tighter. "If the research center gives you grief, honey, you let me know. Your father and I can write letters, make phone calls, and whatever else we can do to make sure your complaint gets heard."

"Same here," Killian added. "And I'm sure Jackie would be eager to help. She's been chomping at the bit for another exposé. But in the meantime, can I get you some ice cream?"

Lila immediately perked up.

KILLIAN HAD JUST PULLED THE RIBS OFF THE GRILL, AND was wiping off his hands with a towel, when he heard another car coming up his driveway. Everyone got up from the picnic table to see who it was. "If it's a tourist, I call 'not-it' on giving directions,"

Branson joked, sweeping his long dishwater blonde hair into a low ponytail.

But when the car came into view, Killian saw red. With a hard snap of his arm, he threw the towel down on the table. What he really wanted to do was punch something. "Oh, you've got to be fucking kidding me."

"It's like she has as sixth sense or something." Branson scratched his head, more amazed then upset. "Like mermaid radar." He nudged Lila with his elbow. "Is that possible?"

She rolled her eyes. "No. That's ridiculous."

Walsh wrung his hands. "Do you think she'll notice their clothes down by the water? Should one of us go down and move them?"

"It's Carrie. Of course, she'll notice."

"I'm on it." Marci hurried down the beach. She scooped up the clothes, and promptly chucked them into the forest before hurrying back.

They gathered at the top of the driveway, forming a line between the meddlesome Carrie Prior and the private cove where Lorelei and Nireed swam. Carrie parked her car behind the others, closer to the forest than his cottage, and exited with the car still running. Dressed in a fitted red suit, it looked like she'd just stepped out of an office in New York City.

She slammed the passenger door and marched right up to Killian. "Where's the mermaid? Where's Lorelei?" There was a crazed look in her eye, and she kept touching her right hip, like she thought she might rest her hand there. Or pull out her phone. But she never did, which Killian found odd.

Lila crossed her arms. "Carrie, what the hell are you talking about?"

Sidestepping, Carrie pointed a finger in Lila's face. "Don't pretend with me. I saw you in the parking lot at the research center."

Marci placed her hands around Lila's shoulders, her tone low, but hard. "You need to calm down, child. And get your finger out of my daughter's face."

"Carrie," Will growled, "I don't care that we're family. Touch my wife, and you're shark bait."

Carrie flashed them both a dirty look but dropped her hand.

Frowning, Walsh stepped between them and motioned with his

hands for her to back up. "All right now, take a few steps back and take a deep breath. You've got yourself all worked up. You're not going to resolve anything like this. And Will, take it easy on the theatrics."

Carrie glared at them all, angry tears glistening in her eyes, but she did take a couple steps back. "I don't know why you're sticking up for them. They're liars."

"What makes you say that?"

She lifted her chin with a haughty expression that made Killian's blood boil. If he didn't need to hear her answer, to know what went wrong, what she had seen or heard, and what she was planning to do about it, he would have just told her to leave and not bother with explaining herself.

"I was at the research center. I'd just gotten out of an interview, and was heading back to my car, when I saw Lila, Lorelei, and that mermaid drive off together." She pointed to Lorelei's car and then Lila. "Here's the car. There's Lila." She said it in this annoying, dramatic tone like she was building up to a grand revelation, a mystery solved, a conspiracy proven, but was giving them one last chance to fess up before she dropped the answer like a ton of bricks. "Where's the mermaid? And where's Lori?"

The group simultaneously exchanged incredulous looks. "Lori?"

She did another waist touch. "What's wrong with you people? How are you not taking this seriously? They broke a flesh-eating mermaid out of the research center. And Lori. There's something not right with her. Last year, with my leg..." She kept droning on and on. Red hair this. Green eyes that. The insinuation should have troubled Killian more, but he was distracted.

Out of the corner of his eye, he saw movement in the trees—a flash of pale skin. When he turned to look, Lorelei's gleaming, predatory gaze stared back at him from the dark shadows of the wood, her sea-drenched hair draped down her front.

As she began to move her lips, he heard his ex's name whispered on the wind, each syllable long and drawn out. *Carrie. Carrie.*

Come into the woods, Carrie.

His ex rubbed her ears. "Who said that?" She took a stumbling step backward. And then another and another, reeled in by Lorelei's song until she backed all the way up to the tree line. She tilted and shook her head like her ears had become waterlogged.

Lorelei appeared behind Carrie, green eyes glowing bright over her shoulder, a wicked grin revealing two rows of razor-sharp teeth. Killian hadn't even seen her move. Staring at the reflection in the window of the nearest car, Carrie opened her mouth to scream. No sound came out, but she reached for her hip...

Eerie crooning filled the air. A wordless song as old as the seas, passed down from siren to siren. Lorelei barely moved her mouth, but he saw the muscles working in her throat. Carrie dropped her hand.

Everyone else reached for their noise cancellation headsets. Once Killian's sat snug over his ears, he checked theirs. All secure. He'd learned his lesson after the incident with Ian.

When Killian turned back to Lorelei, she held his gaze for one long moment before glancing down at Carrie's hip. It was hard to tell, but he thought he might see the faint outline of her phone. Could Carrie be recording all this?

Yanking Carrie's head back by the hair, Lorelei ran a long talon down the woman's throat. Carrie jerked once before freezing entirely. Not even a tremor. The most she could do was blink. "You were told not to come back here. But you didn't listen, did you?"

Nireed flanked from the other side. Killian had forgotten about her. Nostrils flaring wide, the siren audibly sniffed Carrie's hair. "Trespasser," she hissed.

"You've an obsession, Carrie," Lorelei crooned into her ear. "You did more than just come here for answers, didn't you?"

The comms system crackled with static. "Killian, where did you hide it?"

"Hide what? What's he talking about?" Lila's voice was a mix of panic and suspicion.

"It's a rouse," Killian answered Branson.

"What?"

Lorelei met Killian's eye as she slid a hand underneath the hem of Carrie's blazer.

And removed a concealed gun.

Tears streamed down Carrie's face. She mouthed, "I'm so sorry."

Killian took off his headset.

One by one, the rest of the group did, too, none saying a word. They were all too shocked. Pointing the gun down, Lorelei held it out for Killian to take. He took it, checked the safety—Christ, that woman was carrying it around with it off—and promptly unloaded it.

A near soundless choked sob escaped Carrie's lips, followed by a litany of apologies. Was she truly sorry? Or only sorry that she got caught? To bring a loaded gun around family, to even consider shooting Lorelei and Nireed...

Gaze hardening to flint, Lorelei swiped her tongue up the side of Carrie's neck. "Go before the wicked sea witch eats you."

A shiver ran down Killian's spine. But not from fear. *That's my wicked sea witch,* he thought, swelling with pride, and something else. The growing tightness in his groin was a surprising revelation he'd have to examine later.

Carrie stumbled back to her car, her movements stiff and jerking. She wouldn't meet any of them in the eye. Shame and regret lived right beside her fear.

Snaking an arm around the tree beside her, Lorelei dug her claws into the bark, splintering the wood. She didn't blink once, tracking Carrie's return to her car with a predator's focus. As a strong gust of wind blew off the sea, swaying the boughs of pine around her, Lorelei's eyes flashed green bioluminescence. Her lips moved, but the words that spilled out were disembodied. Whispered on the wind. "Forget what I am, Carrie Prior. And never come back here. Never speak of this."

Despite the summer heat, the hair on Killian's arms raised in prickled gooseflesh.

CHAPTER

TWELVE

LORELEI

"Lorelei, what in God's name was all that?"

Wringing seawater out her hair, Lorelei noted Walt's trembling hands. Marci seemed shaken, as well, but Lila was murmuring something in her ear that she was paying close attention to.

"I'm sorry you had to see that." Lorelei's cheeks burned. "Are you okay? Did Carrie hurt anyone?"

"She didn't get past yelling and pointing, thankfully," Will answered, swiping a shaky palm over his face. Aside from Killian, who'd run inside to get towels, he was the only one meeting her eyes right now.

The Walshes had never seen her in full predator mode, and if she could have had it her way, they never would have seen that side of her. She didn't even have a chance to warn them. There hadn't been time. While Carrie was gesturing angrily, her blazer lifted just enough for Lorelei to see the concealed gun she carried at her hip.

And the way she kept touching that gun through her blazer while yelling her suspicions that Lorelei was the flesh-eating mermaid who bit her, and had let loose another, screaming that she and Nireed were a danger to them all, and doing so much too close to family...

It ignited all Lorelei's protective instincts.

The siren blood coursing through her veins demanded that she rip apart the enemy that had trespassed into her home and threatened her family and kin. But she tempered that desire, choosing intimidation instead. The downfall was it wasn't just Carrie she'd frightened.

Killian strode out of the cottage with two fluffy bath towels.

Though his eyes were kind, there was a rigid set to his jaw that highlighted the tension in the group. If anyone had a read on how bad she messed up, it was him.

With shaking hands, Lorelei took a towel and used it to pat down her clothes. She'd found them with Nireed's in the woods when they climbed out of the water. Someone had chucked them in. Judging by the floral scent left on the fabric, Lorelei guessed it was Marci.

Killian offered the other towel to Nireed, but she declined.

Glancing between the group and Lorelei, the siren asked, "Two-Leggers do not defend territory?" Species differences aside, she knew how to read a room.

"Was that what was happening?" Walt crossed his arms in front of himself, wary. "Just some animal instinct kicking into overdrive?"

Animal instinct.

That stung. Walt was the closest she'd ever had to a father, and now he could barely look at her. It would be easy to blame her behavior on "animal" instinct, something he could understand and explain away as beyond her control. But Lorelei wasn't an animal. None of the sirens were. And she hadn't lost control.

Losing control was allowing compounding guilt and work stress eat her from the inside out, eroding her physical and mental health to a breaking point.

Lorelei stalked and attacked Carrie with a clear head, and she did not feel an ounce of remorse for the act itself. Rather, she thrilled at the power her siren song gave her—stopping that dreadful woman in her tracks and feeling every hapless struggle and twitch within her grasp. Eliciting that sweet, intoxicating fear was a delight.

All Lorelei regretted was that it had affected the Walshes, too.

"I had to distract her," Lorelei answered, wrapping herself in the bath towel. "She had a gun. And she kept reaching for it, which means she was thinking about using it."

Marci's gaze zeroed in on her with laser focus, making her squirm under the scrutiny. "Why did you lick her?"

Because I liked scaring her. Because the part of me that isn't human is fierce and vicious, and the part of me that is human loves the power rush.

"I dunno," Branson shrugged, a little less shaky now with his thumbs tucked through his belt loops. "I thought it was all kinda badass, you know, once I knew we weren't gonna be eaten."

Hands flying to her hips, Marci wheeled on him. "William Thomas Branson, that was your cousin!"

"Oh, right. I forgot. Lorelei, next time eat her, so I don't have to put up with her anymore at family reunions."

"William!"

"What?"

The Walshes no longer stared at her with fear and disappointment, turning all their attention to Branson instead to scold him for his insensitivity. Lorelei could have hugged him. She wasn't the one who brought a gun to a cookout.

While they were distracted, Lila snuck over and whispered, "I think we should get Nireed back now."

Just when she thought she couldn't feel more like garbage. Maybe if she'd shown a little more restraint in the Carrie-situation, Nireed could have had more time to spend in the water. They wouldn't have to whisk her away from all the family drama.

Slipping an arm around her shoulders and squeezing, Killian said, "Branson and I've got this."

She slumped against his side. "Are you upset with me, too?"

He leaned in, warm breath caressing her ear. "I'm something but not mad. Far from it." The words, rough and rasping, scraped like sand on skin—burned like swallowed seawater—drowned with a deep, primal yearning. She looked up, startled by the tempest swirling in his eyes. His gaze fell to her lips. "Hurry back, okay?"

CHAPTER
THIRTEEN

LORELEI

AFTER HOURS, THE HAVEN COVE MARINE RESEARCH CENTER should have been dark and quiet. But the whole building shone with florescent light. Past the front entrance glass doors, Lorelei saw a security detail waiting for them—six stocky men standing in front of the reception desk with grim expressions and noise cancellation headsets covering their ears.

Lila clenched her jaw as she slipped out the back passenger door. Though she stood tall with her head held high, her hand shook opening Nireed's door. This little field trip would cost her.

Groggy and nauseous, Nireed exited the car with a moan. She stumbled across the asphalt and caught herself against a nearby light pole, taking in deep lungs' full of air. Before they left Killian's, Lorelei had given the siren a dose of Dramamine, and Lila her front seat, but it hadn't been enough.

Lorelei held back the siren's hair as she began to heave.

When the worst of the sickness passed, Nireed sighed with relief, swiping the back of her hand across her mouth. "I feel better now."

"I'm sorry you had to experience that." Lorelei removed a spare hair tie from her wrist and pulled the dark strands of Nireed's hair, sticky with sea salt, into a hasty three-strand braid. "Motion sickness happens fairly often with humans, too."

Nireed side-eyed the car. "It is awful. Why do Two-Leggers torture themselves this way?"

Despite the gravity of their situation, Lorelei couldn't help but smile a little at that. "It allows us to travel further, faster."

Nireed grimaced, but she kept her opinion on the matter to herself.

Lila was unusually quiet.

As they strode across the parking lot, Lorelei took her hand. The marine biologist met her eye and relaxed her jaw a bit. Raw emotions—fear, anger—churned in that look, but were restrained by grim determination. Lorelei squeezed. Whatever came next, they would face it together.

Jittery with nerves, Lorelei steeled her spine and her expression, and opened the front door. Security swarmed them the moment they all stepped inside.

One of the security guards reached for Nireed. No sooner did his fingers close around her upper arm, did the siren rip it out of his grasp. "Don't touch me Two-Legger," she spat. "I can walk." Sparing a glance in Lorelei and Lila's direction, her fierce expression briefly softened as she signed, "Thank you."

The guard reached for her again, but she flinched away and hissed a warning. He jerked his thumb in the direction of the aquarium. "Move it."

Nireed sneered but marched down the cold tile hallway, her chin high and proud. Four of the six guards trailed behind her at a distance. The siren's confidence almost made them look more like a celebrity's security entourage, rather than guards taking her back to a watery prison.

Lorelei took a step to follow, but one of the remaining guards stiff-armed her. He removed his headset. "You need to leave, Miss," he said firmly. "But you, Dr. Branson, need to come with us. Director Simmons would like to speak to you in his office."

Tapping the employee badge hanging from her blazer lapel, Lorelei reminded them, "I work here, too. I'm going with Dr. Branson." She was not going to let Lila face whatever repercussions awaited alone, even if she had to compel the guards to let her pass.

The guard looked to the ceiling as if a higher power would give him strength. "Fine," he grumbled. Under his breath, he added, "I don't get paid enough for this shit."

Security escorted them both to Phil's office.

The director paced in front of his desk, wearing his usual uniform of tailored dress shirt, slacks, and bespoke shoes, with a glass of amber liquid in his hand. Scotch maybe. He paused when he saw them, and if the color of his cheeks weren't rising to a ruddy red, she might have chuckled at his tie—the thing was designed to look like he'd hung a whole fish around his neck. Lorelei had never seen him so pissed.

Security hadn't even left yet when he began yelling. "What the hell were you thinking sneaking a prize marine specimen out like that?"

In a split second, Lila's nervous expression transformed into mama bear ferocity. The scientist placed her hands squarely on her hips. "We weren't sneaking. We walked Nireed out the front door!"

Phil pointed at her from around the glass he held. "That's even worse! I don't think you understand the gravity of the situation here. She could have escaped."

"Nireed is a volunteer, not a prisoner. She can leave the study whenever she wants, but she stays out of good will. She's our responsibility, and we need to take care of her. And prolonged separation from the ocean is deteriorating her health. That's good for no one."

"Well, the board doesn't see it that way. That creature is property of..."

Rage boiled beneath Lorelei's skin, and suddenly Lila gripped her elbow and whisked her around. Reflected in the glass office door were two glowing green eyes. Talons elongated from her nail beds and wicked sharp teeth pricked her tongue. Lorelei stuffed her hands into her pockets and squeezed her eyes shut. *Shit. Shit. Shit.*

"We'll discuss this another time," Lila snapped at him over her shoulder, all while ushering Lorelei toward the door. She let Lila tug her along.

"I'm not done talking to you, Dr. Branson! There are going to be some changes around here because of this."

Lila's tone dipped low and cold. "And we can talk about them tomorrow morning when you haven't been drinking."

He slammed his glass down on his desk, but screwed his mouth shut. The door closed quietly behind them. "Keep your head down and your hands in your pockets," Lila murmured.

But Phil's secretary, Helen, had returned to her desk, apparently staying as late as their mutual boss. Rising from her chair, she looked up at them from the stack of file folders she cradled. Her jaw dropped.

"Sit down," Lorelei growled. "And forget about it."

Closing her mouth, Helen obediently dropped back into her chair. She blinked several times before shaking her head and trading her files for her computer keyboard.

The command had come so easily. *Too easily.* And the satisfaction that came with, the alluring rush of power, was a slippery slope Lorelei couldn't afford to slide down. She needed to be more careful.

Lorelei and Lila left their boss's office to the sound of clacking keys.

CHAPTER

FOURTEEN

LORELEI

IT WAS LATE WHEN LORELEI RETURNED HOME. KILLIAN SAT on the couch, snoring softly with his head lolled forward. A book sat in his lap with a thumb tucked between the pages to mark his place. He must have tried staying up for her. Easing the book out of his hands, Lorelei bookmarked the page and set it on a side table. She was rifling through the antique sea chest in the corner of the room for a light blanket, when she heard Killian stir behind her.

His joints cracked as he stretched his arms above his head. "How did it go?" he yawned.

Lorelei plopped down on the couch beside him. "Not great," she huffed, picking at the frayed plastic edges of her employee badge. "We still have our jobs, as best as I can tell, but we won't know for sure what the consequences will be until tomorrow morning."

He patted his lap, and she swung up her feet to let him massage away the aches she got from wearing heels all day. Foot massages had become an evening ritual between them, a simple physical connection tethering them together while Lorelei played catch up on her work laptop. There would be none of that tonight. And probably not tomorrow night either. The evening's dealings with Carrie, the security guards, and her pissed off boss, soured Lorelei's mood to all things work-related.

She also had a familial fallout to deal with that felt much more important. "How about on your end? How are Marci and Walt?"

Killian kneaded his fingers into her arch. "They are going to need some time to process."

She tipped her head back against the arm of the couch. Forgiveness seemed so far off. Maybe not possible. She rubbed her chest against the ache of regret pooling there. What if their easy-going family dynamic never returned? All because she got a little carried away with her power trip.

"Hey," he soothed. "It's going to be okay. I promise. You making a scary mermaid face isn't grounds for breaking up the family."

"You know I didn't just make a scary mermaid face. I sung, too." She scrunched up her nose. "And licked your ex."

"Out of context, that would be valid, but it wasn't that kind of lick."

Lorelei arched her brow. "Because the 'mmm, you taste good enough to eat' kind of lick is so much better."

He shrugged. "It is for me."

Pulling her feet from his grasp, she sat, locking eyes with him. He twisted to face her and slung his arm across the back of the couch. "Are you sure about that, Killian? Because I liked it. The taste. Her fear. Using my voice to subdue her. It was such a power rush. And I would do it again if the Walshes weren't around to see it."

Swallowing, he tugged at the front of his jeans and shifted his hips uncomfortably. "You are as seduced by it as I am."

Lorelei blinked, slowly processing his words. "Do you mean that? What happened with Carrie doesn't bother you? The last time I went scary mermaid on her, you were afraid to kiss me for weeks."

He leaned back on his elbows, his back resting against the couch arm. "That was a bite, not a lick. Maybe it should bother me, but once I knew you weren't going to eat Carrie, I…" His cheeks turned bright red. Gone was the fiercely confident man who caveman-carried her into the shower last night.

The only reason he'd be so flustered, that Lorelei could think of, was he was about to admit something. Something he wasn't sure she'd approve of. Or something he was afraid to give voice to. "I think I like seeing you like that. Dangerous but in control. Powerful. Frighteningly beautiful. You're not entirely human, and it turns me on."

Lorelei might have questioned it if his voice hadn't rasped with dark desire—and if he wasn't fidgeting like he was about to burst out the front of his pants. Bracing her hands on his knees, she leaned forward. The cruel set of pointed teeth that hid within her gums slid down and pricked the edges of her tongue, flooding her oral senses with the taste of salt and iron. Her sharp claws elongated across his thighs. "That should terrify you."

"It does, a little," he admitted, licking the seam of his lips. "But I also trust you, and I know that you would never hurt me, or others, just for the sake of it."

"I wouldn't," she agreed, edging close enough to see the green bioluminescence of her own eyes reflected in his stormy gaze. She slowly applied pressure to her grip. Not enough to break skin or bruise. Just a little sting. His breath hitched, heartrate racing one hundred miles per hour. The scent of his arousal filled the space between them in a heady cloud of male heat, sharpening as his blood boiled hotter and hotter beneath her palms. "You really do love lady monsters, Captain."

His eyes flicked to her lips. "Just one."

With the edge of his finger, rough from years of linework, he traced the column of her throat. As callouses rasped against her skin, a pleasurable tingle trickled down to the base of her spine from the quiet reminder of how strong Killian was in his own right. How it was nothing for him to throw her over his shoulder and steer her into sweet, senseless oblivion.

Did he want something of the same from her? To step back from the helm and be dominated?

The path of his touch curved upward, over her chin, to caress the underside of her lip. "Will you sing for me, Lorelei? I want to be spellbound by you."

Heat unfurled between her thighs, and a pleased, low hum rumbled in the back of her throat. The creature in her that belonged to the deep roused at the request. She traced one clawed finger down his front from throat to navel. For one breathless moment, she paused at his waistline before charting a course further down. He twitched beneath her touch and groaned.

Please, his eyes begged, a maelstrom swirling in those pools of blue.

Captain Killian Quinn wanted her to take the helm.

Rising off the couch, Lorelei shrugged off her blazer, letting it fall to the floor. Unbuttoning her blouse, bit by bit, she took one step back and then another, swaying her hips just a little. Twisting on the balls of her feet, she turned toward the front door, and cast a wicked grin over her shoulder. "I'll call for you soon, Captain," she crooned. "Just wait right there."

On her way to the front door, she peeled off her shirt and unhooked her bra, relishing in the feel of his gaze pinned to her bare back. She paused with one hand on the door latch to see how this little show was affecting him.

Lips parted, he exhaled, ragged and heavy, as he pulled down his pants zipper. Relief relaxed his features for but a moment. He stayed seated, as she bade, but as she slid the straps off her shoulders, he swallowed thickly and clenched his jaw, silently begging to be summoned. Lorelei held the lacy undergarment in place, withholding the view, and her song, just a little longer. She had him hook, line, and sinker.

He tracked her every movement with his heated gaze.

Lorelei carried its warmth with her as she slipped out into the cool, summer night air, all her worries about exposure tamped down. Carrie wouldn't be coming back, and the probability of tourists chancing upon Killian's driveway in the dark was slim. There were no streetlights on the road to his cottage. No neighbors. No connecting streets. Just dense pinewood forests that stretched for miles.

She could allow herself this one night to be wholly and unabashedly herself. To explore unfettered bliss with the man who craved even the darkest parts of her. To enjoy a moment of calm before the storm she sensed was trailing the coming dawn.

The moon overhead bathed the beach in indigo, its reflection streaking a path of light in the water out toward the horizon. The seas were tranquil this evening, gentle and languid as it caressed both sand and rock. The tides knew what she needed, and they provided for the daughter of the sea. Whatever it took to coax her back into the ocean's embrace. Although there was nothing that could be done about the cold, Lorelei knew how to keep her man warm.

Lorelei mapped a course for Killian down to the water's edge with shed clothes and footprints in the sand. The sea beckoned, pulling and pulling as it always did, but the aches and pains she'd felt in her bones for months were gone. Her swim that afternoon had been restorative.

As the tide rushed up to meet her, and swirled around her thighs, scales emerged from her skin, and webbing sprouted between fingers. She dove into the water, pressing her legs together to finish the transformation. Skin fused and fins spread out. Though her tail still had a few pink patches, the new growth was coming along.

Lorelei breached the surface and spun back toward the beach, just the tops of her shoulders above water. Her tail waved lazily back and forth beneath the waves, just enough to keep her in place.

It was time for Killian to join her.

Song rumbled up from her chest and spilled from her lips, its haunting melody echoing in the cove, both forest and rock arcing around the beach to create a natural amphitheater.

It wasn't long before Killian's silhouette filled the stone cottage doorway.

She watched him follow her trail of discarded clothes. As he walked, he reached behind him and pulled the short-sleeved shirt he wore over his head, balling it up between his hands before tossing it carelessly to the side. Months of fishing and working outside tanned his skin in various shades, uneven from all manner of states of dress and undress.

Though Killian's eyes had glazed over, as if in a trance, his shoulders were relaxed, and his gait was leisurely, but purposeful—his will in harmony with hers. Medium-wash jeans hung low on his hips, the fly wide open, teasing an Adonis V and a line of brown hair that bridged navel and waistband.

Her song may seduce and beckon, but he compelled her, too.

Killian dropped his pants at the edge where dry and wet-packed sand met. Standing there in tight black boxers, he pried open the buckle to the water-resistance watch he wore. The moment it hit the sand, Lorelei deepened her song to reel him out into the water.

When he waded in deep enough for the water to lick at his upper thighs, he plunged his hands down the front of his waistband to keep himself warm. He didn't flinch until the water reached his groin. Then his core. At his pectorals, his whole body seized up, cold and shivering.

She swam to him then, chin just barely skimming the surface. He reached out for her with both hands, forgetting where he was for a moment, and winced as cold water hit his sensitive bits. She took his hands and pulled him into her embrace. As his arms enclosed around her waist, she cradled his head just beneath her chin and flipped onto her back. With Killian laid across her front, legs floating to either side of her tail, she swam them toward a cluster of sea rock.

Awe filled his eyes as she towed him through the water with ease. "I knew you were strong, but I didn't realize just how strong. There's nothing for me to fear when I'm with you."

Stroking the rounded side of her claws against his cheek, a hum vibrated from the back of her throat. Killian melted in her arms. "The sea can't take you as long as I'm around."

Her body undulated beneath his, generating warmth and friction for them both. Killian nuzzled the dip between her collarbones, and moaned softly, bucking his hips, song and dizzying lust keeping him semi-hard, despite the cold.

The scales that protected her secret flesh parted, stimulated by the rubbing, and a healthy amount of internal wetness gushed out. It was so much more natural lubricant than usual, possibly in response to her environs more so than her desire, although there was plenty of that, too.

Finding an underwater ledge for Killian to stand on, Lorelei pushed him back against weather-worn rock. His torso stretched out in front of her like an offering, rivulets of sea water streaming down his chest, dripping from his hair, as she pinned his wrists overhead with one hand. With the other, she ripped open the front of his boxers and eased him inside her, where she was mercifully warm. Killian tipped his head back, groaning with utter, blissful relief.

Ruining his clothes might become her new favorite pastime.

She laid on top of him, giving him all her weight. "This all right?"

Water droplets glistened from his long, dark lashes as he gazed up at her, such a peaceful, serene expression gracing his features. "I'm exactly where I wanna be."

Her hummed song faltered, then ceased, seeing him so trusting, so ready for domination. He widened his stance, two muscular thighs framing her tail, and his eyes slipped closed, followed by a soft sigh. Lorelei relaxed her hold, just a bit, her lips so close she could feel his breath.

Maybe this was meant to be sweet. She rolled her hips in time with the lapping waves, the torn fabric of Killian's decimated boxers caressing her scales, relinquished control blooming new and delicate between them.

Then his eyes snapped open, fierce, and determined.

With a mischievous grin, he bucked his hips, and wrenched his arms, challenging, testing her strength, trying to throw her off. But she bore down, tightened her grip, thwarting his efforts to break free. The power rush of it raced up her spine, hot and tingling. How she thrilled in this struggle, feeling Killian writhe like an eel beneath her.

"Trying to get away from me?" she hissed. "Such a trouble-maker."

"Stop me," he taunted. The fight in him spurred, his muscles strained against her, but she was immovable. "Make me behave, *siren*."

The responsibility of this fantasy settled over her in a moment both heady and sobering. He was trusting her to draw out every ounce of pleasure through dominance and command, and not hurt him. She needed to take great care in how and when she used her song.

She could satiate the danger he craved in other ways—with the flash of sharp teeth, wicked claws, or the brush of rough scales against his skin—but he demanded to be spellbound, and there was nothing of herself she wouldn't give him.

So, she sang.

With a hooded, drugged look, Killian relaxed, eager supplicant once more, all his hard muscle made pliant on the rocky altar. "So beautiful," he praised.

Hips and piscine tail found a fluid rhythm in the water. They'd christened all manner of surfaces in the cottage and Killian's truck, but ocean sex was new, uncharted territory. Balance, leverage, the basic push and pull they were used to was all thrown off, but she ignored the vain part of her brain that worried how it might look and moved her body in the ways that felt good.

Gripping his hip, she worked his length, savoring each smooth, wet stroke. As her pacing climbed, she got carried away in the bliss of it, and her claws bit in, more than she intended, but he moaned long and deep. Even with hints of blood blooming in the water from pricked flesh, his dick throbbed inside her.

"Fuck, that's hot," he breathed.

Fear and arousal mixed a potent cocktail, flooding her senses, urging her on. "More?"

He tilted his head to the side, exposing his throat. "More."

She pressed her mouth to that tender flesh, feeling his pulse race as she grazed it with her teeth, leaving faint red lines. Lust, not hunger, compelled her to lave the spot, and he quivered beneath her. He tasted so good, something she could admit to herself now without the urge to bite, and moved on, nuzzling the scruff of his jawline. Kissing his cheek.

With a desperate, needy look, he begged her to unravel him, so she gave him the speed he craved, rotating her hips in urgent, feverish circles.

There was no more talking, just determined, frantic coupling as they lost themselves to sensation in the primordial place all life had sprung. The entire Earth had been blanketed by water once, the ocean ruling supreme. And the way Killian stared up at her, forehead pinched and mouth slack, so close to release and begging for mercy, one would think she was its queen.

CHAPTER
FIFTEEN

LORELEI

Hoping to beat the shitstorm brewing at the research center, Lorelei left for work the next morning even earlier than usual. Dragging herself from Killian's embrace at 4:00 a.m. was a herculean effort that took every ounce of her siren strength and willpower. That he held her in a vice grip, cocooning her in comfort and warmth, sleepily asking her to stay, made getting out of bed that much harder. She hated insisting on leaving, especially after the night they shared, but she had to see how Nireed was doing. Make sure she was okay.

She checked in at the security desk.

There were two guards behind it now instead of the usual one, a cheery, young rookie who never seemed to mind that he'd been given the worst shift. Easily charmed that one was, which is probably why he'd been replaced with more seasoned colleagues—two gruff older men she'd never seen before. Neither were open to her lighthearted, early morning banter. Rather they answered her nervous quip "is it a good morning or a goodnight?" with stone-faced silence. Not even a hint of amusement.

That they were here at all, working the graveyard shift, was likely because of mermaid "kidnapping" employees like her. If she was in their shoes, she would probably be grumpy about that, too.

While one scrutinized her ID, and clicked around on their computer, the other pinned her with a searching stare. "You're here early."

"I'm always here early."

The guard with her ID handed it back. "Not this early. Museum work, is it? How's that got you here earlier than the brainiacs?"

Before the people who did the real work, he meant. Lorelei frowned, clipping the badge back onto her lapel. She kept her tone level. "Deadlines. The grand opening is coming up in two months, so I've got a lot of work to do, and not enough hours in a day."

Both guards stared her down. Whether they were waiting for her to elaborate and slip up about her true purpose, or break down and tell them some dark secret, she didn't know. But she wouldn't be baited by awkward silence and pointed stares. "Are we all set then? Can I go to my office now?"

The guard closest to her nodded slowly. "Yeah, all right. Go on."

Lorelei dropped by her office only to offload her workbag before heading to the mermaid lab.

There was one guard stationed at the door. That was new. As she approached, he straightened and crossed his arms, fixing an impassive expression to his face. But he didn't try to block her path. Holding up her ID, she gestured to the scanner on the wall next to him. "Can I just…?"

He nodded and watched her swipe her keycard. The light turned red, not its usual green. She tried again. Same thing. "It worked yesterday," Lorelei mumbled. Phil must have had her access taken away last night. Looking through the window, Lorelei saw Nireed drifting through the tank, arms across her chest and eyes closed. With just the barest flicks of her tail, she stayed in motion, so water passed through her gills and filtered out oxygen while she slept. It was as automatic to her as it was for humans to breathe while sleeping. Tapping on the window, to get Nireed's attention in the aquarium just twenty feet away, Lorelei ignored the guard's commands to step back from the door.

Nireed's eyes shot open.

Even through a wall of water, two sheets of glass, and a room between them, she heard. But that didn't surprise Lorelei. The siren's hearing had to be sharp to survive the dangers of the deep. Lorelei signed, "Are you all right?"

Nodding, Nireed signed back. "Are you?"

Lorelei felt the guard's firm grasp on her elbow, and signed frantically, trying to brush him off without giving away too much of her supernatural strength. "I'm fine, but they won't let me in."

Though Nireed glared at the guard, and snarled, Lorelei saw the worry beneath the siren's ferocity. She was troubled by this development. Maybe even afraid of what it meant. Lorelei was her only tie to the ocean beyond and to her kin. The only one who had any clue what she'd sacrificed to be here. The only one who understood the rush of gliding through the dark brine of a boundless ocean, propelled by one's own fins.

Not only was Lorelei the only person Nireed trusted enough to talk to, she was the siren's last tether to sanity in this sterile place.

The guard puffed out his chest and pushed her away from the door, not by use of force, but by crowding her out with his big, huffy presence. He stood squarely in front of the door now, blocking her view of Nireed. "Ma'am, you need to leave," he said, and not for the first or second time.

A low hum rumbled at the back of her throat, and the guard's stance relaxed, his sharp, hawkish stare sliding out of focus. A little more and he'd step away from the door. A lot more and he'd abandon his post altogether. It would be so easy.

All she had to do was sing.

But the melody died in her throat. It wouldn't be harmless. There wasn't anything she wouldn't do to protect the ones she loved, and she'd already proven what great lengths she'd go to protect herself, but needlessly and flippantly taking a person's will away, just to make things easier on herself, was all sorts of messed up. Carrie had created a dire situation, and Helen had seen too much. But this man didn't deserve to this puppeteering. Not yet.

A dot of red, winking in and out of the top right corner of her vision, caught her attention.

Shit. That was a close call in another sense. There were security cameras installed everywhere. Either people watched the footage, saw the security guard let her waltz in and fired him, or they put two-and-two together that she was using siren song. She'd lose her job, her anonymity, and Nireed would lose one of her only two advocates. Lorelei would never be allowed to set foot in the research facility again.

Or worse. She would never be allowed to leave it.

Neither outcome was acceptable. For him, or for her. She had to let this go—for now.

Lorelei cleared her throat.

The guard blinked, then snapped back to attention. He pointed down the hallway, his jaw ticking from how hard he clenched it. "Go. Or I will physically remove you."

Lorelei held up her hands in mock defense. "All right, I'm going."

She stalked down the hall, contemplating the steep price of freedom.

LILA DIDN'T LOSE HER JOB OVER THE MERMAID FIELD TRIP fiasco. Lorelei never would forgive herself if she had. But there was a cost. Although Lila would remain in charge of the mermaid lab, her access was restricted to 9:00 to 5:00 business hours, and she had to be escorted by either security or a fellow team member anytime she worked with Nireed.

Babysat in her own lab.

It was humiliating.

"Phil, this is ridiculous," Lila seethed. They'd been summoned into his office the moment he arrived. "How many times do I have to tell you that Nireed's not a prisoner? I didn't do anything wrong by giving her the mental health break she needed. You try being cooped up in a tank day after day, month after month. There's a reason why animals in captivity have shorter life expectancies. If anything, it's in your best interests to allow…"

Phil cut her off with a curt remark. "I'll be the judge of that. This isn't up for discussion, Dr. Branson."

Lila sat back hard in the chair next to Lorelei's, arms crossing her chest, fuming.

Lorelei leaned forward. "Why isn't it up for discussion, *Phil?*" She spat out his name as if laced with poison. "The team didn't twiddle their thumbs waiting three months to get signed consent from Nireed for nothing. And you agreed to the plans for an intersectional anthropological study. Now it's straight biology. When exactly did you decide Nireed no longer has personhood?"

"Miss Roth, you forget you've no authority on this subject. Allowing you access to the mermaid lab was a huge oversight, one that's affected your ability to do your actual job as Museum Director, but we won't be making that mistake again."

Digging her fingers into her chair cushion, Lorelei left crescent shaped dents in the leather, but steadied her breathing. She had to remain calm. If she lost her cool, she'd transform right in front of her boss. "I can do both."

"It didn't sound like it to me when you visited my office two days ago to put in a hiring request." His fingertips touched in that annoying steepled pose. "I admire your work ethic and determination, Miss Roth, believe me, I do. But it's plain to see that you've been overworking yourself. Stressed and exhausted isn't the face our patrons should see on opening day."

Blinking back the angry tears that threatened to spill from her eyes, Lorelei clamped her mouth shut, and folded her hands in her lap. That way, she didn't reach across the desk and throttle her boss.

"You keep dodging our questions," Lila managed through gritted teeth.

"Frankly, I don't care. You answer to me, not the other way around." Phil gestured behind her. "If you don't like the way things are done here, there's the door."

Siren song tickled at the back of Lorelei's throat. Just the barest hint of a melody, but Lila grabbed her wrist and squeezed hard. Her eyes flared wide as she sternly mouthed "don't." Lorelei gulped, quieting.

Lila didn't need to explain for her to understand. Just because Lorelei could compel people to do what she wanted, didn't mean she should— even if their boss was being a major tool. That was a nasty slippery slope to go down, and she didn't fight this hard for control over past year to be wholly seduced by the power of her own song.

When Lila didn't get up, Phil continued, "Staying? Good. Now look, I know you're upset, but we've got to stay the course. We're doing cutting-edge marine research here, and we're very close to being recognized as number one in the country, and on track for the entire world. Think about that. This mermaid study is our golden ticket to keep doing the important work our scientists have already been doing for a long, long time. I don't need to explain to you how our research-driven advocacy has led to positive wins for marine life and the health of our oceans and the planet at large."

Accreditation. World-wide recognition. Continued, cushy funding. That's what this was all about. That's what changed. Greed masked by job security and environmentalism.

Lila made eye contact, her lips pressing into a thin, hard line. She'd figured it out, too. But with a small shake of the marine biologist's head, Lorelei stayed quiet. There was nothing they could say to change Phil's mind, especially if the board shared this sentiment, which is where it likely originated. They would have to regroup and plan later.

Phil took their silence as acquiescence. "Good. I'm glad we're all on the same page now. Dr. Branson, if you don't mind, I would like to speak Miss Roth about a museum matter. There's no need for you to stay for that. I'm sure you have plenty of your own work to do."

That was it. Conversation over. And a rude dismissal. Lorelei clenched the arms of her chair, the wood creaking under the pressure. Lila shot her a warning glance, and Lorelei relaxed her grip. She was going to have to keep it together for both their sakes. If she lost her temper and outed herself, Lila would be left alone to deal with the fallout.

And it was Lorelei who got the marine biologist into this mess in the first place with last year's flesh-eating problems. She could hold it together for ten more minutes.

Without another word, Lila stormed out of their boss's office. When she was gone, Phil announced that he hired someone for the Assistant Museum Director's position.

"Hired someone? What—already?" It had been barely two days since she put in her request. "Why wasn't I involved in the decision-making process?"

"Had to move fast. You need help and the board wants to move up the grand opening to September 16, with a soft opening for staff, friends, and family the weekend before. September 15, we'll unveil *The Osprey* memorial..."

Lorelei cut him off. "That's barely a month away! If anything, we need more time, not less, to get up and running." All their previous plans revolved around the date they'd picked in mid-October with the board's approval. Not to mention, September 16 was the day before the anniversary *The Osprey* sank—of which Lorelei was the only survivor. How did Phil and the board of directors expect her to be in any kind of shape to host such a huge event? She could manage a memorial unveiling for her lost crewmates. After all, it was her idea. But she was going to be an emotional wreck those few days.

"Your new assistant thinks it's doable. And it's good timing. The tourists will be back for the fall foliage. School will be back in session for field trips."

It made sense from a shrewd business standpoint, but Lorelei was one frayed nerve away from ripping her hair out. Or his. "But I have to onboard this new person. I don't know what they are capable of, what their qualifications are, or how we'll work together. I don't know anything about them."

"She's got fifteen years of corporate experience, and I can vouch for her personally. There's no one more capable and hardworking than Carrie Prior."

Lorelei sat back in her chair with a hard thump. Sucker-punched.

CHAPTER
SIXTEEN

LORELEI

God have mercy on her soul. Carrie. Fucking. Prior.

Phil opened a desk drawer and plopped a manila file folder in front of her. With trembling hands, Lorelei opened the front flap to reveal Carrie's professional life on paper. An impressive resume. A stunning portfolio. Impeccable references. And glowing recommendation letters. As for Lorelei's own character reference—based on personal interactions outside the workplace? Utter fail. But not even considered in this sham of a hiring process.

"You've got to be kidding me," she muttered under her breath.

Phil pinned her with an exasperated look. "I'm not. What's the problem now?"

Oh, nothing. Just, your new hire brought a gun onto my fiancé's property yesterday and thought about shooting the first mermaid she saw. Squinting at the file, Lorelei kept her mouth screwed shut. If it weren't for Lorelei and Carrie's personal issues, hiring the woman would have been a no brainer.

She desperately needed the help. But was she this desperate?

The looming September 16 deadline threatened to push her answer into the 'yes' category. But Carrie as her colleague, let alone her second-in-command, could create more problems than she solved. While the woman wouldn't remember anything from yesterday's encounter, there was still bad blood and the threat of a restraining order between them.

To Phil's credit, he wouldn't know about all that. There was an opportunity to rectify this.

"There's something I should mention to you, for transparency's sake," she said and explained that she was not only engaged to Carrie's ex, but Carrie had stalked them while they were dating to the point that they'd had to warn her off with a potential restraining order.

Rubbing his fingers across his temples, Phil expelled a heavy, aggravated sigh. "I'm sorry to hear that you two have had personal issues, but without an actual restraining order, I'm afraid there's nothing concrete enough to disqualify a stellar candidate who's otherwise had impeccable professional references. I'm talking glowing praise from her prior firm's executives and Fortune 500 clients. If we need to get HR involved for mediation, we will, but please, try to set aside your differences, and make this work like mature, professional adults."

Clenching and unclenching her fists, Lorelei bit back the urge to call him a jackass, but instead said, "Trespassing and stalking aren't petty issues. Those are legal concerns. And what I can't figure out is why, as your *colleague*, is my voice worth less than people you don't even..."

He cut her off. "It's your prerogative to find Carrie annoying, and to find this situation awkward. But I *know* Carrie, and I can personally vouch that she's harmless. I'm not asking you two to be best friends, like you are with Dr. Branson. I'm asking you to be civil and professional. Carrie has had an illustrious career in New York City, and we need her extensive corporate marketing experience. She knows how to reach the international patron-base we have the potential to attract as the soon-to-be *only* natural mermaid history museum in the world. Whatever issues you have with each other, work them out."

For fuck's sakes. "She's not the only person qualified for this position, and if you'd included me in the hiring process from the start, I would've helped you find other candidates."

"Carrie's local, and frankly we don't have time for another equally qualified candidate to put in two weeks' notice and relocate to Haven Cove. The grand opening is less than a month away."

Recalling her recent bathroom run-in with Carrie, and the easy acceptance Phil received her hiring request, Lorelei fired back, "You hired her before I even requested an assistant, didn't you? Getting my input was never a consideration."

Jaw clenching, Phil's expression hardened, the insufferable mule. "I'm sorry we couldn't extend you that professional courtesy, but like I said, we didn't have time to dilly dally. And anyway, it's a done deal. The board's already unanimously approved her for the position."

A board which Lorelei suspected had even more of Carrie's family on it.

Just like with Nireed, there was nothing she could say that would make a difference, not when her bosses never cared to have her opinion or approval in the first place. That much was painfully obvious.

"Fine," Lorelei said through gritted teeth, glaring daggers at the ground. If she looked at his ignorant, nepotistic face another second, she might claw it off. Just considering it made her stomach twist on itself, reminding her that she hadn't eaten breakfast yet.

"I'm sorry for shutting you down like that," Phil added, his tone softening. It jarred Lorelei how quickly his mood flipped the moment she stopped arguing. "But it's my responsibility to oversee this project, and having someone like Carrie onboard is a great win for us." When she didn't reply, Phil continued, having the nerve to sound cheerfully optimistic. "She can put you on the map. Just imagine, your museum becoming one of the greatest oceanic natural history museums in the world. It's too great of a possibility to pass up. You'll see. I've saved us both a lot of time and stress by expediting the process."

Lorelei could only nod, barely maintaining a hold on her temper and barely tamping down the transformation prickling beneath her skin. *Don't Hulk out. And don't eat your boss.*

"She starts first thing tomorrow morning."

Rage pooled in her belly, saliva in her mouth.

Before she could do something regrettable, Lorelei replied

"understood" with the last shred of professionalism she could muster and rushed out of his office. Her stomach growled on her way out the door.

Within the safety of her own office, Lorelei dug into her purse for a tin of canned pork to abate the roiling people-eating hunger tying her stomach in knots. She turned her computer monitor so she could hide behind it while she ate her fill.

Working side-by-side with Carrie Prior was a recipe for disaster. A toxic workplace nightmare come true. Tossing the empty can into the recycling bin beside her desk, Lorelei buried her face in her hands and groaned audibly. "Fuck."

THE LATEST DEVELOPMENT OF THE CARRIE VS. PEOPLE-eating mermaid saga needed to be shared. Lorelei strode the stretch of hallway between her office and Lila's, heels clacking against the tile, fighting off the hysterical laughter that bubbled up at the back of her throat. This day was so bad, it was almost funny.

The mental fog that plagued her just a few days before, hadn't returned. She floated above it, watching her work life crash and burn before her with an eerie sort of detachment. Or denial. Only a small town could boast this level of drama.

She found the marine biologist crying behind her desk, half turned away from the door in her swivel chair. Lorelei's need to vent vanished. Hurrying inside, she closed the blinds over the door, so her friend had the privacy she herself needed just days ago.

As the blinds dropped, Lila looked up from the crumpled tissues in her hands. In their absence, tears-streaked cheeks. Lorelei pulled a chair around to sit beside her and plucked more tissues off the desk. "Lila, what is it? Is Phil giving you more shit?"

Taking the tissues, Lila blew her nose loudly. When she was done, she pumped hand sanitizer onto her palms, a fierce glint in her eye. "No more since that fucking meeting. But I am just so angry." She clenched her fists and let out a frustrated growl. "And betrayed, to tell you the truth. I started working here, because I really believed in the leadership and the research and environmental advocacy work HCMRC was doing. I could have gone to any number of higher ranked research facilities across the country, but I stayed home, because this place just blew me out of the water with their integrity and commitment to real environmental change. It was energizing. Inspiring. I LOVED coming to work every day. And now…" Lila double flipped off her office door. "I was afraid this would happen. But I kept telling myself to give HCMRC the benefit of the doubt. It would be different. I could talk sense into Phil about Nireed, then the board. I stayed up all night thinking last night was all just one big misunderstanding that could be resolved with clear heads and a logical conversation. But deep in my gut, I knew they were going to be hypocritical pieces of shit. I don't know how to go about my job with that. I don't know how to fight for Nireed and the scientific code of ethics without hurting the whole institution."

"We're going to figure this out. I don't know how yet, but you're not alone in this, Lila. You've been there for me so many times in the past year, and in ways, even my best friend couldn't be. I want you to know that I'm here for you, too. Whatever happens, whatever they try to pull, I'm not going to let them steamroll you."

"I know. And thank you for backing me up in Phil's office. I appreciated it. I'm just accepting that we're not going to make any headway with him, and I seriously doubt the board will be any different. The mermaid limelight is getting to their heads. And now, with the new restrictions on my lab access, I've been getting cutthroat vibes from some members of my team. I went into the lab this morning after the meeting to check on Nireed, and Dr. Jerry Nedry was fucking smug the whole time he followed me around, playing babysitter. Don't know what high horse he thought he was trotting around on. Maybe he's gunning for my job." Lila groaned into her hands. "The nerve of mediocre old white men. What a shark. Can you do me a big favor and like… eat him?"

Tempting. Almost as much as using her siren song to get her way. But Lorelei shook her head, a wry smile on her lips. "People keep asking me to eat their problems away," she teased. "It's becoming a pattern."

A smile cracked across Lila's face. She reached under her desk and pulled a bag of individually wrapped chocolates from her purse. After taking one for herself, she offered one to Lorelei. "I guess the phrase 'eating your feelings' hits a little different now, doesn't it?"

Lorelei snorted, unwrapping the candy, and biting through its soft caramel center. "I did almost rage eat Jerry when he was being a dickhead to Nireed."

Lila popped hers into her mouth, and closed her eyes briefly, taking a moment to let the decadent dark chocolate melt on her tongue, savoring it. Then she pushed it against her cheek. "I remember. Kinda half-wishing you did."

"Probably would've given me indigestion," Lorelei joked. "Would've been worth it though. And speaking of eating our feelings and problems away, take a wild guess who Phil hired to help me out with the museum. And without my input, of course."

Tapping a finger to her lips, Lila ran through a gamut of possibilities.

"You're thinking too hard. It's literally the worst person you can think of. It sounds too bad to be true, but it's very much true."

Eyes sparking, Lila leaned forward. "It's not *her*, is it?" Lorelei pinched her lips together, merely nodding. "Oh my God. *It's Carrie!?* Are we living in a soap opera? This is too much. Why can't my kicks for juicy drama stay in front of the TV screen?"

"First Carrie, now Phil. Does a cloud of drama and angst follow that family around—everyone except Will?"

Lila smirked, popping another piece of candy into her mouth. "Don't let Will fool you. I love my husband, but he's a little drama queen. Gobbles up gossip like I gobble up candy. He's just a lot more down to earth about life than the rest of them and has a good sense of humor."

"Glad he's on our side with this whole mermaid business then."

"He really thinks you're cool. Which you are. But he's dorky about it, like you're his favorite comic book hero, especially after that wild as fuck gun situation with Carrie. I'm not going to lie, we were all nervous about how you were going to deal, but you've reconfirmed your hero-status to Will."

Lorelei blushed. "I'm no hero. Got more of the villain vibe—the claws, the teeth." She gestured to her throat. "The song."

"Pssht. No. That's bullshit. Folks always demonize women for using their voices. It's about how you use it and when. Great power means great responsibility or however it goes. Sure, you might get complacent, and yes, you're probably going to mess up. If I see it, I'll let you know. But slipping up doesn't make you a villain or a monster or whatever. Hell, you're more of a Jedi, and they make plenty of mistakes. We still root for them. It's all a part of being a person."

"Do Jedi lick to intimidate though?"

"Okay no, that was a bit much, but my point still applies."

Lorelei picked at the hem of her blazer. "I think when your parents look at me, they see force-choke Darth Vader."

"No, I mean, they're trying to wrap their heads around it, but believe me when I say they were more freaked out by Carrie carrying a gun. It might not have seemed that way, but they focused on the piece of that situation that they could process easiest. It's disturbing as hell, but scary mermaid shit is low-hanging fruit compared to the threat of gun violence."

Lorelei exhaled, breath ragged. Lila was right. That was super messed up. "And now Carrie's going to be a colleague."

"Yup," Lila said, popping the 'p'. "But I feel safer having you around, and that's no small thing. You used that siren song of yours when we needed it most, and I know you'll use it again to protect those who need it. My parents will come around in time and realize it's not you they have to fear."

There was so much about being a mermaid Lorelei had to figure out for herself. And that day in the driveway was full of uncertainty. It was perfectly reasonable for Marci and Walt to be afraid of her. But that Lila felt safer around her...

Lorelei would guard that trust with her life.

Waving a hand in front of her face before reaching in for another chocolate, Lila continued, "Anyway. Does it look bad if we hit up happy hour twice in one week?"

"It's probably going to be three times after tomorrow. And I don't care one bit."

Lila gestured between the two of them. "See, this is why we are friends."

As Lorelei reached for another chocolate, Lila pulled the bag away, wagging her finger. "Uh-uh-uh. Can't have you spoiling your dinner. You've got at least three people to eat by the end of this week."

Darksider.

CHAPTER

SEVENTEEN

KILLIAN

Leaning against the doorway, Killian watched with amusement as Lorelei danced around the kitchen with a serving spoon in one hand and a drink in the other. She'd gone out for happy hour again with Lila—and despite the day's pile-on of turmoil and drama—was in a good mood when she breezed in through the front door. He'd been about to make dinner, but she playfully booted him out of the kitchen, throwing together homemade salsa and grilled chicken salad.

And now she was shaking her hips and singing along to one of her feel-good songs. Something about how haters were gonna hate. Killian liked seeing her like this. Happy. Carefree. Twirling about the kitchen like she was high on life. And—he sipped from the glass he was holding —taking lemons and making the best tasting lemonade he ever had in his life.

He loved this woman. And he loved to listen to her sing. Even if it was usually off-key. A sea siren who couldn't sing. And now it sounded almost...good? "Have you been sneaking singing lessons?" he joked.

Lorelei stuck her tongue out, face scrunched up with cute

disgruntlement. "Sorta." She shrugged one shoulder and explained how Nireed speed-trained her vocal cords.

"I'm gonna miss the terrible singing."

She playfully swatted his arm. "They pass down their siren song, just like language and stories and traditions."

Stepping away from the doorjamb, he helped Lorelei set the table. "Would you teach me? The sign language they use, I mean."

He didn't think Lorelei's mood could brighten even more, but it did. Her smile dazzled like shimmering sunlight on water. "You really want to learn?"

"Of course, I do. I want to be able to tell you how much I love you in every language you know."

Grinning from ear to ear, Lorelei ducked her head, a blush creeping up her cheeks. When they finished setting the table, and began tucking into dinner, Lorelei paused to point at herself, then crossed two closed fists over her chest, and pointed to him. "That's how you sign 'I love you' in ASL. The sirens use it, too."

"How do I sign your name?"

"You can either finger spell it or use my name sign." She showed him both.

He signed 'I love you, Shorewalker' first. "Can you show me how to finger spell your name, again?"

She slowly went through each letter, waiting for him to copy her before moving on to the next one. When he messed up 'R,' she reached for his hands across the table, not quite touching him. "May I?"

He nodded, letting her gentle touch coax his pointer and middle fingers into the correct crossed position.

"Knowing what the sign feels like helps me," she said. As he slowly put it all together, another 'I love you,' followed by the letters that spelled Lorelei's name, happiness shone in her smile, glowed on her skin.

When he finished signing, she drizzled a sweet homemade vinaigrette across their salads. "You learn quickly," she beamed, setting the pitcher back on the table. Dressing ran down its side, which she swiped up with a finger.

Killian winked, clasping her hand, and drew the finger into his mouth. He sucked it clean, then kissed the tip. "I have a pretty teacher that I want to impress."

Her blush deepened. "You did that ages ago."

"Doesn't mean I'm ever gonna stop."

Just because they were engaged, and soon to be married, didn't mean he'd stop showing her how special she was. He hated when guys at the gym whined about their wives, like marriage to them was a shackle or a chore and not the best damn thing that ever happened to them.

When Killian put that ring on Lorelei's finger, he did it with the promise that he would spend the rest of his life earning her love. Showing support and participating in the things she cared about was a part of that promise.

Honesty was important, too.

He didn't think now was the time to tell her about Branson's tranquilizer gun under a tarp in the barn, not while she was so happy and focused on teaching him something as personal and intimate as her kin's underwater language. But he'd have to tell her soon. He hated keeping a secret between them.

Sign language lessons continued between bites of food. Just a few conversational basics like 'thank you' and 'please,' and signs with occupational relevance, such as 'fish,' 'ocean,' and 'boat'—the latter of which the sirens always coupled with the sign for 'loud.'

"How about 'mermaid'?"

When she showed him, worry wrinkled her brow. Something about the sign sparked a memory or idea that shifted her mood to pensive. "What is it?" he asked.

"I just remembered something. The mermaids that boarded your boat—they were led by Nireed's older sister Aersila." She explained what she had learned from Nireed.

Apparently, Aersila and her Merry Band of Murderous Mermaids didn't intimidate his crew just for the sake of it; they were looking for the shore-bound siren and retaliating against Undine. There was some kind of mermaid drama between the two.

She showed him how to sign Nireed's family name, the sign for peace, and how to finger spell 'Aersila.'

Killian got the sense that family name signs were a big deal, and not shared lightly. Especially not with Shorewalkers or Two-Leggers. And a shift was beginning to take place in Lorelei about how she felt about her oceanic kin—one from anger and disgust to acceptance, maybe even pride.

The tides were changing.

She nudged his knee under the table. "Something's bothering you, too."

He rubbed his hands across his face and huffed out a breath. He didn't want to do this now but lying again and saying everything was fine was a wicked bad idea. "Yeah, I have a couple confessions to make. Well, one's more an announcement than a confession."

While Lorelei was at work, the contractor came by to take measurements and begin the groundwork for building the privacy fence. If Killian could keep it a surprise he would, but soon he wouldn't be able to hide the construction taking place on their property—between all the vehicles, the workers, and the noise.

But now that he thought of it, he wasn't sure how Lorelei would feel about him making major changes to the property without her input. They weren't married yet, but he'd long considered this slice of paradise Lorelei's home, too. And so did she.

He'd start with the fence first, then work up to the tranquilizer story.

"I want you to be able to feel like you can be completely yourself in your own home—that means the mermaid bits, too. And this past year, you've been suppressing that part of yourself. For safety. I don't want that to be what the rest of your life here looks like. Not if I can help it. So, I hired a contractor to put up privacy fencing around our property." A smile crept back into Lorelei's expression. "It's been a whirlwind week, but I probably should have told you the moment I seriously considered it."

He told her how it would run along the tree line on the left side of the property, down the driveway path to the road, and into one of two pillars that would frame a security gate. Maine forests were dense, and

Killian wanted to cut down the fewest trees possible. The right side of the property was bordered by cliffs, so the privacy fence ran along the road around them, then cut in to block off access.

Lorelei nodded along, in thought, as he laid out the plans. "I'm going to miss being able to see the tree line, but..." She looked out the window at the ocean. "Last night was everything to me, and I want more nights, and days, like it. If this is the way to do it, I'm on board."

When she looked back at him, there were tears in her eyes and a smile on her face. "It makes me so happy to hear that you think of this as 'our' property. And that you thought of this solution. I've been so wrapped up in work and guilt that I couldn't see anything else, and I got tunnel vision. Thank you for looking out for me, and for telling me about the fencing plans now. You're right about this week being a whirlwind. If I wasn't feeling so good now, I might be reeling from the emotional whiplash." She reached across the table to take his hands and squeezed. "Change is coming. And there's going to be a lot more challenges ahead, but I'm glad that I'm facing them with you. Despite what a shit day this started as, I'm feeling hopeful, because I have faith in you, our friends, and myself. We're going to figure this out."

He squeezed back. "We are."

And then she went right for his jugular.

"So, what's the second confession?"

He wasn't sure she'd think so warm and fuzzy about him after this one. But it was time to spit it out. He didn't want secrets between them. "Branson brought a tranquilizer gun with him to the cookout yesterday."

The confession hung in the air, blunt and heavy. Lorelei didn't say anything at first, but the hurt and anger he expected didn't come. She looked more inquisitive as she studied his face than upset.

"That was smart," she said finally.

"What?" Did she just say it was 'smart?' That couldn't be right. Maybe she misunderstood who and what it was for...

"Killian, do you remember last year, after I bit Carrie, that I said I would never hold it against you, or others, if you defended yourself against me? Neither of us knew what was going to happen after reintroducing Nireed and myself to the ocean. But Will found a humane way to deescalate what could have been a very bad situation. Thankfully, it didn't come to that, but it was a very real possibility. I'm not upset that he thought ahead and took measures to protect his family. I would never forgive myself if I lost control and hurt any of you. Getting shot with a dart and knocked unconscious isn't a big, horrible thing but especially not in comparison to the alternatives."

His shoulders slumped.

Though her answer brought some relief, it wasn't just having a tranquilizer gun that bothered him. It was that he insisted on being the one to use it—to stare down the black barrel at his future wife. If he would have squeezed the trigger at all. He wasn't sure what he would have done in the moment. He might've frozen.

"Ah. I see." Lorelei came around the table to hug him from behind, resting her chin on his shoulder. "It's not a real gun, Killian. Don't think of it as 'shooting me.' Just a little sting from a dart and putting me to sleep. No bullets." She kissed his cheek. "There's nothing to forgive. Not a single thing. But I am glad you told me, so that I could assure you of that."

Killian leaned into her touch, threading his fingers through hers. "I don't think it will ever sit right with me but knowing that does help."

"So, we're good then?"

"You're asking me? I was the one with truth bombs to drop."

"Yeah, well, they weren't really bombs, so..." She shrugged. "I'm good, if you're good."

He smiled. "Yeah, I'm good."

CHAPTER
EIGHTEEN

LORELEI

TODAY WOULD BE A TEST OF LORELEI'S PROFESSIONAL
mettle.

Each new day this week sought to upstage the last for the reigning
title "Workday from Hell," and Lorelei doubted Carrie's first day would
upset the pattern. Still, she could put on a front of civility and
professionalism, and with the list of tasks and onboarding notes she'd
put together, nobody could say she was unprepared.

Lorelei propped the door open to her office. While on one hand, it
gave an 'open' and 'welcoming' vibe her colleagues would expect for a
new employee, Lorelei hoped the threat of eavesdropping would keep
her interactions with Carrie tame.

She was reviewing her notes when a cleared throat snapped her
attention to the door.

As always, Killian's ex was impeccably dressed and styled—like she
still worked in NYC advertising. Makeup on point, and not a hair out of
place. If her new employee was literally anybody else, Lorelei would
have asked for tips.

Carrie looked smug, not fearful, so it seemed reasonable that the woman didn't remember anything that happened two days ago when Lorelei went full scary mermaid on her ass.

"Didn't know you were interested in museum work, Carrie, but Phil says you're great with customer service and promotions, not just advertising, so why don't we just jump right in and come up with a plan." Lorelei gestured to the empty chair in front of her desk. "I'll tell you what I've got worked out so far, where I think you should step in, and we can go from there. It's all up for discussion."

Carrie sauntered across the room and sat down, that smug smile, broadening. "Well, well. Look at you, Lori. Playing the part of someone's boss. It's cute, but honey, I was working Fortune 500 accounts in New York while you still had braces and were scooping ice cream for bad tips."

What a ridiculous thing to say, and how dare this woman be spot on. "First off, my name is Lorelei, not Lori. And secondly, why did you want this job, Carrie? If it was to get paid to harass me, I am going to have to firmly, but respectfully, ask you to leave." *Before I fucking bite your face off.*

They barely made it one minute into their working relationship and Lorelei was already pissed off enough to do it.

Carrie held up her hands in defense and had the gall to look like Lorelei was out of line. "Geez, okay. Don't get your underwear in a twist. But some friendly piece of advice, if you're going to be the director of anything, you're going to need a better sense of humor and thicker skin."

Honorable Greta Roth, give me strength before I do something super illegal.

Channeling her mother's courtroom calm, Lorelei took a deep breath and swallowed her anger at Carrie's words, and how they twisted everything. "Anyway." Lorelei pivoted, drawing out the word. "Here's what still needs to be done."

As Lorelei talked, letting herself get lost in work, and the passion she still had for it, the smug smile on Carrie's face faded. Bit by bit, it was replaced by rapt attention. At one point, Carrie reached into her purse and pulled out a notepad and pen. She scribbled furiously as Lorelei spoke, occasionally asking her to stop and repeat something or ask a clarifying detail.

Finally recognizing that it was time to roll up their sleeves, put their heads together, and get shit done, Carrie was slipping into work mode, too. It was like night and day, this shift. Forgetting who each other was for a bit, while working out a manageable plan and timeline, was kind of nice.

Maybe even energizing.

Lorelei had to admit that Phil was right about Carrie knowing exactly what she was doing. She had great ideas and was already solving thorny problems Lorelei secretly agonized over. If she kept work-focused-Carrie on task, she wouldn't have to deal with the infuriating-ex-girlfriend side.

This whole crazy work situation might turn out okay.

By the time the workday ended, Lorelei wasn't even all that mad when Carrie said, "See you on Monday, Lori."

It had been an extremely productive day. And decidedly not the worst day of this hellfire week. She could live with a hated nickname if that was the worst she'd have to put up with from Carrie. For all intents and purposes, this day was a success, and Lorelei was going to ride that high all weekend long.

With September 16th just around the corner, grand opening day would be here in a blink of an eye. But even with Phil's asinine deadline, maybe, just maybe, they could actually pull this off.

CHAPTER
NINETEEN

KILLIAN

Stopping the engines in siren territory was dangerous.

But Killian needed to clear the air with Nireed's older sister Aersila and come to an accord with the siren on his own terms. The sooner he nipped this aggression in the bud, the better. They were only worried about Nireed, after all—or so Lorelei seemed to think. The sirens would only grow bolder with time as they waited for Killian and his crew to make another mistake—waiting for another opportunity to rescue their kin. He didn't want to contemplate the consequences of being caught unawares again, but it was exactly the sort of thing that kept him up late at night.

His crew wasn't happy about his plan to let the sirens onboard for a peace talk. Only years of built-up trust kept them from walking off the pier and never coming back. While Killian was sure he could keep them safe, he wasn't sure he'd have their trust after this.

He hadn't expected them to be pleased with this plan, but he thought they'd at least follow his logic. Most didn't think the sirens could be reasoned with. Even Walsh and Branson were wary. The only other siren those two had ever dealt with was Undine, and as far as they were concerned, her willingness to negotiate might be more an exception to the rule, rather than a model for typical siren behavior.

Killian would have to make it up to everyone with extra time off and hazard pay.

But it wasn't just his responsibility to his crew's long-term safety that fueled this effort to broker peace. Killian empathized with the siren, too. She didn't know what happened to Nireed and likely assumed the worst fate possible. Imagination could be cruel in its tendency to fill in the missing gaps with all sorts of ugliness.

He knew what that was like.

When he was fourteen, and his mom didn't come back from her weekend mountain climbing trip, he had assumed the worst. Only, the worst imaged scenario had actually come true. Delaney Quinn hadn't hunkered down somewhere, waiting for a storm to blow over. She hadn't been injured, or stuck, waiting for rescue.

While park rangers were eventually able to recover the body, she'd fallen from a great height. Quick and painless, they'd said. Dead upon impact. A small mercy he supposed, for her, but the stuff of nightmares for him. She had to be cremated. They couldn't even have a closed casket funeral.

So, Killian knew all too well what Aersila must be feeling in almost a year of waiting for her worst fears to be confirmed. What he would have given to have had his own fears proven wrong twenty-five years ago. But he was powerless to rewrite the past. The present, however, he could do something about.

He could give Nireed's sister the peace of mind she undoubtedly needed.

Maybe his crew sensed the empathy in him, and it scared them, because they didn't understand where it came from—why he'd take the risk with people he knew for years for creatures more likely to try to eat him. But for better or worse, these sirens were Lorelei's kin. And from what he saw of his fiancée's interactions with Nireed, she hoped to someday build a relationship with them, which would soon make them his kin, too.

The scrape of claws against metal heralded the arrival of Aersila, and her Merry Band of Murderous Mermaids. There hadn't even been a disturbance in the water. Nor singing. They'd come quietly up to the boat from the deep.

Listening to that awful screech of metal, Killian ground his teeth, a surge of irritation replacing nervousness. He'd have to repaint the boat again when they got to shore. The last time they encountered sirens, they scratched the side of his boat to hell when they climbed onboard.

Killian alone stood in front of the open crates of potted meat, with a tranquilizer-shooting pistol holstered at his hip, and Branson's rifle strapped across his back. Most of the *Dawn Chaser's* crew stowed away below decks, their noise cancellation headsets firmly in place—Ian's triple checked. Only McAdams, who was locked away in the pilothouse, ready to turn on the boat's engines and thrust the throttle forward at a moment's notice, wasn't with them.

Killian wore his own headset around his neck, so he could give orders when needed but still hear his surroundings. Only Lorelei's song affected him, so he didn't need to cover his ears, except for show in front of his crew.

Clawed hands reached over the side, and seven dangerous beauties hoisted themselves over. Aersila's amber glare fell on him first, as abrasive as barnacles, meant to cut and shred. She hissed, simultaneously flashing a wicked set of teeth. Her hard, lean muscle flexed as she perched on the gunwale in a half-shifted state, naked save for the bracers and upper arm cuffs she wore made from hammered out potted meat cans. That, and the long dark-hair, streaked with white, that covered her chest.

Unlike Nireed, who had softer features, Aersila's facial structure could have been chiseled from sea rock, her cheekbones prominent and jawline cut sharp. Scars—some slashes, some crescent-shaped—covered her arms and flanks. Her belly featured both ripped muscle and stretch marks...from childbirth? Killian couldn't picture this siren in a nurturing, motherly role.

While Lorelei could be fucking scary, Aersila looked like she regularly ate sharks for breakfast and picked her teeth clean with their skeletal cartilage.

The aluminum can adornments only slightly dimmed her terrifying appearance.

Steeling his nerves, Killian slowly worked his way through the signs he practiced with Lorelei—the family name sign, Aersila's name, the word 'peace.' The glaring and hissing stopped. But Killian continued to sign, introducing himself and fingerspelling his name, followed by his relationship to the "Shorewalker."

Aersila cocked her head to the left. "You know our language." Spoken word rasped uncomfortably on her tongue.

"Nireed taught Lorelei, who taught me." The siren slinked down onto the deck slowly, watching him carefully. Killian held up his hand. "That's far enough." He kicked the crates of canned pork behind him with the heel of his boot. "This is for everyone, not just you and your friends."

Aersila's jaw clenched, but she stopped, holding a crouched position. "I want my sister back."

Judging by the mature cut of her cheekbones, the weathered, wary look in her eye, and streaks of white in her hair, Killian would have placed the siren as twenty years older than Nireed, at least. A whole generation between the sisters. Killian himself was an only child, but he could relate to the protectiveness the siren felt for a loved one. If their roles were reversed, he would be doing the exact same thing to get back someone he cared about. "I know. And she's sorry she didn't tell you that she wanted to go."

Aersila hissed. "You lie. No one chooses the shore. No one."

Killian shook his head. "She's just trying to help." He jerked his thumb behind him. "This stuff isn't a permanent solution. But Nireed's helping us find one."

Aersila slapped her hands together, the gesture too angry to be a clap. "Choose another. I want my sister."

As Killian studied the siren, thinking of what to say to put her mind at ease, he remembered what Lorelei had said to him about Nireed and her focus on personal merits and the greater good. He made a couple quick, hopefully spot on, assumptions about her. "Look, I know you love your sister and want to protect her. That's what big sisters do. But Nireed is old enough to make her own decisions, and right now she's trying to prove herself worthy to you and all your people. To earn their respect in her own right, as I imagine you have."

Furrowing her brow, Aersila listened closely and asked him to repeat some parts. And as he clarified, she slowly began to nod along with what he was saying, but her anger wasn't abating. "Nireed has our respect. But even if she didn't, she wouldn't choose this path. It is madness."

"Then how do I know who you are? And your family name?" He signed it again for emphasis. "If she didn't agree to this, didn't think this was the right thing to do, why would she share those details with us?"

The siren paused.

"Perhaps you speak true, Two-Legger." She sighed, signing the siren name for humans. When she followed that up by fingerspelling his name, surprising him, hope sparked in Killian's chest. That the siren bothered to remember and use his name, even in anger and frustration, felt big—a sign of respect.

Aersila climbed back up onto the gunwale and twisted her torso so she could peer at him over her shoulder. "Nireed must trust you and the Shorewalker a great deal to share what she has about our family and our people. I don't like it, but this is her path. I must let her see it through." The siren touched her fingertips to her chin and lowered her arm toward him. Then she flipped off the side and dove into the sea below with hardly a splash.

Her mermaid compatriots silently followed, surprised looks on all their faces.

Killian exhaled loudly, slumping back against the crates. He was a little surprised, too, at how smoothly the conversation had gone. How in the hell was dealing with vicious, people-eating merfolk easier than dealing with his ex-girlfriend? The lengths that woman went to stir trouble—using family ties to insinuate herself into Lorelei's department.

One wrong move, and they were getting a restraining order. Director Fucking Phil wouldn't be able to ignore that.

Slipping his headset over his ears, he turned his mic back on and told McAdams he could restart the engines. The helmsman's voice crackled through. "Captain, are you okay?"

"Yeah," he said, shakily running a hand through his sweat-damp hair. "That went really well. They won't be bothering us anymore. We came to an understanding."

There was a pause, punctuated by the sound of *Dawn Chaser's* engines rumbling back to life. "I can't figure out if you're crazy or brave, Quinn."

Killian let the comment hang unanswered as he heaved the crates into the ocean.

CHAPTER
TWENTY

LORELEI

THREE WEEKS OF MUSEUM PREP PASSED BY IN A WHIRLWIND.

Except for the occasional snide comment from Carrie, there wasn't enough time to bicker and trade cutting remarks with each other. The one thing Carrie was more committed to than taunting Lorelei, thankfully, was her job. They barely kept their heads above water as the finish line raced to meet them. But they were ready. Or as close to it as they were going to be. As long as they put on a good front for patrons— and they would—no one would know how frantic and rushed things felt behind the scenes.

Ticketing staff and docents were scheduled and rehearsed. Flyers were posted across town, in any street corner or business entryway claiming foot traffic, and mailings to research center donors and local schools were sent. The exhibits had been ready for a while and Lorelei was fine tuning her opening remarks. She'd likely fiddle with the language right up until opening day and practice her delivery every night in the bathroom mirror. Nothing like staring at herself to beat out the worst of her public speaking anxiety.

One thing Lorelei learned from Carrie in the past few weeks, just by watching her take meetings with donors and influential community leaders, was the art of faking it until you make it. Although, the seasoned advertising professional would probably scoff at the phrasing. Fake it? Carrie Prior did no such thing.

While Lorelei had come a long way since last month's breakdown, she could learn a thing or two from Carrie's professional confidence and poise. Styled hair, a full face of make-up, and a bright smile went a long way. And as much as Lorelei thought Carrie was a bitch outside of work, that woman knew how to wield 1,000-watt charm like a weapon. Donors and potential patrons gobbled up everything she said and made generous promises as if she, too, had been gifted with siren song.

On the evening of the soft opening with family and friends, Jackie Gaten from the *Haven Cove Daily*, would arrive an hour early for a private tour of the museum. She planned to do a feature piece on the Haven Cove Museum of Oceanic Discovery that would run in the Sunday paper, along with a profile piece on Lorelei as the first museum director.

Waiting for the reporter, Lorelei hovered near the museum foyer, keeping an eye on the entrance and another on Carrie as she drifted from exhibit to exhibit, refamiliarizing herself with the layout and displayed information. She'd also be interviewed. Then Phil. Thankfully, the research center director wouldn't drop by until just before the event began. The past three weeks had done nothing to dull Lorelei's desire to strangle the man.

Pausing in front of a display detailing the sirens' dietary range, which was based on observations of Nireed, Carrie folded her arms across her chest. "Why the hell do mermaids love potted meat so much?"

"'Cause it tastes like people," Lorelei mumbled under her breath.

"What?"

Lorelei bit her tongue, a smirk fighting for dominance.

With Jackie due any minute, she had to be on her best behavior. Carrie had just begun pestering her for an answer, when the reporter strode up to the door, fluffy cloud of hair bouncing up and down in time with her step.

Plastering a smile on her face, Lorelei ignored Carrie and met Jackie at the door. She held out her hand, but the petite woman surprised her by pulling her into a tight hug. Acquaintanceship in small towns demanded more than a stiff handshake. Jackie pulled away to get a view of the room. "Wow, this is really something, Lorelei. The design's more on par with what you'd see in a big city, not little ol' Haven Cove."

Money was no object. The museum had been almost wholly funded by the mermaid research. Once Lorelei knew just how big her budget would really be, she spent weeks researching her favorite museum exhibit designs, redesigning her exhibits in SketchUp, and contacting the manufacturers who could bring her new, revamped vision to life.

"Ah, well, you know HCMRC. We don't do anything in half-measures," Lorelei joked lightly. "Come on. I'll walk you through each of the exhibits. Give you the run-down."

Jackie followed Lorelei about the museum, furiously scribbling notes in her notepad, periodically asking questions. At the end of the tour, the reporter withdrew a professional-grade camera from the bag slung across her hip and took shots of the exhibits and a few ones of Lorelei posed in front of a mermaid display case. Then interviewed her for the professional profile piece.

Judging by Jackie's focus on her accomplishments, young age, and a quip about nominations for 30 under 30 lists, it was going to be a glowing article. But more than that, it was affirmation that Lorelei, for all the bumps it took to get here, and all the career ladder rungs she skipped past, she was the real deal and worthy of notice.

Take that imposter syndrome.

She would have to call her mentor Susan Lennard after the event to let her know how it went. She would be proud. And so would Mom, if only she were alive to see this.

Blinking to clear the mist from her eyes, Lorelei waved Carrie over so Jackie could get more quotes for her article. With just fifteen minutes until the event started, she probably should have emailed Phil, too, to let him know to come down, but she could honestly have cared less whether he made it into the article. It was petty, but he also deserved it for being a dick to Nireed.

At 7:00 p.m. the friends and family of select Haven Cove Marine Research Center staff, as well as prominent community leaders, began filing in through the front door, paired up with Lorelei's colleagues. With a smile pinned to her face, Lorelei welcomed everyone as they came in, while anxiously gauging their reactions. Just over 200 guests, including the town mayor and his family.

She was met with wide smiles, firm handshakes, and heads on swivel, taking in her work with awe. As the guests approached various display cases their expressions shifted. Natural and local marine history unfolded before their eyes—reading placards, videos, and artifacts neatly packaged together to give visitors a glimpse of the mysteries of the sea. Some nodded along as they absorbed the information. Some mouthed the words as they read. Others stood with their arms crossed, or stuffed in their pockets, or linked arm-in-arm with a spouse or date. The ones with young children towed them along by the hand or carried them on their hips, pointing to the more visual bits of the exhibits. There was laughter. Enthusiastic chit-chatting.

Awe returned to the faces of those who wandered into the mermaid exhibit.

Jackie threaded through the groups of people, introducing herself, and asking if she could take pictures. The catering staff Carrie hired wove their way around, as well, offering refreshments and hors d'oeuvres to the guests.

The people she wanted to see the most arrived fashionably late.

It had been planned. Killian, Lila, and Branson brought up the vanguard so that when they stopped to chat with her, they wouldn't hold up the receiving line.

They arrived together, all in cocktail hour attire. Killian wore a tie and button-down shirt tucked into fitted slacks, a broad grin spanning face. He'd rolled his sleeves above his elbows, all neat and crisp lines, to show off those corded forearms of his. The tease. She'd never seen him dress so sharp, and for one misty-eyed moment, she imagined how handsome he would look on their wedding day.

She wiped the happy tears from her eyes. The successful culmination of a rewarding but grueling project made her emotions especially fragile tonight.

"This is cool." Killian beamed, thumbs hooked in his belt loops. His gaze traveled across the room, lingering on every detail, his stormy eyes twinkling. The way his fingers twitched, she could tell he was itching to touch her, but wasn't sure if he should at her workplace. "This is really cool."

"It's phenomenal," Lila jumped in, pulling her into a tight, rocking hug. "You've done top-notch work here, Lorelei. I am so proud of you."

Killian hugged her next, and pressed a kiss to her forehead, the friendship PDA putting whatever doubts he'd had about showing affection at her work event to rest.

When they parted, Branson lifted his hand for a fist bump, a big smile adoring his face, too. "Bring it in."

Chuckling, Lorelei bumped his fist. "Thanks, guys. It's wild seeing it like this—not just finished and ready for public viewing, but actually seeing people walk around in it, looking at my work from this bonkers year…it's just so surreal." She pressed her hands to her cheeks. "This is really happening."

"You've earned it ten times over," Killian said with a grin. Their friends nodded in agreement, before leaving them by the front door to go explore Lorelei's museum themselves.

Lorelei craned her neck to see past Killian. "Are Marci and Walt coming?"

His jaw ticked. A wide range of emotions flashed across his face—disappointment, anger, resignation. "They weren't feeling up to it. They…need more time."

Her heart sank. It had been more than three weeks since the incident with Carrie. While she didn't expect blanket forgiveness, she thought they might at least be on speaking terms by now. Yes, this was the soft opening, and not as big of a deal as the grand opening, it was meant for friends and family. And Lorelei thought they were hers. It hurt that they weren't here.

She'd poured blood, sweat, tears, and soul into building this museum from the ground up. It was her proudest achievement. She hoped to make Walt and Marci proud, too. But even more, she hoped that maybe if they saw the mermaid exhibit, they would finally understand and accept all her layers. Even the vicious ones.

"It's not just," he stepped closer and lowered his voice, "the scary mermaid stuff. They're upset with Carrie, too, for the shit she pulled. Knowing how unstable she can get, they want to keep their distance, at least until they can be certain she's getting the help she needs." He took her hand and rubbed circles across the back with his thumb. Soothing and centering.

Keeping her voice to a whisper, Lorelei replied, "She's asked me a few times to leave the office for therapy appointments."

"Your compulsion worked. Completely."

Lorelei nodded. Everything she'd said to Carrie that day on the beach —*Forget what I am, Carrie Prior. And never come back here. Never speak of this*— the woman obeyed it all. "Is this mind-controlling people thing still bad if used with good intentions?"

"I think there's a very fine line, but if you ask me, you haven't crossed it. Carrie's situation was a dire emergency. It's important to remember that. She was out for blood and ready to hurt someone, possibly more in the crossfire."

Lorelei searched the crowd for Killian's ex and saw her schmoozing the Mayor of Haven Cove with expert charm. Despite their past differences, Lorelei begrudgingly admitted that she was good at her job and had been integral to the museum's successful launch.

Taking a cue from Carrie, Lorelei excused herself with a kiss to Killian's cheek and worked the crowd.

The soft opening had been a good idea. While Lorelei didn't know nearly everyone in the room, there were a lot of familiar faces from town and amongst fellow staff. A nice stepping-stone outside her comfort zone. Drifting from group to group, and chatting folks up, gave her the opportunity to nail down her spiels and tease out conversational kinks. Not only was it good practice, it boosted her confidence in her ability to master next week's public events.

Over the course of the night, Lorelei noticed that people spent the most time in the mermaid exhibit. She had predicted it would be the most popular and designed it to accommodate greater volumes of foot traffic. It comfortably held tonight's crowd, but the grand opening could be a squeeze when both locals and fall-color-chasing tourists could attend. A busy launch would be fantastic, but hopefully not so much that they'd have to turn people away at the door.

Things were looking up.

CHAPTER
TWENTY-ONE

LORELEI

After parting remarks to the museum's first visitors, Lorelei wasn't ready for the night to end. Even Phil's presence beside her, and microphone hogging, hadn't annoyed her enough to dim the buzz of excited energy she felt from an event gone well. A small after-party with close friends was just what she needed to come down from this social high.

Once clean-up and lock-up were taken care of, the Branson duo followed her and Killian home for drinks. They kicked off their shoes, passed around bottles of beer, and didn't quite make it out of the kitchen. They were too busy recapping the night to even think about sitting down.

During a break in conversation, Will lifted his bottle of beer and said, "To Lorelei. Our badass mermaid friend and museum expert extraordinaire."

"Aww, Will."

"Cheers!"

"I'll drink to that!"

They clinked their bottles together. Her friends' beaming smiles warmed her just as much as the alcohol. Eventually they drifted to the kitchen table and settled into seats all around. Lila raised her bottle to her lips and took an extra-long pull. "I have some good news and bad news. But good news first."

The cheery mood sobered.

Lorelei wrapped her hands around her own beer, centering herself in the cool touch of glass. She could guess what the bad news was about—something to do with Phil, the board, and Nireed. And if it gave her friend pause about sharing even the good news… "Lila, what is it?"

"The good news is that the virophage we gave Nireed a couple weeks ago worked. She hasn't been having human-flesh cravings. I wanted to tell you sooner, but I thought it would be better to wait until my team knew for sure. I didn't want to get your hopes up. But we can begin treating the merfolk population."

"That includes me, right?"

Lila hesitated, her eyes darting to Killian. Neither liked the idea of her participating in the clinical trial, but it wasn't their decision to make. Her body, her choice, and all that. "If it's fine enough to use on more of my siren kin, it's fine enough for me to volunteer."

"But…"

Lorelei leveled Lila with a firm look. "I want the injection."

The marine biologist puffed out a breath. "Okay."

If bad news hadn't been promised, Lorelei would be soaring right now. No more insidious hunger. No more potted meat. She'd be completely in control again, and never have to worry about the dire consequences of a skipped meal.

Judging by the grave look on Lila's face, Lorelei wouldn't like the price. She twisted the beer bottle in her hands. Killian settled his hand over hers, and she stilled. With a small smile, he gently pried the bottle from her grasp. Siren strength carried over into human form, and she could easily break the glass.

Lorelei wrung her hands underneath the table instead. "So, what's the bad news?"

Regret pinched Lila's lips as she tugged on one tight curl, pulling it straight. "You know what? Tonight's your night. It can wait until tomorrow."

Will smoothed circles across his wife's back. "It's a little late for that now, hon."

Peace already disturbed, Lorelei voiced her agreement. Should that state of mind continue, better it be with the truth than an unanswered question.

Killian reached under the table and steadied her hands, saving them from their own punishing grip. That man missed nothing. "She'll be up all night wondering," he said, taking her hands into his and massaging away the stress.

With a heavy sigh, Lila gave in. "Nireed took a turn for the worst last night. It's not virophage related. That's been in her system for a couple weeks now. But she knows now that the research center is never letting her leave alive. Overheard some idiots talking about it yesterday in front of her. And she doesn't know we plan to break her out. I've been trying to sneak messages, but Jerry's been watching me like a fucking hawk."

"Took a turn for the worst? What does that mean? I thought she was healthy."

"She's been on a slow, but steady mental and physical decline since we brought her to shore. The field trip last month gave her some life back, but since...she's not been doing well, Lorelei. How she looked before our ill-fated field trip is nothing to how she looks now. It's bad. Real bad. And now she's crashing. But when I pointed that out to leadership—" Lila's voice began to rise. "How we're isolating her, and screwing her mental health to hell, they just say it's an unfortunate, but inevitable result of life in captivity. My team's doing what they can— making sure she gets enough fluids and nutrients, but it's not enough. We're petitioning to have the tank drained and refilled with new seawater, but it's been denied as 'an unnecessary and outsized expense.' The whole lab's too scared to do anything more drastic, what with the NDAs they signed. They don't want to put their careers on the line for her, and while I can't make that call for them, I can't just sit around and do nothing. Nireed doesn't even swim in her tank anymore, just drifts.

It's horrible, and even if I could access the Mermaid CAM to show you, I wouldn't."

The men swore under their breath.

They were killing her.

"Her lungs are going to go out. She's been away from the ocean too long." As she shared what Nireed told her, Lila nodded along as if she'd already deduced as much, and said, "Phil doesn't give a shit."

But Killian stiffened beside her, jaw clenched. "You conveniently left that part out when you refused to return to the sea." Although his hold on her hands tightened, it wasn't painful. More clinging. The scent of fear mixed with anger rolled off him in droves. "Were you just going to let yourself asphyxiate and die?"

"No," she answered but it sounded weak even to her own ears.

Given her mental state at the time, anything could have happened, but she wouldn't have let herself die, would she? Lorelei pulled her hands from Killian's to rub her temples, her mind racing a mile a minute. No, she wouldn't have. Itchy, irritable skin was easy enough to habituate to. Difficulty breathing was not, and it would've snapped her out of it, which she voiced to Killian.

"That's still taking it way too far. Letting your skin and tail deteriorate as you had was taking it too far."

Their friends agreed, faces engraved with worry.

"I know." Lesson learned. No amount of guilt or grief or self-loathing justified jeopardizing her health, but there wasn't time to linger on this. "What Phil and the board are doing doesn't make sense. It's in their best interests, fucked as they are, to keep Nireed alive and well. The mermaid study is what's attracting most of the funding streams, and she's the only one the institution has."

"I think they're afraid of how 'human-presenting' she is." Lila swiped angry tears from her cheeks, leaning into Will as he wrapped an arm around her waist. "They're getting unnerved that they can't just look at her and see an animal. She understands what we're saying and can talk back. Very sassy about it, too, might I add. Savvy viewers can probably pick up on some of that by watching the Mermaid CAM, but now Phil and the board are talking about getting rid of the restrictions I placed on the public's access to the mermaid lab. They're talking about doing daily, public-access tours. It's gonna be a circus."

Lorelei's blood ran cold. "But that doesn't make any damn sense either. Are you saying they're trying to kill her by neglect? Why would they do that if they're planning on showing her off for tours?"

The marine biologist hugged herself. "I think they're afraid of what she can and might say about her treatment; they're actively trying to live capture more mermaids. They haven't been successful, even with using potted meat as bait. My best guess is the mermaids are too smart, and we keep them too well fed. But the virophage...I'm afraid that delivering it is going to be a trap. I think they want to replace Nireed with a mermaid that hasn't learned our language."

Well, shit. Lorelei pinched the bridge of her nose. None of this was adding up. "But why would they think kidnapping other sirens would solve their problems? They have personhood, language, and culture. I mean I guess we don't really know how many sirens speak human languages, but the sign language Undine's school uses is very similar to ASL. I don't know how the research center plans on hiding that."

"True..." Lila drawled out, then shook her head. "I don't know what the hell they're thinking, but it doesn't really matter. It doesn't change that I want to stop them."

Lorelei took a long pull from her beer. "I think it's time to start planning Operation Jailbreak."

"And Operation Steal All the Virophages," Branson chimed in. "Do you know where those are stored?"

"The refrigeration unit is in the lab."

A grin broke out across Will's face, a mischievous glint entering his eyes. Rubbing his hands together, he said, a little too giddily, "I've always wanted to plan a heist."

Lila arched her brow at her husband. "You're only saying that because *Ocean's Eleven* was on TV last night."

He shrugged.

Lila rolled her eyes, but a smile crept up her lips. Some of the night's earlier cheer returned to the group. But Lorelei was thinking, planning.

The sooner they got Nireed out the better, but they had to be smart about it. Her own song would play a pivotal role in getting them past security and curtail anyone else who might stop them. No discussion was needed for her to know that much. But she didn't know the limits of her song, and a building full of people was a lot. With stakes like this, she couldn't afford to mess up. They needed a distraction. "I think the time to do it is on the museum's Grand Opening Day. Everyone's going to be busy and distracted by that. It would be relatively easy for us to sneak away, invent a family emergency."

"I'm fairly certain either one of my parents would fake a fall for the cause," Lila offered. "You know. The good 'ol life alert trick."

Covering his mouth with a hand, Will mumbled, "Not sure if I'm supposed to laugh at that or not."

Concern deepened the creases beside Killian's eyes, not a shred of humor to be found. "You sure, Lorelei? That's a big day for you. You've worked so hard for this, and you deserve to enjoy it."

Lila nodded. "We can do it another day. Figure something else out."

"I'm sure. How can I design a museum meant to educate the public on merfolk, but stand by as one suffers in captivity one building over? None of it will mean anything to me as long as Nireed isn't free. She did her part. Now we keep our promise. Besides, the next big event on the calendar is the Winter Gala, and that's way too far off."

Folding his hands on top of the table, Killian leaned forward. "Okay. Let's get planning."

CHAPTER
TWENTY-TWO

KILLIAN

STARS PEEKING OUT FROM THE CLEAR, TWILIGHT SKY, Killian steered *Dawn Chaser* into siren territory. Alone. He hadn't asked his crew to come along this time, and nor was he here to fish. No one could know why he was here, apart from his co-conspirators.

Long-time family friend and *Haven Cove Daily* reporter Jackie Gaten had been helpful. Maybe instrumental after getting her Nireed's health records and documentation of HCMRC's corruption. For weeks, Lila had snuck around compiling the file, contending with a pest of a colleague. "Fucking Dr. Jerry Nedry," Lila had cursed, hovered over her shoulder anytime she came anywhere near Nireed, muttering how she should've been fired, but thankfully, he watched less closely when she sat at her lab computer. And not at all when she was in her office.

It required patience, but Lila found openings. And the reverse camera and zoom features on her phone had become her best friend— great for stealth photographing Nireed's declining physical health.

That asshole colleague couldn't watch her every second of every day.

Shutting off the engines, Killian darted down onto the decks below.

He heaved an offering of canned pork over the side, and a climbable net, and waited for the sirens to come.

The rope of the net pulled taut when they reached the boat—that's the only way he knew they'd arrived. Their ascent was silent, but it left *Dawn Chaser's* latest paint job intact.

He was surprised to see not just Aersila, but Undine as well, slink over the side and crouch down, dripping seawater puddles onto the deck. Nireed had mentioned to Lorelei tensions between the two, but whatever differences they might've had, they evidently had been set aside.

The glint in Jackie's eyes as she pulled rubber bands off the thick file folder he delivered, reminded Killian of that vicious look that Aersila, Undine, or even Lorelei, sometimes got. Predators coiling to strike, savoring their prey's obliviousness to impending death.

It was more than hunger. It was glee in the kill.

Killian had no doubt HCMRC's piss poor leadership would get their comeuppances once Jackie was through with her reporting. But that's not why he was here in the middle of the ocean, alone with two murderous sirens.

Lambent blue and amber eyes stared back at him in the waning light. Waiting.

He signed Aersila and Undine's names and said, "We need your help."

CHAPTER
TWENTY-THREE

LORELEI

THE ANNIVERSARY OF *THE OSPREY* TRAGEDY REOPENED Lorelei's wounds and packed salt into them. She was supposed to give remarks at the memorial unveiling. Her best friend Katrina had even flown up from Boston to support her, but sandwiched between Kat and Killian, as she sobbed her frickin' eyes out, she knew she couldn't do it this time. And wouldn't. She just didn't have it in her.

While the crowd was a lot smaller than the one that gathered in the church in Portland a year ago, it consisted entirely of locals, not the families who lost their loved ones.

For her crew's friends and families, she would have tried.

Carrie was there, too, unexpectedly but mercifully quiet and humble with her hands clasped in front of her and her head bowed, as if in prayer. She kept her distance and hadn't said a word to either Lorelei or Killian since the event began. Some might say Carrie should have offered sympathies, despite their differences, but Lorelei was grateful she kept them to herself. Genuine or not, Lorelei didn't have the energy to deal with any kind of interaction from her fiancé's ex.

The crowd of people pressed in from all sides with their pitying stares and phone cameras. They encircled Lorelei, and the stone obelisk before her, the memorial structure erected outside on the ocean-side of the Haven Cove Marine Research Center, to commemorate the lives lost.

Forty-nine names were etched into its surface—eighteen permanent crew members and thirty-one sailing trainees. Like her. But only not like her. There should have been fifty names carved there, but the siren blood in Lorelei's veins and the hidden gills along her neck kept her name off the stone.

She stared at those names, listening to the breaking of ocean waves against rocky shore, behind the din of the people surrounding her.

At least at the memorial service at the church last year, everyone gathered was bonded by the same abyssal grief that swallowed them whole. There was also a podium she could grip and a wide stretch of space between her and the first row of pews.

And no cameras.

Someone's phone clicked to her right, mimicking a camera's shutter sound as they took a photo. Lorelei startled at the sound. The person responsible turned beat red and mouthed the word 'sorry.'

A gruff voice rose from the crowd. "Put that away," the man grumbled, mirroring Lorelei's mood exactly.

When Lorelei looked up, she made eye contact with Ed Knutson, a retired Portland Press Herald reporter. Not all locals then. He nodded to her with a small, weary smile as he nudged his way through the crowd to stand with them. Though his eyes were puffy and red, his face had filled out since the last time she saw him. He looked healthy, not gaunt, nor sallow with grief.

Touching her hand to her chest, Lorelei made sure Mackenzie's silver necklace was tucked away beneath her shirt. She wouldn't be able to explain to Ed how she'd gotten this remnant of his niece. It was all that remained of her from her time onboard *The Osprey*. Drowned and eaten by a mermaid you knew just wasn't something you told people.

Phil took the lead on the event, telling the gathered crowd why they were here today. She wished it could have been anyone other than him, a local minister or priest, but he'd insisted that it be him if Lorelei couldn't do it. And she couldn't. She was just too much of a mess.

Choked sobs clogged Lorelei's throat.

It was too much. She just wanted to honor and grieve in peace without an audience. If it weren't for Killian and Kat's arms around her, she would have felt so open and exposed in front of all these people—reliving those horrible hours spent out on the open ocean in an immersion suit, certain she would die.

Ed occasionally blew his nose, but his tears were silent.

A part of her resented that she was the only one crying loudly at this event, drawing attention, when this wasn't about her. This was about *The Osprey* crew who lost their lives on that fateful, stormy night. The way people stared at her openly and dry-eyed made her feel like she was making a scene.

But she wasn't. She had every right to this grief.

When Phil finished his remarks, he looked to Lorelei, his expression over-schooled with faux sympathy and asked if she would like to say some words. She'd prepared some. They were written on a piece of paper folded up in her pocket, but her thoughts on whether she could give them hadn't changed since the event began.

She shook her head and gestured to the towering obelisk with a tissue-crammed hand. The only words that she could manage were, "I wish they were here, and this wasn't."

Phil pushed, and she felt both Killian and Katrina tense on either side her. Before they could raise their voices to defend her, she leveled her boss with a hard look. "No."

He blinked several times and looked around him, trying to gauge who else heard. Those closest to them seemed a little affronted by her bluntness, but she didn't care if it made her look like an asshole. She was ready for this event to be over and for these people who didn't really care about *The Osprey* crew to go away.

Their families had been invited, but Haven Cove was too far, and the hurt too big to make the trip. And maybe they had sensed better than Lorelei had that their grief would have been turned into a spectacle. For their sakes, she was glad they hadn't come.

But Ed came. And when the event was over, she gave him a tight hug.

When the crowd left, Lorelei lingered, finally having her peace. She asked Killian and Kat to wait in the car for her. Kat rubbed her shoulder and Killian kissed her cheek before leaving together. Even Ed went with them to give her privacy and space.

Rubbing Mackenzie's necklace between her fingers, she touched her other hand to the stone and said the words she couldn't in front of the others. The words that weren't even written down on paper. "I am so sorry for what happened to you that night. That your last moments were spent in utter terror and agony. I'm sorry that my kin..." *Ate you.* She couldn't say those last two words, even to the dead, amongst whom there were no secrets. "And I'm sorry that you were never laid to rest."

Tears rolled down her cheeks as she made her confession. "I didn't know it at the time, but I'm like one of the monsters you saw in the dark. Only, they aren't monsters. Not really. I used to think so, too, but not anymore. I'm still angry about what happened to you. None of you deserved any of it, but I'm not angry at them anymore. I think you would understand if you could see what I see and know what I know about them. That they're just like us—human and flawed but capable of better. But, of course, you're perfectly in your right to just tell me to shut up and fuck off."

Inhaling deeply, she pushed her residual guilt out with her breath. "I can't undo what happened, but I still wish you could be here and be a part of this world that knows mermaids exist. Mackenzie, you would like Nireed. She's fierce and sassy, but I can see you making it your personal mission to make her laugh. I have no doubt you would have succeeded."

She traced her fingers over their names and whispered a prayer in German that her mother had taught her. The last time she'd said it was at her mother's funeral.

After one final touch, she turned around to face the Haven Cove Marine Research Center. She couldn't see through the glass, but just beyond on the other side was the mermaid lab, and within it, Nireed in her tank. She had no idea if the siren could see her—or was even looking—but Lorelei signed anyway. In English, it roughly translated to, "I am coming to get you."

CHAPTER
TWENTY-FOUR

LORELEI

THE GRAND OPENING STARTED IN JUST FIFTEEN MINUTES.

Within the privacy of Lila's office, Lorelei said, "Are you sure you want to do this? You don't need to come. I can do this on my own." She tapped her throat. With most of their colleagues congregating in or around the museum, Lorelei didn't think she'd have a problem pulling off the jailbreak and virophage extraction singlehandedly. Her voice could knock out a few security guards and Jerry. "If we get caught, you'd lose your job over this."

Lila shook her head vigorously, folding her arms across her chest. "Last year, on *Dawn Chaser*, we made a vow to free Nireed if her health failed, and I fully intend to keep it. Besides, I know how to properly handle the virophages, and you'll have your hands full with Nireed."

"If you change your mind, I won't be upset..."

"Lorelei," Lila said firmly, giving her arm a reassuring squeeze. "It's my choice, and I'm helping."

"Okay," Lorelei puffed out her breath and shook out her arms, her nerves along with them. After two deep breaths, she schooled her features, and fixed a bright smile on her face, the one she used in professional settings. She called it her customer service smile.

"Wow, that was a scary transformation."

"You've seen far worse."

Logging out of her computer, Lila said, "I prefer the teeth and claws, actually."

"One of the few who do. You ready?"

"Lead the way, Museum Director."

Lorelei chuckled. "What did Will call this—Operation Badass Babes?"

"Yup. But I think Badass Bitches fits the tone better for what we're pulling off today."

"All right, Bad Bitch. Let's get this shit done."

Doorbuster was a good word to describe the day's event. All the rooms were already jam-packed and pushing max capacity, and it was little after the museum's 9:00 a.m. opening. Carrie stationed herself at the door with security to hand out discount vouchers to guests they had to turn away at the door. If Lorelei didn't have a mermaid rescue and virophage heist to pull off, she would've taken a moment to triumph in this great success.

For the first hour, Lorelei worked the room hard. One because it was her job, and two to make sure she was well seen and heard by patrons and colleagues. But especially Phil and members of the board.

At 10:00 a.m., Lorelei began weaving through the crowd toward the back, as if making her way to the bathrooms. It was Operation Badass Bitches go time.

"Ms. Roth!"

Shit. Spinning around, the customer service smile firmly in place, Lorelei saw Phil heading her way. He seemed tickled pink—pleased by the success of the event and revenues streaming in no doubt. While he was likely only going to congratulate her, she didn't have time to get caught up in conversation with her boss.

They needed every bit of the next two hours to get Nireed and the virophages out the marine research center and out to sea, well before anyone trickled back to their offices for lunch and realized what they'd done.

Before anyone could come after them and stop them.

Just as Lorelei opened her mouth to say she had to address a family emergency, her friend Katrina practically launched herself out of the crowd to intercept Phil. "Hello, Director Simmons," she said cheerily, holding out her hand. "I'm Katrina Lovera. I work for Regent PR in Boston. This is just a fabulous event, and I'd love to talk to you about…"

Opportunistic glee shone in his eyes.

With Phil properly distracted, Lorelei silently thanked her friend for the rescue and disappeared out the back to where Lila was already waiting. The scientist leaned against the building's red brick wall, arms crossed, wearing black sunglasses and a "don't fuck with me" attitude. She looked positively fierce.

One shared look and some of that fierceness ignited in Lorelei.

Pushing off the wall, Lila joined her and together they walked to the main building, their strides in sync, with all the energy of Wyatt Earp and Doc Holliday heading to the O.K. Corral.

Marine biologist. And people-eating mermaid.

Badass Bitches.

They slipped in through a side door, near the video surveillance room.

The security guard stationed inside spun around in his chair and began to rise from his chair. "Hey, you can't be in here!"

Lorelei hummed, the eerie tune of her people's song filling the room. The guard's shoulders relaxed, and a serene expression fell over his face as he sat back down. "Erase the footage of us coming in here and then shut off all the cameras for one hour," she bid. He complied without resistance.

"Anything else?" He smiled up at her, shy and eager to please. She had this strange man completely and utterly in her thrall. He would do anything she asked. It made her stomach queasy that he might lose his job over this, but a literal life was at stake.

"Forget that you saw us."

He turned back to his workstation to stare at a wall of black screens.

They strode past empty offices and down quiet hallways leading to the mermaid lab. Lorelei dispatched the security officers posted outside the mermaid lab door in the same fashion as the video surveillance guy.

Let us in. Look away. Forget.

As the door swung open, Fucking Jerry the Scientist looked up from his computer, startle quickly turning to outrage. Lorelei took quick stock of the room. He was the only other person in the lab. Jumping up from his seat, he pointed a finger at her. Of all the scientists on Lila's team, Jerry always seemed to dislike her the most. "Dr. Branson, she's not allowed in here."

"Don't care, asshole." Lila whisked by him, wasting no time with the virophages. She ran over to the refrigeration unit and began loading them into the coolers they'd been delivered in from the manufacturer.

"What are you doing? You can't..." Jerry sputtered, cheeks growing red. "Are you seriously stealing right now? Unbelievable. Just wait until I tell Phil about this! You can kiss your job good-bye. And finally, too, if you ask me. You should never have had this position. People like you..."

"Close your fucking mouth, Jerry," Lorelei snapped, advancing on him.

As she moved, wicked rows of teeth emerged from her gums and talons from her nail beds. She got right up in his face—close enough to see the glow of her ferocious glare reflected in his eyes—and jabbed a claw into his chest. Not enough to do serious damage, but enough to draw blood.

He squeaked.

"If you ever disrespect Dr. Branson again, I will rip your heart from your chest and eat it in front of you. Got that?"

Sinking into his chair, he nodded meekly. The sharp scent of urine filled the air.

Glancing down, Lorelei noticed a dark patch spreading down the pants leg of his khakis.

"Gross." She spun his chair around, with him in it, so that he faced his computer and not her. "Forget you ever saw us here today and go to sleep." He slumped forward, forehead clunking against his keyboard. Whatever email or document he'd been typing in would soon be filled with keyboard smash gibberish.

Lorelei left Fucking Jerry to his piss-soaked oblivion and hurried over to Nireed's tank.

It had been weeks since she made the climb up its grated, open-backed stairs, but she swallowed her fear of heights and darted up. When she was at level with Nireed, where the siren floated inside, she held onto the railing and stretched over to rap the glass.

Nireed was just as bad as Lila had said.

Eyes closed tight, the siren didn't even register Lorelei's presence. The once vibrant oranges and metallic silver coloring in her fins were washed out and dull. Nireed drifted about the tank, her tail occasionally twitching, just enough to keep her moving and breathing. The siren's grey and gaunt skin mirrored the color of death.

Lorelei rapped against the glass again but with more force. "Wake up, Nireed."

The siren's eyes shot open. Two glowing amber gems stared back at her from the dark shadows of the tank. Their light fluttered as Nireed blinked and shook lethargy from limbs and tail.

Lorelei leaned over the railing to press a hand to the glass.

With more life than she'd shown just moments before, Nireed raced over. She drew up short of collision and pressed her hand to where Lorelei's rested on the other side. Hope shone bright and desperate in her eyes. She pulled back and signed, "Get me out?"

Lorelei nodded and pointed up.

Without further prompting, the siren sped toward the top of the tank, and Lorelei dashed up the rest of the stairs after her. When she opened the hatch at the top of the tank, she choked on the thick cloying scent that wafted up. Not a dirty, soiled odor, nor decomposition. The water reeked of despair.

Trapped in the same recycled water, Nireed was left to stew in her own pheromones, feeding a vicious cycle that could only be broken by dredging the tank and piping in fresh, new seawater. She was never intended to thrive here.

Nireed breached the surface and scrabbled against the opening of the hatch, trying to pull herself out. But she was too weak to support her own weight out of water and kept slipping. Reaching inside, Lorelei grabbed Nireed by the arms. While Nireed had lost her strength these last few weeks, Lorelei had regained hers. Careful not to grip too hard and bruise her, Lorelei hauled Nireed out. She tried to keep her upright, but the siren collapsed on the metal grating, breathing heavily, the passage of air rasping against her throat like ripping paper. Just the effort of leaving the tank knocked the wind out of her.

Their descent down the stairs was slow and clumsy, reminiscent of the first time they'd ever made the journey. Nireed's legs were as weak and wobbly as a newborn foal's. Partway down, after a few too many heart-stopping near-falls, Lorelei lifted the siren into her arms, taking each step down slow and steady, stomach lurching and thighs burning as she tried to maintain her balance.

As soon as they reached the bottom, Lorelei sat her in the nearest chair. Even with the help, the siren reclined back, wheezing. "Arms up," Lorelei instructed. "It helps." While Nireed held her arms in the air, Lorelei ran to grab the tote bag Lila stowed underneath one of the desks and passed the marine biologist on the way.

"It's all packed," Lila said as she lifted one of the coolers. "I'm going to start taking them out to the truck."

"Great. I'll help you as soon as I've got Nireed situated." When Lorelei returned to Nireed, the siren's labored breathing had subsided. She withdrew a pair of flip flops from the tote bag and helped the siren put them on, followed by a dress that she pulled over her head. "Come on," Lorelei said, hooking an arm underneath Nireed's and hoisting her onto her feet. "We're almost there. Just need to get you out the door and into the car."

"Car," Nireed groaned, her complexion already draining. But she shuffled forward, spurred undoubtedly by the promise of freedom, despite her hatred of the moving metal contraption, and the effort it took to breathe.

"We've got you, every step of the way." Lorelei hoisted the siren into her arms, making use of that supernatural strength. "I promise, you'll never see this facility again. Just focus on breathing, ok?"

Closing her eyes, Nireed drew in air as deeply as she could, each breath rasping painfully in her chest.

"Kat's leaving," Lila announced, looking up from her smart watch as she passed Lorelei to get another cooler. "She just planted the family emergency story in Phil's ear."

They wouldn't be returning to the party.

Lila was going to administer the virophages today, and it was Lorelei's job to convince the sirens to accept it.

CHAPTER
TWENTY-FIVE

KILLIAN

He kept his truck running in the small lot behind the back entrance of the mermaid lab, mind racing a million miles an hour wondering how the ladies were fairing inside. What if they got caught, and Lorelei's song couldn't save them? What if her bosses and colleagues found out she was a siren? Would they kidnap her and throw her into that tank with Nireed for study? Poke and prod her with needles and parade her before all of Haven Cove and the world like some zoo exhibit?

He clenched the steering wheel, twisting his hands over the hard plastic. It sounded insane, but he wouldn't be shocked if their worst fears came true. If those people dared touch Lorelei, he would burn that fucking place to the ground to get her out.

A nudge to his ribs jolted him from his rage-filled thoughts. "Hey man," Branson said. "I don't know what just crossed your mind, but you look like you're gonna kill something. Wanna talk about it?"

Killian shook his head. "Just imagining a worst-case scenario."

His friend clamped a hand on his shoulder. "They're gonna be fine.

It's Operation BADASS Babes, remember? We're just the sidekicks. If anyone's gonna need help or rescuing, it's us."

Huffing with half-hearted laughter, Killian released his stranglehold on the steering wheel. "Yeah, you're right. They've got this." But the sick feeling in his stomach didn't go away. Not knowing what was happening in there was stressing him the fuck out.

At 10:36, Lila burst through the back door, hustling but determined, not alarmed. Killian exhaled, and Will hopped out of the truck to go help his wife with loading in the virophages. The lab's back entrance door locked as soon as it closed, and couldn't be accessed by keycard, so they wedged a rock between the door and its jamb.

Lorelei and Nireed exited via the lab's back entrance door a few minutes later. Even with Lorelei's restored strength, carrying Nireed had her red-faced and breathing hard. Killian itched to help, but as their getaway driver, he had to stay where he was and keep the engine running, ready to peel out of there at a moment's notice.

Setting Nireed on her feet with a grunt, Lorelei opened the rear passenger door and instructed the siren to brace herself against it, promising she'd help her inside after shedding a layer. Looping her arms through the open window, Nireed clung tighter than barnacles on a ship hull, making the metal creak even in her weakened state.

"Easy," Lorelei warned breathlessly, shucking her blazer into the front seat. "Don't break our means of escape."

Nireed loosened her grip, cheeks pink. "Sorry, Shorewalker."

Swiping sweaty strands of hair away from her eyes, and tucking them behind her ears, his fiancée continued, "It's okay. Now, I'll give you a boost, but you're going to want to step here." She pointed to the step rails. "Then grab that handle above your head and pull yourself up onto the seat."

The cautious way Nireed peeled away from the door maintaining at least three points of contact, made the whole endeavor look more like rock scrambling than entering a vehicle.

Nireed was half in, half out of the truck, with Lorelei boosting her hips, and Lila and Will stacking coolers outside the back door, when cheerful whistling made them all freeze.

A middle-aged man wearing grease-smudged coveralls turned the corner, toting a toolbox in one hand and jangling a key ring in another. The name "Glenn" was embroidered across his shirt pocket in neat, white lettering. No one moved in inch, each of them gripped by a panic-induced delusion that if they remained still maybe he wouldn't notice.

But Glenn stopped, whistling cut short. Swiveling his head from the lab's open backdoor to the siren half hanging out of Killian's truck and dripping aquarium water everywhere, his expression grew serious.

A beat passed. Then two.

"Nice day to go for a swim, yeah?" Glenn asked after a time, surprising Killian with his jovial tone.

It was a brisk fall day in Maine. Not even the lake water would be warm enough.

"Um, yeah," Lorelei agreed. "Great day for a swim."

Glenn nodded once, and although his serious expression didn't change, tiny hints of a smile crept in at the edges. "Be safe out there," was all he said before walking away, whistling the classic cartoonish tune of "nothing to see here!"

"I might've shit myself a little." Will laughed, lifting one of the virophage coolers and duck-walking it over to the truck.

Nose scrunched with distaste, Lila replied, "Better hope not, or you're riding in the bed. No one wants to sit next to your stinky ass."

Will's gait smoothed out. "Skid free, baby."

Lila rolled her eyes.

"Kind of nice not having to use my song on someone," Lorelei added, getting Nireed settled inside and buckling her in. "Restores my faith in humanity a little."

Once Nireed was situated, Lorelei ran to help Lila and Will with the virophages, forming an assembly line from the back door to Killian's truck bed. Between the three of them, the coolers were loaded in, strapped down, and tarped over within minutes.

"Let's get out of here before we have anymore unwanted visitors," Killian called out.

Lorelei ran to the front passenger seat, Lila and Will to the back. As soon as they all piled inside and closed the doors, Killian hit the gas. A little too hard. A collection of oofs, ows, and one hiss rose all around him as his comrades lurched forward from the sudden change in inertia, knocking limbs into each other and various parts of the interior. Despite having planned this get-in-the-car-and-floor-it getaway ahead of time, none of them seemed to have been ready for it.

He apologized.

"I'm gonna feel that one in the morning," Lila teased, rotating her shoulder. "But well worth it. I mean is it truly a heist experience if you don't burn some rubber at the end?"

Half the people in this vehicle were pushing forty, and while that wasn't by any means close to old, he supposed they were maybe getting too "old" for these kinds of Hollywood movie dramatics.

Sitting back with a huff of laughter, and buckling her seatbelt, Lorelei cheered. "We did it!"

Branson whooped, pumping his fist into the air. "Operation Badass Babes for the win!"

"It's 'Bitches', Will. We changed it," Lorelei laughed as she reached around her seat to dole out high-fives.

In his rearview mirror, Killian watched Lila show Nireed how to join in. "Not too hard," she said, arching her brow, all while holding out her hand for Nireed to slap it. The siren looked bewildered, but she clapped her hand on top.

"It's not over yet," Killian cautioned, but he couldn't help but smile, too. The hardest part was behind them.

From the corner of his eye, he saw Lorelei rub her elbow and wince. "You okay?"

"Just hit my funny bone on the dash is all."

"You sure?"

Lorelei smiled, glancing briefly back at Nireed, where she sat sandwiched in the backseat between Lila and Branson. "Never better."

Checking his review mirror once more, some of the tension coiling in his stomach eased as he watched the marine research center shrinking behind them. Save for the hubbub over by the museum, the campus remained calm and quiet. No shouting, no sounds of alarm, no security guards hopping into SUVs with black-tinted windows to chase after them. HCMRC might be a state-of-the-art research facility, and its security might have amped up in the last year, but this was still small-town Haven Cove. Heists here weren't flashy. Not like in the big cities, and certainly not like in the movies.

"Where are Aersila and Undine?" Lorelei asked. He glanced over. Her head was bent while she tapped something out on her phone—likely texting Katrina that the coast was clear, and to meet them at the docks as planned.

"Back at home," Killian replied. "They're sticking close to shore, waiting for us to bring Nireed."

"Good." Lorelei lowered her voice. "And they're aware she's in bad shape?"

"Yeah, I gave them a heads up, so they'll be prepared and hopefully won't eviscerate us when they see her."

She rubbed her forehead. "I hadn't thought of that possibility."

"I mean they weren't pleased, but they weren't outraged either."

Nireed spoke up from the back. "Aersila and Undine are together?" She sounded surprised.

"Yeah, they seem to be working together," he confirmed. "I think they're both really anxious to get you back."

Once they cleared town, and turned onto the country road, he sped up, sailing past the speed limit. No one might be following them now, but he didn't want to take the chance. The more distance they put between themselves and HCMRC the better. The sirens still needed to take Nireed and get her back to the deep. And this ragtag crew needed to follow them in *Dawn Chaser* with the virophages. With any luck, Lorelei, the only mermaid in the group, could convince them to go through with it.

Operation Badass Bitches wasn't over yet.

CHAPTER
TWENTY-SIX

LORELEI

Sirens waited for them in the cove, bobbing along in the grey, choppy water. A light fog had rolled in, and seven pairs of lambent eyes stared out from the haze. Each tracked Lorelei and her companions as they exited Killian's truck.

When Nireed slid out from the back seat, with help from herself and Lila, the sirens dipped beneath the surface. Swimming to shore no doubt. Lorelei's stomach tied itself in knots at the quick approach of her kin.

But were they kin? That word once accompanied horror and disgust, but now Lorelei feared she didn't have a place amongst these vicious ladies of the deep. They shared siren blood, yes, but Lorelei had always been a shorewalker. All that bound her to them was a deal she made with Undine under a year ago. Not respect.

An amber-eyed siren who shared Nireed's features, just aged, sloshed onto shore. Her movements, though clumsy, were quick and determined. Despite walking being new and unfamiliar, she pushed herself up the beach, picking herself right back up each time she stumbled and fell.

Nireed let out a cry and raced down the sand. A surge of adrenaline and the downward slope propelled her onward, lending her tired body the momentum it couldn't produce on its own. She collided with the siren, bowling her over, sand and limbs flying as they tumbled together down the beach. They rose to their knees clutching one another, their bodies shaking with tears and laughter. This must have been Aersila. Lorelei followed at a distance, letting the sisters enjoy their reunion without disruption. She heard the others trail behind her.

"Aersila," Nireed sobbed. "I am sorry I did not tell you."

Her sister hugged her tighter. "It does not matter now. I am just happy to have you back. And you speak Two-Legger now. You learned so fast." Pride shined in Aersila's eyes.

Nireed withdrew from her sister's embrace, rolling her own. "I was surrounded by them every day."

Undine and the others crawled up the beach to join them. The leader of the sirens pinned Lorelei with a firm look. "It is done, Shorewalker?"

"We've got the cure," Lorelei replied, gesturing behind her to Killian's truck. "And we'll bring it to your territory by boat—just like with the canned pig."

Undine turned to Nireed. "Is it true? You no longer crave Two-Legger flesh?"

Nireed nodded, a weak smile spanning her face. "I am free." As she said the words, she tried standing up, but wobbled back, the adrenaline rush fading from her limbs. Lorelei caught Nireed before she fell, and gently lowered her to the sand.

Worry wrinkled Aersila's brow as she turned to the other sirens and began to sign. With her back turned, Lorelei didn't catch what she'd said, but two broke off from the group to pull something out of the water by two long pieces of rope. As they dragged it up the beach to where Nireed sat ashen-faced and winded, Lorelei saw that it was a stretcher made from whale bone and woven seaweed.

Together, they helped Nireed onto it, moving quickly, but tenderly. They cradled her head as they laid her down and strapped her torso to the stretcher. Aersila signed some more. *Rest, sister. We tow you. You've done more than enough.*

Every siren bowed their heads, signing 'thank you' and resting their fists over their hearts to express deep gratitude and respect. Lorelei joined them.

Nireed nodded, a beaming smile stretching her face from ear to ear as she closed her eyes. Lorelei couldn't help but smile, too, at seeing Nireed so happy and triumphant to be honored by her people.

While six of the sirens towed Nireed into the ocean, Undine lingered on shore. Her electric blue gaze locked onto Lorelei's as she rose onto her feet, slowly, but steadily, standing in front of Lorelei face-to-face. With a slight shake of her head, Undine grazed the underside of her chin with her thumb, then cut down in a slicing motion, brushing the fingertips of her other hand, which she held flat, palm facing her chest. *Unfinished.*

"We will see you again soon, Shorewalker."

Then she too disappeared into the waves.

That might have seemed threatening to some but not to Lorelei. The reminder hewed her sense of purpose to a sharp point. Undine upheld her end of the bargain. Now it was time for Lorelei to uphold hers and prove to her siren kin that she didn't make empty promises. And that she was worthy of their trust.

"I CAN'T BELIEVE I'M ABOUT TO MEET A BUNCH OF mermaids."

Lorelei looked over to where Katrina leaned over the gunwale, long brown curls whipped back by the wind. Her skin was deeply tanned from regular weekend trips to Cape Cod, its olive complexion taking to the sun far better than Lorelei's own fairer, ivory tone. While Lorelei didn't easily burn—possibly a trait that stemmed from her oceanic origins—she was quicker to freckle than tan.

While this expedition was far from a pleasure cruise, she wasn't worried about bringing Katrina along. Not a shred.

Will brushed past with a crate of potted meat, working the deck for now. He'd trade places with Killian at the helm when they got close to siren territory, since her fiancé was immune to every siren song but hers. Over his shoulder, Will said to Katrina, "I'd say you get used to it, but... I'm not there yet. I mean, Lorelei's cool." He paused, tipping his head toward the sea. "I just don't think the others see us as friends yet."

"Well, after today, at least we won't smell like food," Lila called from the middle of the deck, where she set up a pop-up clinic. At its center sat a gurney, the wheels locked in place, so it wouldn't roll away, though the seas were steady and calm. They had gotten lucky. Administering intracerebroventricular injections required not just a steady hand, but a steady workstation. Lila also had a table set up with antiseptic wipes and a numbing agent to make the injection as painless and comfortable as possible.

Donning a pair of latex gloves with a snap, Lila added, "Humans are friends, not—"

"Stop," Katrina interrupted, meeting Lorelei's eyes as she scrunched her face. "I *really* don't like thinking about this boat as a floating charcuterie board, but that's where my mind just went, and I think it's going to get stuck there for a while."

Lorelei shook her head slightly, a ghost of a smile on her lips as she joined Katrina at the railing. Her friend's growing fear did not touch her. Slinging an arm across Katrina's shoulders, she gave her a squeeze and hoped to press some of her own confidence into her.

They had Undine, Aersila, and Nireed on their side, as well as the sirens' mutual desire to wrestle back their self-control from the hunger that consumed them. Siren blood primed her instincts, but nothing resembling dread or ominous foreboding gripped her. She was a little nervous, yes. Dealing with a small group of mermaids was one thing. But a whole community? They had a rough estimation of how large Undine's pod was from talks with Nireed—just under one hundred, children included.

One hundred people-eating mermaids, clambering onboard for a fresh start and a chance to save their species. All putting their trust in the hands of a bunch of Two-Leggers with a medical procedure that was invasive even to Lorelei and her friends—and completely foreign to them.

No one could say for sure how this expedition would go, but Lorelei was hopeful. Excited even.

Watching her closely, Katrina's shoulders relaxed beneath the drape of Lorelei's arm. "You're practically glowing, Lorelei."

She couldn't hold back her sudden need to smile, full and bright. A phrase sprung to mind, one she heard both in the context of Ernest Hemingway and a *Jurassic Park* sequel. "This isn't a moveable feast. It's a new beginning."

Kat pulled her into a one-armed hug and rested a cheek against hers. "I like your version much better." They stood together in companionable silence, letting the wind tangle their hair and coat their cheeks with salty ocean spray, as *Dawn Chaser* smoothly cut through the afternoon's grey chop. Between the boat's speed, weight, and the wide spacing of the waves, they barely felt any bounce.

"Hey, Lorelei. I'm just about done setting up over here. You ready for your shot?"

Ready? She was more than ready. But when she turned to face Lila, and saw her holding up a syringe, its long metal tip glinting, she paused. Maybe it would be good if the other sirens witnessed her getting it. So that they knew what to expect. And to quell any fears or doubts. If it was safe enough for the Shorewalker to get it, it would be safe enough for them. When she voiced as much, the marine biologist popped a finger gun and returned it to cold storage.

Undine was the first to come onboard, trailed by a group of ten. Many, many more waited in the water, silently bobbing up and down along the waves. It was a mixed group. Some of the sirens bore the hardened demeanor of warriors, like Aersila. Others, though softer and more curvaceous, carried or towed children with fierce, protective expressions. All were offered cans of canned pork to appease their hunger.

Still and tense, the sirens watched the human crew with wary eyes, tracking every movement on deck as they slowly ate their meal. "Thank you for coming," Lorelei said, both signing and speaking the words out loud. With Undine's translation help, she communicated to the group what was going to happen next—they would be strapped down to the gurney, their head locked in place with thick padding, cleaned, numbed, and then receive an injection to the back of the neck, at the base of the skull.

Wariness turned to interest when Lorelei announced that she would go first and show them all how it was done. Nodding to the syringe that Lila lifted for all to see, Lorelei made the sign for 'injection,' and said, "It's a sharp pinch. We might feel sore after, maybe a bit tired like Nireed did, but that's normal for this kind of medicine."

Placing her hand in Killian's, she climbed up on top of the gurney and laid facedown, while Lila quickly immobilized her head and strapped her in place. The padding blocked out all light, shrouding her in a cocoon of darkness. All around her, she heard murmuring siren voices—some English, some percussive clicks and whistles like dolphins. The ocean breeze kicked up, cooling the nervous perspiration accumulating on her back, followed by the touch of Lila's fingers as she sterilized her neck with a wipe, then applied the numbing agent. The back of her neck tingled then lost sensation bit by bit as the serum dried —it was the only place she could no longer feel the wind. "Do you feel that?" Lila asked.

"Feel what?" Lorelei mumbled, voice muffled by the padding. Thick and calloused fingers laced through hers—Killian's.

"Nothing then? I just tapped your neck."

"Nothing," Lorelei repeated and then hissed, sucking her teeth. Despite the numbing, a sudden sharp pinch in her deep tissues made her spasm, followed by the unnerving sensation of needle sliding in at the base of her skull. Beyond the brief initial pain, the injection didn't hurt, but it felt weird as hell; she'd never been more aware of that part of her body. "It's almost over, love," Killian murmured, placing a hand on her lower back. "She's pushing in the serum." The best Lorelei could describe the sensation was a slow trickle of cool liquid. A shiver ran down the length of her spine.

Next thing she knew, the pressure from the straps and padding lifted, and light returned to her vision. She blinked back the light's sting. Hands supporting her head and back, she was rolled over onto her back and was met with Lila's and Killian's beaming smiles shining down at her. Lila squeezed her wrist. "You did it. The worst is over. Just hang tight for ten minutes and try to lay still."

"How do you feel?" Killian asked, rubbing soothing circles across her temple.

As she laid there, smiling up at her fiancé, the virophage was already at work, attacking the brain virus that had come to control her life and the terrible hunger that demanded she consume human flesh. When she stepped off this boat, her loved ones would finally be safe from her beyond any shadow of doubt. No more chance of slipping up and making an irreversible, horrifying mistake. "That was a little weird, but I feel great." Gaze flicking to Lila, who was busy disposing wipes and syringes into a biohazardous waste disposal container, Lorelei said, "You did great, too. You've come a long, long way from last year." She touched her stomach where scars from siren talons lay beneath her shirt.

Lila twisted her mouth at the gruesome memory. While she hadn't stitched those wounds, she cleaned and dressed them before taking Lorelei to the hospital. It understandably freaked her out, both grossed out by the task and completely out of her depth in attempting it. But Lila got the job done, and in the time since, she stepped outside her wheelhouse and learned how to do intracerebroventricular injections under the supervision and guidance of HCMRC's marine veterinarian. She'd done this procedure a dozen times, determined to practice away her squeamishness, and it showed. "I wanted to be ready when this day came," the marine biologist said, brushing back curls the wind blew across her face.

When it was okay to get up, Lorelei eased herself off the gurney, and finally took stock of the awaiting sirens. They had all gone quiet, even the children. They stared back at her with troubled expressions. Perhaps even a little fear. She looked to Undine and signed, "I'm fine. Some pain and weird feelings, but not too bad. Sirens have faced worse, I'm sure, following attacks by sharks and other predators."

Undine nodded, speaking and signing at once, "This is new to us, but if you can bare it, we can, too." She then motioned Lorelei forward and took her by the shoulders, spinning her around, back to the rest of the group. Rough, taloned hands pushed up the hair covering the back of her neck. "Tiny, tiny wound," she said, and dropped Lorelei's hair. Smirking, she spoke and signed, "It's my turn now, and best believe I won't make a sound, unlike our soft Shorewalker friend here."

Undine winked at Lorelei as she climbed onto the gurney next. She may have called Lorelei soft, but there was no insulting sting. Glancing at the other sirens, Lorelei saw that many of them had straightened, chins lifted in determination. Undine had just issued them a challenge, calling upon their competitive natures, and told them to buck up.

When Lila pushed the long needle in, Undine made not a sound. She barely even flinched. Just as she boasted.

They administered injections late into the night, requiring use of *Dawn Chaser's* deck lights, and a spotlight that Katrina and Lorelei took turns holding. After Undine got her injection, other sirens stepped forward, eager to prove themselves. Adults and juveniles alike offered one another comfort and support. Mothers sang lullabies to their young children, putting them into relaxed stupors, not unlike the trances humans fell into when hearing siren song. Some returned to the water right away. Others lingered to poke around the boat and chat with the others over extra cans of potted meat. "You're as white as fish's underbelly," one teased, elbowing another who was holding onto the railing in a death grip, either afraid of the boat, or the injection to come.

Lila's little pop-up clinic had become a siren community event, and Lorelei couldn't be more relieved.

When the last member of the siren pod slipped back into the water, returning to the dark depths of their watery home, the deck grew quiet, absent of jovial siren chatter. Only Undine remained onboard. She turned to Lorelei and her gathered friends, each bone-tired and swaying back and forth on sore feet. Undine's eyes and limbs glowed blue with bioluminescence in the dark shadow of night. She bowed her head and pressing a closed fist to her chest, over her heart. "Thank you,

Shorewalker child, and Cure Creator," she said. "You kept your promises."

Lila's lower lip trembled. She had been given a siren name.

"Our work today is done, but there is still more to do," Lorelei said, gesturing to the unopened coolers with virophage injections. "We have enough to give to at least some to your men, but we can discuss that at another time."

Undine smiled, nodding. "Yes, another time. Soon. But tonight, we celebrate, and you rest Two-Legger friends." She climbed up onto the gunwale and paused. Looking at them over her shoulder, she said, "No matter what comes next, our people will always remember this day, for as long as we swim the seas."

Then the siren queen disappeared over the side and into the black abyss.

CHAPTER
TWENTY-SEVEN

LORELEI

MUMBLING AN EXHAUSTED GOODNIGHT TO HER FRIENDS, Lorelei watched Katrina and Lila shuffle down the hallway toward the crew's quarters. They leaned into one another, swaying from side to side with tiredness, not a lack of sturdy sea legs or a steady boat. In the middle of a murmured conversation of who would take who's bunk, Lila yawned long and loud.

When the two disappeared inside, Lila to Will's bunk, and Katrina to Walt's, Lorelei ducked into Killian's snug little cabin, clicking the door shut. She was eternally grateful to both of those women. They faced one unknown after the next with her. Loved her and supported her at her worst. Didn't run screaming from a boatful of murderous, people-eating sirens. She couldn't have two braver friends.

Lifting Killian's mattress to reveal the hidden compartment underneath, Lorelei pulled out a sweater and a large pair of charcoal grey sweatpants, the same ones she wore a year ago today, after Killian plucked her half-frozen out of the ocean. She smiled a little at the memory and how tenderly he'd cared for her in those early days, when they were little more than strangers.

The sound of boots clomped down the deck stairs and paused just outside the door. A quiet rap on the door followed, along with Killian's voice. "Hey, Lorelei. It's just me. Will's taking the helm first. May I come in?"

Setting down the bundle of clothes, Lorelei crossed the tiny cabin to open the door. Killian stood just outside, sleepy-eyed, hands shoved in his pockets and his sweater rumpled. "Good timing. I was just about to get ready for bed."

"Need some help?" He winked, following her inside.

Pressing the back of her hand to her forehead, she sighed. "Oh Captain, I am so exhausted, I can scarcely raise my arm to swoon. How will I ever manage to take off my clothes?"

"You're ridiculous," Killian laughed. "Come here." He pulled her to him by the waistband of her jeans. His warm, calloused hands roved up her sides as he lifted her shirt. "You were so brave and amazing today."

Lorelei arched a brow. "Me?" If anyone was brave today, it was this man for willingly inviting a pod of murderous mermaids onto his boat. And her friends for being on a "floating charcuterie board."

He tugged the shirt over her head and swept her hair free of the neckline. "Yeah, you." His fingers brushed lightly over the skin at the base of her skull. Even that barest touch felt sore, the numbing agent having worn off. But she didn't mind. "That injection was gnarly. You saw how long that needle was, and where it was going, but you stayed calm, because for any of this to work the sirens had to be willing to get it. To let their children get it. You read the situation and did what was needed."

"You've always done the same for me." She gripped his shoulders, giving a little shake to emphasize her point. "You always know just what to do or say, and I couldn't have done any of this without you."

"Well." He chuckled, thumbing open the button of her jeans. "It's felt more like flying by the seat of my pants, at times, but I've always been certain that we're better together. Life's full of unknowns, and you've opened my eyes to a literal sea of them. There's no one I'd rather face it all with than you."

"There you go again," Lorelei breathed, standing on her toes to press a kiss to his lips. "Knowing the right thing to say."

He smiled against them and, with a wrapped an arm around her waist, pulled her flush, hand smoothing up the length of her back. On the downstroke, he unhooked her bra with the flick of a wrist. "Think we can make this one bed thing work?"

"We have before."

"But this time you'll be staying."

Piece by piece, they stripped off the rest of their clothes, and fell onto the tiny mattress together, meeting with slow passion, their mutual exhaustion set aside for a time.

After, she lay draped across Killian, back to the wall, her cheek pressed to warm, dewy skin, head tucked just beneath his chin. They were all entangled limbs, but it was the only way they were going to fit on the tiny twin mattress together. For a time, he traced lazy lines up and down her side.

He fell asleep before she did—his hand coming to a rest at her hip. The rise and fall of his chest, the beat of his heart, all slowing. He was a master of falling asleep quickly, a necessary skill as the captain of an offshore fishing boat. It was a demanding job, the hours long and rough. Sometimes there wasn't time for it, or weather conditions required all hands on deck. He'd learned to take sleep whenever he could get it.

As his skin cooled, and he curled into her more snugly, face nuzzled in her hair, she pulled a blanket over them both, and tucked him in. She slowed her breathing to match his, sleep edging the boundaries of her consciousness.

The sound of waves lapping against the metal hull was soothing. Just one year ago, she had thought the ocean sought to claim her. It had. But not in a way she could have ever imagined. She was a daughter of the sea, and it had called her home.

Killian shifted in his sleep, jostling her neck, which was already at a precarious angle. Wincing, she readjusted, tucking a bit of pillow between herself and Killian. She was sore and stiff, but that was a small price to pay for her loved ones' safety and her control. She reckoned a larger debt was due—Nireed's disappearance from HCMRC's mermaid lab would not be a quiet affair. Not to mention her vanishing act during the museum Grand Opening. Even with the security cameras disabled, and a family emergency story planted, it didn't take a scientist to put two and two together. But whatever troubles her return to work might bring, those were worries for tomorrow. Tonight, she would rest easy, knowing that Nireed was home once more and would heal under her pod's care.

And more so, Lorelei also had Undine's gratitude and respect. One day she might even be welcomed by the siren queen and the others as one of their own. A family above the waves and a family beneath them. What more could she want?

Burrowing underneath the blankets, Lorelei let the steady beat of Killian's heart, and the low, rhythmic hum of *Dawn Chaser's* engines lull her into a deep, blissful sleep.

CHAPTER
TWENTY-EIGHT

LORELEI

SECURITY ESCORTED HER AND LILA TO PHIL'S OFFICE. ALL they'd gotten when they arrived together was a gruff explanation from a guard about a theft and that every employee was being asked to speak up about anything strange they might've seen or heard. There was no mention of Nireed or the virophages or even the mermaid lab in general, but there was no doubt in Lorelei's mind what this was about.

Phil must've wanted to keep it under wraps.

For now.

The director was perched on a corner of his desk when they entered, reviewing something on an electronic tablet, brows furrowed, but as they approached, he looked up, face shifting into an impassive mask. "Dr. Branson, Ms. Roth, please have a seat," he said cordially, gesturing to the two chairs in front of him.

"What's going on?" Lorelei sat, playing the part of clueless employee. "All we were told was that something was stolen."

"That's correct." Folding his arms across his chest, Phil tucked the tablet under his arm. The screen was pressed against his body, so she couldn't see what he'd been looking at. "We had a major security breach during the Grand Opening yesterday."

She shared a look with Lila, both feigning surprise, and then her friend asked, "What's been compromised? Was it a cyberattack?" The marine biologist's concern was palpable, as would be expected, but it didn't ring false. She was the picture of a scientist fearful for her data and intellectual property.

Something flickered across his gaze, but Lorelei couldn't read the emotion, and it was gone in the blink of an eye. Drumming his fingers along the back of the tablet, he shook his head once before rounding the desk to collapse in his chair, air pushing out of the cushion in a puff. "Did either you see or hear anything weird? Maybe someone not from town?"

"Yesterday was a bit of a whir." Lorelei paused, making show of thinking. "There were people everywhere—chatting, wandering through exhibits—but no one stuck out to me as peculiar."

"Not even when you disappeared just one hour into the event?"

Silence fell upon the room, so succinct you could hear a pin drop.

But they'd expected this question and prepared for it.

"My mom called," Lila said, her voice low and grave. "She was hysterical over the phone—I've never heard her so upset. Eventually, I was able to get out of her that my dad had been working on the roof and fell. And by that point, I was too freaked out to drive, so Lorelei took me."

"I'm sorry to hear that." Phil frowned, steepling his hands, as he leaned back in his chair. "How is he?"

"Badly bruised. Sore, but not as bad as we feared. He got lucky. We thought for sure he'd broken some bones."

"That's interesting..." He trailed, a smirk forming. *Was he amused by this?* Only outright laughter could be a more inappropriate response.

"Excuse me?" Lila clenched her chair's armrests, pitch climbing, even though Walt was unharmed and completely fine. "What's interesting about my dad getting hurt?"

"I'm sorry to hear about your father's accident, truly, and normally, I wouldn't ask for a doctor's note, because honor and trust between

HCMRC colleagues, right? But I'm not feeling particularly trustful right now. You say you left for a family emergency—a story your friend Miss Lovera affirms—but what I can't wrap my head around is why you wouldn't be there to help him."

He flipped the tablet in his hands to face them, a still shot of the mermaid lab timestamped 10:13 a.m., and pressed play.

Lorelei stared at the video footage, too numb to feel dread. The camera didn't catch her transformation, but the "theft of HCMRC property" was pretty damn clear. There was no mistaking that was her, Lila, and Will on screen, taking the siren and cases of virophage. Killian had never come into the lab, instead staying behind the wheel of their getaway vehicle, so the cameras didn't catch him. *Thank God.*

She hadn't expected this when she came into work today. Suspicion and a grueling interrogation, yes. A call to the Walshes to confirm their story, also yes. But hard, irrefutable evidence?

The shot was taken at about hip height over by the computer monitors, and not the usual bird's eye view of the security camera's they'd shut down at the start of their mission. Phil explained how he'd installed the secondary, back-up camera, one that was not connected to the main surveillance system. A measure against "tampering," he called it.

What an inconvenient bit of foresight.

The director wasn't smirking anymore. Whatever initial amusement or triumph he leeched from catching them in their lies had vanished.

"Dr. Branson, Ms. Roth, I think it goes without saying that you're done here." Though his tone was even and low for the sake of professionalism, it hid none of his fury. "I'd demand you forfeit the virophages, and give you a chance to rectify the situation, but I suspect they're long gone by now. So, we'll be pressing criminal charges against you both to the fullest extent of the law for theft of lab property, as well as Mr. William Branson, for his part to play."

An anguished cry escaped Lila's lips.

Numbness gave way to stifling panic. Heat swept up her chest to her face and spread through all her limbs, rendering them tingling and rubbery. Lorelei gripped the edge of Phil's desk, using the last bit of strength to keep herself from falling over.

This was the true price of helping the sirens. And the true cost of her friendship. They knew they were risking their current positions, but criminal charges? Forget about being gainfully employed ever again. Would Will and Lila see jail time?

Anger ripped through her at the thought, steeling her bones and her resolve. They would not get in trouble for this, *for her*, not if she had anything to say about it. And she had plenty.

Lorelei leaned across the desk, lengthening claws biting into the wood and carving out splintered furrows. Phil jumped back in his plush office chair with a yelp, eyes wide, but not without snatching his office phone first, jerking the base across his desk by the cord, no doubt calling for security.

With one clawed finger, she pressed down on the switch hook, ending any attempt to make a call. "You wanna press charges, Phil?" Lorelei hissed through pointed teeth. "Fine. But leave the Bransons out of this. The only guilty party here is me."

Fingers closed around her upper arm. "Lorelei, what are you..." She shook Lila off, giving her a firm look. The marine biologist bit her lower lip, fear creasing her brow.

Lorelei turned back to their boss and narrowed her eyes. "Director Simmons, you're aware of siren song. It doesn't matter how many degrees you have, how strong your willpower is, or how tight a grip you have on sanity. It will always bend a person to its will. Even someone with the mental fortitude of Dr. Branson. I compelled her and her husband to help me. They didn't have a choice but to obey my siren song."

Phil trembled. "You're a...you're a..."

"That's right." She hopped on top of the desk and plucked the phone out of his hand, returning it to its cradle. "You made a huge mistake thinking the sirens are just animals. You've had one working for you right under your nose all along. That says something, doesn't it? That you had no idea. We could have continued working together, honor and trust between colleagues, right? That is, until you stopped caring about

Nireed's health and autonomy. What was I supposed to do—stand by while you abused my siren sister? And held her here against her will? The legal system might not know what the hell to do with this case, but that's a blatant ethical violation I'm sure the scientific community would love to hear about. So go right ahead and press charges against me Director Simmons. Do your worst." She tapped her talons against the desktop. "But just know that these aren't the only claws I have, and I don't need siren song to destroy you. You're not the only one who can collect hard evidence of a crime."

She slid off the desk, and without a parting glance, stormed out of Phil's office.

There was nowhere to go but home. But home was sanctuary.

She funneled her anger into badly rage singing in the car—an eclectic playlist-mix of heavy metal and Carrie Underwood. "Before He Cheats" had no situational relevance, but the tone was chef's kiss, and she knew all the lyrics. Slashing tires, keying cars—or clawing desks—was the most vengeful fun a pissed off gal could have. By the time she parked next to the cottage, more askew than usual, she'd sung herself hoarse.

Kicking off her shoes and flinging them further than necessary, Lorelei plopped down in the sand near the water's edge and let out a loud aggravated screech. As the waves rolled over her feet, simultaneously cooling her body temperature and her temper, her phone pinged three times. She glanced down to see if any were worth responding to.

One message was from Phil's secretary, a missive instructing her to schedule a time to come in and clear out her office. Good fucking riddance. That didn't take long. They were probably going to have her escorted by security. She fired off a curt date and time for later that week. Helen didn't deserve her ire, but she was too prickly to care.

The second message came from Lila: *Wow. You really just did that. And it worked. The asshat did an about face—he apologized to me and offered "hazard pay" which smells a lot like hush money—but no criminal charges for me and Will. But WHY did you out yourself, Lorelei?!!*

Lorelei replied: *You've protected me all this past year. Now it's my turn to protect you. Besides, with that case file you put together for Jackie, it's only a*

matter of time that Phil and the board get theirs. And once they are (hopefully)
ousted, HCMRC will need you to pick up the pieces and rebuild, so that nothing
like this ever happens again.

Lila's typing started and stopped several times before she evidently
decided on a simple 'thank you.' Sometimes words were inadequate, but
Lorelei felt the full weight of those two.

She scrolled to the last unread message, this one from Jackie Gaten.
'Call me when you get this,' it said. Falling back into the sand, Lorelei
released a bitter huff of laughter. The last time Jackie said 'call me now'
to anyone within their circle a teenage boy had gotten video footage of
her in mermaid form. She was half tempted to roll herself into the water
and swim away.

Instead, she tapped on Jackie's name and phone number. The phone
only rang twice before Jackie picked up. "Lorelei, I'm glad you got back
to me so quickly. We've got a bit of a situation."

"Figured. What happened?"

"I just got a call from Director Phil Simmons, claiming he had a
scoop. 'That mermaids walk among us.' He explicitly outed you. Of
course, he didn't know I already knew, but with all the 'villain' talk, it
was obvious he was on a discredit and destroy mission. It's a PR tactic
I've seen before. He was trying to control the narrative by getting his
version of the story out first."

"Wasted no time," Lorelei grumbled, burying her toes into the wet
sand. She kicked a clod into the water. It landed with a satisfying *plunk*.
She hadn't exactly thought through all the ramifications outing herself
to her boss would have. All that mattered at the time was keeping Lila
and Will out of jail. She could've wiped his memory, and saved herself a
lot of trouble, but she was decidedly trying *not* to do that, plus an
optimistic part of her had hoped the blackmail would be enough. "What
did you say to him?"

"I told him to go 'fuck himself.'"

She sat up straight. "For real?"

"Hell yes. My exposé is mostly written thanks to Dr. Branson.
Already sold it on spec, too, to a national paper with syndication across
the country, so the coverage will be far and wide. Soon everyone will

know about the sleazes running HCMRC. Got some update texts from Lila today, so I'm also including that you and Dr. Branson freed the mermaid Nireed from inhumane captivity and were fired for it—initially in the doc's case, permanently in yours. That'll undercut his credibility and make whatever he tries to say about you suspect. I don't know if your secret will stay a secret when all is said and done—hopefully it will be nothing more than a local rumor—but if the worst happens, the news cycle is fast and intense, but it will blow over quickly."

Drawing swirls in the sand, Lorelei digested Jackie's words. "It's my word against his," she began. "He has no hard proof about what I am..." Except for ten deep gouges in his desk. *Shit.* "Oh wait, I fucked up his desk. I was too angry to think straight." She puffed a strand of hair out of her face, waiting for the panic to hit. But nothing. Just...relief? Maybe it was denial, but now that her worst fears had come to pass, it was kind of freeing. "I don't think I'm all that upset about it actually. I've worried for so long that people would find out, that I made myself sick over it, but now that the cat is out of the bag, I feel like I can just get on with my life. If I get calls, I'll ignore them. If people start showing up at my house, our new fencing will keep them out."

"It's a big accusation. Most people aren't as quick to believe such things as you'd think, and it flies in the face of what people think they know—shifter mermaids born and raised on land? They don't know Shorewalkers exist, and they have no reason to. Sure, it might get some conspiracy theorists and cryptid-seekers speculating, but the masses aren't going to be clamoring for you. And when you say fucked up his desk, are we talking Hulk smash or...?"

"I scratched it up."

Jackie chuckled. "You're probably not the first person to take a *knife* to their boss's desk."

Now why hadn't she thought of that? She'd just listened to a song about this kind of vengeance. "That's probably true."

"Also, I'm real sorry you lost your job in this mess. But you did good sticking it to the man. And shit, that was a bang-up job with the museum! You've got talent; don't let anyone tell you any different. If it's any consolation, you can still count on my feature running in the Sunday paper as planned. Your professional profile, too."

"Thanks, Jackie. That does make me feel better. I think I'll frame them both."

"You should." Her affirmation was followed by a rhythmic staccato in the background—possibly the tapping of a pen or pencil against a desk. "Well, I'll let you go. I just wanted to make sure you were aware of Phil's schemes. Pour yourself a stiff one, all right?"

"That's not a bad idea. And thanks for the warning. I really appreciate you looking out for me, yet again."

"Sure thing, kiddo. Oh, and one more thing. If Phil is found half-eaten before this week is out, it was bears, okay?"

Unexpected laughter erupted from Lorelei's chest. "Sounds about right," she said before hanging up. Damn it was good to have Jackie on her side. With any other reporter, that phone call might've been a nightmare.

Tossing her phone to a dry patch of sand, safe from the waves, Lorelei stood, and shucked off her blouse. It was time to celebrate "sticking it to the man" with a long swim.

CHAPTER
TWENTY-NINE

LORELEI

GIVEN THE HOT SEAT THEY'D ALL JUST RECENTLY SAT IN, Lorelei didn't expect to see Lila and Will standing at the front desk, flanked by security, when she returned to HCMRC to clear out her office.

"Just in case things get sketchy," Will said, explaining their presence. Her confusion must have been obvious. "Lila insisted we be here when she heard through the Carrie-grapevine that you were coming in."

Tapping an empty cardboard box against her leg, trying not to cry, she nodded. The emotional support was needed. It wasn't every day one got fired from their one-time dream job.

Taking quick stock of the lobby, she noticed that it was completely empty. Not even the regular receptionist sat at the front desk. Between visitors and staff, there was always someone here in the middle of daylight hours.

Lila hadn't acknowledged her arrival yet, too busy glaring daggers at the guards.

Leaning over, Will whispered in his wife's ear. Not that the security detail could hear anything he was saying—they were all wearing noise cancellation headsets. "Honey, take it easy on the scary eyes for the corporate minions and save them for the big, bad siren who made us do bad things. Remember we agreed on 'supportive but pissed friends?'"

Lila rolled her eyes and turned her stare on Lorelei. "I can't believe you used us like that," she deadpanned, her falsetto dripping sarcasm. "And before you make excuses, you terrible, terrible friend you, I know what they were doing to Nireed was wrong. But you should have trusted us with your secret and let us help without forcing us to with your wicked cool siren powers. There was a better way to handle this, and it wasn't going behind the backs of this facility's corrupt leadership." She arched her brow at Will. "How was that?"

He made a caricature of an angry face and shook a finger in Lorelei's general direction. "Probably a good thing the cameras only get video. Lorelei, you are a bad, bad friend. Shame on you."

Lorelei bit her lip hard enough to draw blood, but it kept her from laughing. "You're both ridiculous," she mumbled, hanging her head. "I'm sorry I'm a real asshole."

Spinning on her heels with a fake huff, Lila gestured that Lorelei follow. "We need to work on your apologies, girl. But more on that later. Let's just get this over with. And heads up, Carrie's lurking in your office."

"Are you frickin' kidding me?" Typical Carrie. "She came to gloat?"

"Oh, it's so much worse," Lila seethed, balling her fists. No fake anger there. "She's your replacement."

It was all Lorelei could do to keep herself from punching the nearest wall. Not that there was much of an audience to create a spectacle in front of. Save for her friends and this silly security escort, the hallways were empty. The offices, too, for that matter. "Of course, she is. Does she know now that I'm a...?"

"No. Phil hasn't spread that around yet, at least, not beyond his attempt to get Jackie to write a smear piece on you. And Carrie doesn't remember."

So not everything was going to hell in a hand basket.

They passed yet another empty office.

Odd.

"Where the hell is everyone? Was there some kind of professional development training today that I forgot about?"

"No, they cleared out this part of the building earlier this morning and put it on semi-lockdown. Carrie's not supposed to be here, but she doesn't listen to anybody for shit, and Will's my personal muscle and emotional support, which is the official reason why he's here. Breaking up with your super powered work wife is some serious business."

Lorelei stopped abruptly and the security guard directly behind her nearly bowled her over.

"Keep moving!" he barked, louder and more forceful than necessary.

Rather than give him a piece of her mind, she bit her tongue and continued walking. Wasn't like he'd hear her anyway. "Is this because of *me*?"

"Yup."

That put a new spin on the phrase "armed to the teeth." She was lethal by default—teeth, claws, and potent siren song. But if Phil really saw her as a potential threat, why didn't he just have someone mail her belongings home? Less fuss, and she could've stayed home in her pajamas and demolished her stash of chocolate. It really would have saved everyone so much trouble.

Wait. No. Wait...

They wouldn't just lure her here and—shit. Will did say Lila insisted they both be here in case things got sketchy. Sketchy like upper management forcing her to become Nireed's replacement in the mermaid aquarium. That caliber of fuckery was only supposed to happen in movies.

As they approached her old office, Lorelei thrust her hands inside her trouser pockets to hide their trembling. The guards waited outside as she entered with Lila and Will.

While Carrie's smug smile wasn't a healthy distraction from the thought that her previous employer had possibly plotted to kidnap her, it was a distraction. She centered her energy on ignoring the woman as she made a b-line for her desk.

Plopping the cardboard box next to her computer, Lorelei opened the top drawer and began unceremoniously dumping her belongings inside.

Nothing within was so fragile or precious that it couldn't take the rough treatment. The sooner she got out of this hellscape, the better. The only things worth being gentle with were the picture frames of her and Killian, but those she'd lay on top.

"Must have been nice while it lasted, having a title you weren't qualified for. But every dog gets his day."

Lorelei looked up to find Carrie "casually" inspecting her nails.

Any charitable thought she'd ever thought about the woman vanished in a puff of smoke, recent events whittling her patience and restraint down to toothpicks. *Every dog gets his day—that snooty, insufferable bitch!*

"I don't know, *Carrie*." She spat her name as if it were a curse word. "I did a damn good job for being short-staffed. And I wouldn't be slinging dirt if I were you. You're the poster child for nepotism."

"Oo, burn!" Will called, but Lila cut him off with a sharp glance, shaking her head. Translation: don't get in the middle of this.

Carrie stuck up her nose. "At least I was qualified for my job."

Every nerve in her body bristled. She could bite that woman's face off.

"Seriously, Lorelei, you should see this as a blessing in disguise. You were in way over your head. It's a real wonder the board hired you. 'Underqualified' was putting it lightly. I mean, come on. You had a semi-relevant internship at a museum. Once."

Lorelei clenched her fists so hard she cut crescent moons into her palms. If this were a cartoon, steam would be shooting out of her ears. Her whole body twitched as she struggled to think of a proper comeback. "Yeah, well," she began, her thoughts frantic and frazzled. "You taste like SPAM!"

Carrie blinked. "What?"

A beat passed. Then two of dead, awkward silence. Only the low din of the building's central cooling system punctured the quiet.

Will's face contorted into comedic bliss as he busted out into laughter, the kind that makes your eyes water and your stomach hurt. He bent over his knees, wheezing. Lila looked between all three of them with a horrified expression.

"Shut up, Will," Carrie snapped, stealing a piece of scrap paper from Lorelei's desk. "It's not funny!" She balled it up and threw it. It bounced off his forehead, which only made him laugh harder. If anyone knew how to unarm Carrie, it was Will.

Growling with frustration, Carrie whirled back on Lorelei, jabbing a perfectly manicured finger into her chest. "And what did you just say to me?"

Lorelei saw red. She might be cured of her cravings for human flesh, but that wouldn't stop her from biting the damn thing off. "Don't touch me," she hissed, slapping Carrie's hand away.

Carrie lifted her hand again, like she was going to keep poking her, but paused. Fear flashed across her face, followed by a dawning realization. Her mouth hung open for one long moment before every emotion was replaced with rage. "Oh my god. It WAS YOU! You're the sea bitch who tried to eat me!" Carrie took a bold step forward and shoved.

Fucking shit fuck. Lorelei caught herself on her desk, claws and teeth elongating. Pushing off, she got into Carrie's face, gleefully watching the woman's pupils shrink. "Still might if you touch me one more time," she snarled.

She didn't even need to use her siren song. Carrie backed off.

"Why are you two just standing there?" Carrie yelled frantically at Lila and Will. "Call in security!"

"Um. How about you just leave?" Lila folded her arms across her chest and nodded pointedly toward the door.

"Are you serious right now? She's a flesh-eating monster. We need to report her to the authorities."

Will rolled his eyes. "Yeah, okay. We'll get right on that, Spamela."

Carrie shrieked. "What the fuck did you just call me?!"

"Spam-e-la, rhymes with 'Pamela.'"

"You are unbelievable. How can you side with her? She literally ate a piece of me! I'm going to have trouble walking for the rest of my life!"

For once, he didn't have a clap back. There really wasn't one for that.

Sobering, Lorelei pinched the bridge of her nose. She'd always feel terrible for tearing a chunk out of Carrie's leg, no matter how much this woman infuriated her, but she didn't hate herself for it. However, now that the cat was out of the bag, she could finally give the apology Carrie was owed.

If only she'd stop yelling long enough to listen.

"How's it right that she gets away with this?" Carrie continued, gesticulating wildly. "What if I'm not the only one she's done this to? What if she's a mermaid serial killer..."

Taking a deep breath, Lorelei cut into the clamor. "I'm sorry."

The apology surprised the woman enough into momentary silence, so she continued, likely to never get the chance again. "I'm sorry for taking a chunk out of your leg. I hate that I did that, and would take it back if I could, but as much as it's unforgiveable, that happened during a time when I couldn't control myself. I had a brain virus, one that's kind of like rabies, and it hijacked my behavior, cut my decision-making down to base instinct, and drove me to do things I wouldn't ever do otherwise. But I'm as good as cured now." Cured was putting it loosely, but she wasn't about to try explaining how virophages worked. "So, you don't need to be afraid that something like that will ever happen again, at least, not from me. We might not like each other, but you didn't deserve that."

Mouth screwed up into a tight line, angry tears streamed down Carrie's cheeks. With the heel of her hand, she swiped ferociously at them. "I've been scared of my own shadow, every small creak in my house, for a whole year now. I don't sleep. But when I do, they're filled with nightmares. You took away my peace, my sense of safety."

"I know, and I'm sorry for that, too."

"What the hell am I supposed to do with 'sorry'? Sorry doesn't give me back the year I lost. Or my health."

"I know," Lorelei repeated, queasy, and at a loss for words.

What could someone say to adequately apologize for that? Or do to make appropriate amends? Saying sorry was easy, but saying sorry in a way that meant something? That took time. And it wasn't abundantly clear to her yet just how to go about doing that.

Carrie wasn't done.

"I even bought a gun—and I hate guns."

There it was. Now that, too, was out in the open.

A sharp, strangled cry erupted from Lila.

"What?" Carrie snapped.

Was she seriously that obtuse?

The glacial stare Lila leveled on her in-law was positively lethal. "You don't remember *anything* about crashing the cookout at Killian's?" Each ice-cold word pricked goosebumps along Lorelei's skin, and she wasn't even the object of ire. "Why my parents and I haven't replied to your texts?"

Not all of Carrie's memory had been sung away. Just the mermaidy bits. Everything else, Lorelei left intact. There was no supernatural reason why Carrie wouldn't remember barging into the family BBQ, yelling, getting into peoples' faces, all while reaching for the gun she had concealed under her clothes. Out of line, out of control, and on the dangerous path toward escalation, and Carrie had the audacity to say she hated guns. And she *should* remember, *should* learn from such a fuck-up, so she could get help and never pull shit like that ever again.

"What cookout..." A dark, panicked look crossed Carrie's face. "I've lost some time recently. I swear I'm not drinking, but it's like a brown out, I get snippets of memory, but with the insomnia and the nightmares, I just thought it was just a dream, a terrible, terrible dream."

Watching Carrie's face turn sheet white as she put it all together, pieces of a fractured mind meeting to form a horrifying puzzle, was painful. Had she truly not realized? Was she this unaware of the harm she'd done—and what more she could've done, if left unchecked?

"Oh my God," she whispered, cupping her hands over her mouth, as tears refilled her eyes. "Oh my God."

Lifting a finger, Lila opened her mouth to say something more, then shook her head. "Mm, nope, not dealing with this." And without another word, she stormed out of the room.

Will's face was inscrutable when he asked, "You seeing a therapist again?"

"Yes." Carrie collapsed into the nearest chair, drawing her knees up to her chest. "And I promise I'll talk to her about this."

"Good."

"I'm so, so sorry, Will." Her face crumpled. The tears fell heavier now, words tumbling out in choked sobs. "Please believe me. I've not been myself. This isn't who I want to be."

With a heavy sigh, he crouched down, getting on eye-level with her. "Getting help's the first step. Focus on that, okay?"

The advice was firmly given—no nonsense or room for argument—but it was the closest thing to tender Lorelei had ever seen between the two of them.

Whisking her box of belongings off her desk, Lorelei edged toward the door, meaning to give the cousins space. "The office is yours," she said quietly.

Carrie nodded dimly.

CHAPTER
THIRTY

KILLIAN

THE STARING WAS BAD.

People crossing the street to avoid them on the sidewalk was much worse. Though his beautiful woman held her head high, Killian wrapped a protective arm across her shoulders, and glared right back.

They'd just wanted to get lunch in town.

Mermaid. Siren. Witch from the Sea.

Dangerous.

Lorelei's old boss had been running his mouth and the town listened. The only people who'd brushed the claims off were his crew. After seeing what they had at sea, they couldn't even fathom that the rumors might be true. Perhaps that was for the best. He might lose them if they believed.

"Still good with getting lunch, or would you like me to take you home?"

"I have nothing to be ashamed of," she replied fiercely.

And that was answer enough for him. "Your pick then."

She steered them into a sit-down restaurant with a moose head sign, not an unusual motif in these parts, even though the animals mostly lived more inland.

Though the waiter inside the restaurant gave them funny looks, he took their orders for sandwiches and lobster bisque, and was professionally polite enough. But notably, no one was seated at nearby tables. It made Killian angry, but he kept his cool for Lorelei.

It didn't matter that she'd brushed shoulders with the town's residents many times before, and no harm befell them. People feared what they did not understand.

While they waited for their food to arrive, Lorelei checked her phone. Nose scrunched, she murmured, "I just got a LinkedIn message."

"Someone you know?"

She shook her head, eyebrows lifting as she scrolled.

"You sure you want to be reading messages from strangers right now?" His stomach clenched thinking about what terrible things random folks on the internet might say.

"It's quite sweet actually," she said, smiling a little to herself, cheeks getting rosy. "A woman from my home state wrote to say that she took the virtual tour of the museum—guess they put one up on the website. She says it's fascinating and that she learned a lot just from looking around online and wants to make the trip out to see it in person. Then there's some stuff about making history and that she's proud that a fellow Michiganian built the first real naturalist exhibit for merfolk."

That did sound nice. He watched Lorelei type a response.

"She seems a bit nervous though," she continued. "She's asking if the coastline is safe. She's read Jackie's articles about Lila's work, and knows about all that, but seems to need more reassurance."

Once Lorelei finished drafting, she showed him the original message, and the assurances she sent about safety. He scrolled.

Annaliese Kruetz. That was the woman's name.

But no profile picture. And though it was a premium account, the profile looked barely used. There was a university listed with a graduation date but little else.

Odd.

It was almost as if this person had made the account just to talk to Lorelei.

Every protective nerve in his body was on high alert, but he kept his unease to himself. If the original message hadn't been so kind and complimentary, he would've recommended she block the sender, because the rest of it looked suspicious.

But perhaps their interactions in town soured his view of humanity.

Was it really that unreasonable to think that someone might create an account just to say something nice to a person whose work they admired? From an outsider's perspective, the job networking platform was genuinely the only way to get a hold of Lorelei professionally. She'd lost her museum work email right along with her job.

After all her hard work—the long hours, the sleepless nights—only to have her pride and joy yanked out from under her, Lorelei deserved all the praise and credit only an overenthusiastic fan could give.

CHAPTER

THIRTY-ONE

LORELEI

AFTER DONNING A THICK KNITTED SWEATER, LORELEI stepped out into the chilly, early October air, a cup of tea in one hand, a book in the other, and a smile on her face. It was nearly noon, but she still wore her pajama pants, fuzzy slippers, and a messy over-the-shoulder braid from yesterday. Comfy was her usual attire these days.

Plopping down in the rocking chair she bought for the express purpose of outside reading, she thumbed open the book. Slow lazy days were heaven. While she missed her museum, not having to work fourteen-hour days was heavenly.

She'd begin looking for a new job eventually, but she had more than earned this time off, and she was going to enjoy it. Besides, she wasn't sure anyone local would hire her just yet.

People in town whispered about the shore-bound mermaid by the sea.

Jackie's exposé released days after she was fired. She was named, but not outed. Phil, however, issued his rebuttals and had no problem doing so. All her social media accounts were set to private, and she ignored phone calls from numbers she didn't recognize, but there weren't as many as she feared.

As for the news itself, she ignored it—ignorance is bliss, after all. Katrina monitored it for her, only sharing highlights and "need-to-knows" like legal steps taken toward prosecution against HCMRC leadership.

Katrina's assessment of her media situation was heartening.

Most of the world thought Director Phil Simmons lost it, especially considering the hard proof cited in Jackie's article of the unethical research practices his leadership fostered, but the residents of the rural, coastal town Haven Cove were superstitious by nature. They grew up too close to the sea, its foggy, murky waters, spooky maritime stories, and Stephen King books not to be.

The scientific community was properly outraged, which Lorelei and Lila both felt vindicated by.

Home life remained quiet. But only because the newly constructed gated driveway and privacy fencing around the seaside cottage kept out the busy bodies. Turns out the world perceiving, or at least suspecting what she was, wasn't the hugely horrible thing she built it up to be. People might give her weird looks, or attempt to infringe upon her privacy, but there were ways to block it out.

Like being a hermit.

People would eventually forget about her…Lorelei shrugged off the thought and rocked the chair back and forth, finding her escape in the book she held.

An hour passed, maybe more, and the sun dipped behind a cluster of clouds.

Sloshing down by the shoreline ripped Lorelei's attention from her reading. It wasn't the sound the tide made when it came rushing it, rather movement through the water. She had a visitor.

A dark-haired siren popped to the surface, a toothy smile, and amber eyes glowing. She waved with her whole arm.

Lorelei shot from her chair. "Nireed?" She could scarcely believe it. The mermaid was free now, why the hell would she ever come back to shore?

"Hello, Shorewalker!"

A smile broke out across her face. She set her book down and joined the other mermaid at the water's edge. "What brings you here?"

"We came to invite you to our home."

Lorelei touched her chest, heart thumping against her palm. "We?"

Two more sirens bobbed to the surface.

One had dark-brown skin, brown topaz eyes, and a halo of tightly coiled hair. The second was pale like Nireed, white skin with an almost translucent, pearly sheen, but had golden hair. She held a clawed hand above her eyes and squinted, so much so that Lorelei almost didn't notice her eye's light blue hue.

Both sirens dipped their heads in greeting.

"These are my friends Melusina," as Nireed spoke, the dark-skinned mermaid pointed to herself, "and Delphine."

Lorelei signed, "Nice to meet you."

Grinning, Melusina and Delphine repeated it back to her, but the latter notably closed her eyes when she used both hands to sign. As soon as she was finished speaking, she went back to shielding her eyes with her hand and squinting.

"Do either of you speak Two-Legger English?" She signed the words, as well.

Delphine shook her head, but Melusina answered, "Some. Nireed teaches me."

"Most of us don't know it," Nireed explained. "The oceans became noisy—one hundred fifty years ago or so—when the Two-Leggers traded their wooden ships for hard metal. We dove deeper to escape the noise. Did not surface so much and lost your language."

She must have been talking about the Industrial Age—the rise of machines—a significant historic event to sirens and humans alike, but for two completely distinct reasons. Innovation for one. But noise pollution for the other, followed by other ills in the decades to come like overfishing, ghost nets, sonar, and drilling. Humans didn't realize it, but they had forced the sirens of legend down into the deep, to the point where they had become nothing more than maritime myth, coastal aesthetic, and fantasy.

"I was very small," Nireed continued, signing as she spoke, "but seventeen years past, the ocean became quiet again." Melusina nodded along, signing the word "spooky," coupled with a troubled, almost frightened expression. "It was almost the same time of year as this but a moon cycle before. Even in the dark deep, I had never heard it so quiet before, and never again since, but my great foremother said her mother swam in seas like that. She thought maybe the Two-Leggers left the water for good. Or died in large numbers on their shores like many of our fish."

Lorelei did a quick mental calculation. This time of year, but a month before, meant September. Then 2018 minus…

A chill ran down her spine. 2001. Nireed was referring to 9/11. Even the sirens had known something big had happened that day—all epipelagic life would have for that matter. In an underwater world, where sound travels faster than it does in air, the silence would have been sudden and all encompassing, impossible not to notice by hearing-sensitive creatures.

Lila had told her once about a whale study her college professor had been involved in that measured their stress levels. They significantly dropped during 9/11 when all air and ocean traffic halted. Though whale populations had once more habituated to the ambient noise when human travel resumed, the truth was the poor things were low-key stressed all the time.

In Lila's research of Nireed, she learned that sirens were high-frequency hearers like dolphins, meaning they heard a wider, higher range of sounds than humans did. And they were hearing sensitive, which explained their initial aversion to engine and propeller sounds—something they had habituated to over time as they began ascending to the surface to take canned pork from *Dawn Chaser*.

"Some still speak Two-Legger languages," Melusina signed, bringing the conversation back around. "Very few."

Nireed nodded. "Our foremothers passed them down to some, but less and less so as the years passed. Undine and Aersila learned because they are leaders." Then gesturing to Delphine, she added, "Some of us have never even surfaced. I had only just begun doing so when we first met. Adjusting to all the light was the hardest bit. This is Delphine's first time."

Oh gosh. That explained all the eye shielding and squinting.

"Let me write Killian… my, uh, 'mate' a note so he knows not to worry while I'm gone. I'll be right back. You can wait for me below the surface if you'd like to rest your eyes."

Delphine smiled with relief. "Thank you," she signed and promptly dove. The others followed. Pulse racing from excitement, Lorelei jogged up the beach to the cottage to shuck her clothes and scribble the note. This was really happening.

She was going to see the home of her siren kin.

THEY ZOOMED THROUGH THE WATER, FOLLOWING NIREED'S lead, using the currents to propel themselves forward, streaks of bioluminescence in the murk. Green, amber, topaz, and light blue. Just like the colors of their eyes.

A cheerful melody—at first a hum, then song—rose from Delphine, her voice sweet and bright as it permeated the water around them. It grew in volume as each one of them joined in—first Melusina, then Nireed. This was not a song meant to lure prey or a mate. It spoke of friendship, sisterhood, and love of the ocean. A song meant just for them.

Lorelei listened closely to the tune, inner ear absorbing resonance, internalizing pitch, getting a feel for the sound. As her own voice rumbled up from the back of her throat, she let the vibrations guide her and poured her heart into joining her siren sisters in song. This was one of those moments remembered forever, more for the soaring feeling of companionship and sense of belonging than anything else. Having simple unadulterated fun.

Nothing could touch such joy.

Her first swim with Nireed had been energizing, but this was next level. Save for brief, playful brushes with harbor porpoises last year, this was Lorelei's first time swimming as a part of a pod. And pod was family.

They stayed close to the rocky sea floor, its formation much like the clusters of boulders that made up Maine's shoreline, but broken up by patches of muck, silt, and seagrass. The landscape of the ocean with its mountains, valleys, plateaus, and gorges had all the same kinds of geographical features as Acadia National Park, just sunken. And instead of trees, there were seagrass forests.

The sea floor gradually sloped deeper and deeper the further they swam.

Nireed's pace slowed as they approached the edge of a seaweed forest. When she spun in the water, a swirl of soft amber light, they drew up around her. Bioluminescent nodes, like glowing fireflies in the night, dotted her hands and fingers so that when she began to sign, they could see that she had said, "Almost there, Shorewalker. Just through this."

Seaweed towered above them, some fifty-sixty feet high, its individual strands gently swaying back and forth in unison. With the flick of her tail, Nireed dipped down, hands brushing along the sea bottom and kicking up a cloud of silt. Arching back up in one fluid motion, she flicked her tail again, and plunged herself into the thick of the underwater forest.

Lorelei followed—Melusina and Delphine at her back.

Thick was an understatement. More like pushing through a pliant, slimy wall; 360-degrees of seaweed. It would be so easy to get turned around and lost in here, and yet, Nireed kept pushing on with purpose. How did she know which direction to go? Lorelei glided along, right on the siren's glowing tail fins, almost close enough to get smacked in the face by them. She barely dared to blink, lest she lose track of Nireed and her way.

Nireed's arms moved forward then backward over and over again, but it was no front stroke Lorelei had ever seen. If she didn't know any better, she would have said the siren was hauling line.

Something that was too rough to be seaweed brushed the underside of her tail. She jumped, her green bioluminescent nodes flashing brighter. But upon a quick, cursory glance down, Lorelei saw that was exactly what Nireed was doing. She had picked up a thick length of frayed, braided rope. Probably an old bit of sail line.

Hand over hand Nireed pulled herself along, following the trail it marked.

Calming, Lorelei's personal lantern light dimmed to a soft glow once more.

Bit by bit, the sea forest began to thin out, enough to see strips of ocean through the waving seaweed stalks. Nireed dropped the rope, darted forward, and swept aside the final strands, like opening a curtain. But the view beyond the window baffled Lorelei. It was just more open ocean.

She swam off to the side to let Melusine and Delphine through, and signed, words in green motion. "I thought home was just through this forest?"

All three sirens grinned, then pointed down.

Lorelei complied, staring down at chasm of dark water. The sea floor had dropped away completely. She swam out a little and saw humanoid bioluminescent figures flitting in and out of the rocky cliff face fifty additional feet down.

Her three siren companions waved their arms, the universal sign for 'come on,' then dove together in 'V' formation. Lorelei trailed behind them, rapidly closing the distance to where the other sirens swam.

With just one flick of her tail, she descended ten feet, coasted to her internal twenty-foot marker. Another flick and she was at thirty, now forty. She gasped, taken aback at what lay just fifty feet below the seaweed forest.

A whole city was carved into the cliff face, roughly the size of Haven Cove proper. It reminded her of the mountain side communities in Italy and New Mexico. Thin streams of light glinted against the granite structures.

Here in the lowermost portions of the epipelagic zone, the water was dark, pitch black to the human eye. But a siren's eyes picked up so much more underwater, biologically evolved to catch the smallest amounts of light that filtered down from the surface to even these depths.

Delphine whistled, short but sharp.

Sirens of all ages and bioluminescent colors swam out of their homes and lined up into two rows, forming a gauntlet with synchronized precision. One hundred sirens living in a place big enough to hold one thousand. This was what was left.

"Come," Nireed signed. "We say 'welcome.'"

Wide-eyed, Lorelei followed Nireed down the opening between the two rows, watching as every mermaid made eye contact with her as she passed and pressed their fists to their chests. She didn't need to have a clue about siren culture to understand that a procession through the entire siren community was an honor.

Undine and Aersila waited for them at the end of the rows. "Welcome, Shorewalker," Undine signed, a broad smile bowing her lips.

"Thank you for inviting me. I'm honored."

Aersila chimed in, pointing at Lorelei. Like Nireed, her bioluminescence was amber. She made a 'C' shape with her hand and dragged it from the base of her throat to her chest. "Hungry?"

Lorelei nodded, clutching her stomach, rumbling beneath her palms. The last she'd eaten was breakfast, and all that swimming had worked up a healthy appetite.

THEY SWAM THROUGH THE ROCKY CHANNELS OF THE underwater city until they reached Undine's personal abode. A seaweed curtain draped over the narrow doorway, topped by a shark jaw nailed above its mantle. A grin tugged at Lorelei's mouth. Who would have thought she and Undine shared taste in décor?

Inside was cavernous.

High ceilings and a wide room cut deep into the mountain. Other ocean creatures crammed themselves into nooks and crevices, but not the mermaids. They needed space to stretch their fins and keep water moving past their gills. Shelves made of whale bone lined the walls, all of Undine's belongings on display. Some looked like they might be trinkets reclaimed from ship wreckage, but most seemed utilitarian—foodstuff storage and tools.

The floor was packed with muck from which a thick, neatly trimmed kelp bed grew. Someplace soft to lay and rest. At least, that's what Lorelei felt compelled to do when she saw it.

When Undine swam toward the ceiling, Lorelei followed.

At the top, there was a circular stone slab, suspended from the ceiling by rusted iron hooks and thick rope as wide as her wrist. She glanced at Nireed, and the siren made the signs for "table" and "eat," then pointed up.

Craning her neck, Lorelei looked up. A glittering mosaic of a many-armed kraken spanned the ceiling, made from tiny pieces of white, blue, and green tile. "Huge," Lorelei signed, her eyes wide from awe. Prehistoric. A leviathan.

"Ocean Goddess," Nireed replied, hands moving quickly. "No one's seen her since before the sickness."

Though that sounded ominous, Lorelei couldn't help but be relieved. A leviathan was not someone she wanted to stumble across. She'd be little more than a snack to such a creature.

Undine brought over a circular silver-plated tray with braided etching around the rim that may have once belonged to a tea service from the 1800s—either a wreckage find or a family heirloom, possibly a gift an ancestor received from a sailor lover in the days before the flesh-eating brain virus. Strips of thinly sliced meats fanned the platter's circumference. Upon closer inspection, Lorelei noted the initials U.S.N. engraved into the center—United States Navy. The piece had once belonged to a naval officer.

Lorelei sniffed—haddock, tuna, and something else she couldn't place.

Nireed tapped Lorelei's shoulder to get her attention. "Shark," she signed. "Big. Aggressive. From last pod hunt." Lorelei pinched a strip between her claws and took a bite. She chewed thoughtfully. It might be a new favorite.

Undine set the tray down on the table.

When Aersila described the shark's size, grey top, and white underbelly she gulped. Great White. Rare in the Gulf of Maine, but not unheard of. Ballsy of the sirens to go after it. Ocean animals didn't usually hunt things bigger than them, but then again, sirens weren't animals. And humans had hunted things bigger than themselves since the Stone Age.

Great Whites were also a protected species, illegal for humans to hunt. Not that the sirens were beholden to human law, and to this siren pod, a Great White would be an invasive natural predator. Still, she probably wouldn't tell Lila about this part of the trip, and at a later point, she might suggest to Undine that they try to chase out the next one they saw instead. If anyone understood first-hand the significance, it would be the sirens who were themselves an endangered species.

"How long have you lived here?" Lorelei signed.

"Not long," Undine replied. "Grand foremothers built this place when our men drove us out of the deep."

"Is this not deep?" They had to be about 600 feet down from the surface, far enough that storm effects no longer touched them.

Undine's bioluminescence dimmed a bit. She shook her head, a motion seen because of two glowing eyes and lambent nodes at her temples and down the length of her nose. She pointed north of where they were now and began describing what sounded like a huge pit in the ocean floor.

Hands moving through the water, graceful as dance, but imbued with language, she said their people had carved cities into its walls going down and down and down. The oldest ones, now abandoned ruins, were built closer to the top. The louder and more dangerous the Two-Legger's oceanic activities became, the deeper and deeper they built to get away from it all. But when their people got sick—the sirens craving human flesh, and the mermen turning against their own kind—their grand foremothers fled to escape the growing violence.

Recalling the topographical maps Lila showed her, it sounded like she was describing Georges Basin. Or something like it. Hundreds of miles wide, and hundreds of miles deeper than surrounding areas, its depths crossed into the mesopelagic zone.

X-rays of Nireed's ribcage showed that it was much, much thicker than a human's but also flexible. Like the sperm whale's it allowed merfolk to swim to great depths without being killed by the pressure. They had powerful, collapsible lungs, too, for the same reason. Between Lila's research and building Haven Cove Museum of Ocean Discovery's mermaid exhibit, Lorelei had learned a lot about her species and the Gulf of Maine.

She took another strip of fish from the tray—tuna this time.

"There's something we'd like to say." Undine's bioluminescence dimmed, flickering softly. Why did the siren seem sad? "The cure has given us..." She paused, rubbing her forehead. "More clarity than we had before about your ship friends. On behalf of the pod, we are sorry."

Lorelei swallowed, rubbing her chest against the building pressure. Undine had apologized to her before for what happened to *The Osprey* crew, but it hadn't been sincere. At least, she hadn't understood Lorelei's grief and anger a year ago and didn't think the pod had done anything wrong.

"Coming to the surface began as storm play," Undine continued. "Letting the waves toss us around. Feeling sky water hit us from above. But then we smelled the Two-Leggers, their fear, and saw the wooden boat tipping from side to side in the waves. It surprised us to see what our foremothers told us in stories—a Two-Legger vessel that barely made sound. Thought it was just stories." Undine touched the back of her neck, the spot where the virophage had been injected. "Shorewalker, you helped us remember that Two-Leggers could be friends. Then gave us back the ability to choose. We know our mistake now and have put your friends to rest, their bones wrapped in seaweed the same as our own dead. If you wish to pay your respects, Nireed will take you to them."

Lorelei clutched her hands to her chest. Should she do this? Was she ready? Human burial practices were hard enough. Could she handle the sirens'? If she saw individually wrapped bones and skulls, she might scream. But if it was more of a shroud, she could maybe do that.

She didn't have to stay long. And a quick visit might give her the closure she never imagined she could ever have, and the peace of mind that she would never accidentally stumble upon their bones or *The Osprey*'s wreckage in her ocean explorations.

She nodded slowly.

They swam to another section of the seaweed forest, just Lorelei and Nireed, miles away from the cliff face city. She followed her siren sister through, though it was far less dense here. She could easily weave her way around the stalks of seaweed.

Twisting back, Nireed signed, "Close," and Lorelei appreciated the warning.

They came to a circular cluster of seaweed stalks that grew closer and more densely together. Some shoots looked younger than others, as if they had been nurtured to grow there. And tethered to each stalk by rope, floating in place ten feet up from the sea floor, were humanoid cocoons made of seaweed. Grave bundles? She didn't know what else to call what she saw. Mummies maybe. The seaweed wrappings reminded her of them, but that's not what they were.

Lorelei swam just a little bit closer to examine them, but not too close. She had no desire to touch them, afraid of what lay beneath. Bones couldn't hurt her, but knowing that they had once supported a life, a soul, now gone, cut too deep to bear.

It stunned her how intricate and complex the weavings were of the seaweed wrappings. A lot of time and a lot of hands must have gone into threading these burial shrouds. Little trinkets hung from each grave bundle—carved bits of driftwood and stone. Like wind chimes that caught the current, not air. Each were different from the next. Mementos. Markers. These graves were art as much as they were a display of respect. A craft imbued with sorrow and regret. An apology.

Her chest tightened and her eyes began to sting.

Some additional seaweed had been cleared away in front of the grave bundles, so that there was an open path encircling the site. She could swim right up to each to visit and pay respects without having to bend around seaweed stalks. Such a simple physical task, but mentally she couldn't do it. Maybe someday she would have the fortitude to swim right up to them and lay a hand upon the woven shrouds, but not today. This was close enough.

Nireed wrapped an arm around her waist and rested her head against hers. Lorelei returned the one-armed hug, unable to feel the touch of her own tears, all claimed by the ocean the moment they fell.

She didn't regret seeing the siren's grave bundles for her crew. There was closure in it, but it was still hard.

There was something unnerving about paying respects to a body, much less a whole crew's worth. She had never liked open casket funerals. The departed never looked real to her, a macabre imitation of the person they once were in life, as cold and motionless as a wax museum figure. When her mom died, there had been enough funds for a casket and a traditional burial, but she had her cremated. She couldn't bear the thought of her mother in a casket—open or closed. Instead, she gave her ashes to the wind and Lake Superior.

Lowering her gaze, Lorelei took a moment to herself.

Gold lettering caught her eye.

The section of ship that bore *The Osprey's* name rested at the base of the grave site, scratched and faded, but propped in place by sea rock. She clasped a hand across her mouth, another choked sob escaping her lips in a cloud of bubbles. This wasn't just a grave site. It was a memorial.

Spinning in the water, she pulled Nireed into a hug. "Thank you," she said, though the sea took words, rendering them nothing more than moving lips and bubbles. But the siren squeezed her back, swaying them from side to side in the water, and Lorelei thought she probably understood.

CHAPTER
THIRTY-TWO

KILLIAN

DAWN CHASER HAD BECOME A COMMON MEETING GROUND.

A group of ocean-born sirens sat on crates on deck, interspersed between the humans. There were five in total—three Killian knew, two he didn't. Lorelei handed one of them a pair of sunglasses to wear and showed her how to put them on.

Killian was at a loss for how they were going to get the virophage into the mermen. The brain virus affected them more severely, and unlike the sirens, they couldn't exactly be reasoned or bargained with. They were utterly feral. Baiting and attempting to capture them like they had with Undine would be dangerous, and he had a nauseating suspicion that simple human blood wouldn't lure them.

More sinister cravings drew them from the deep.

Because why else had they never been seen before?

Heavy sedation would be involved—he knew that much—even before Will pulled out a case filled with tranquilizer syringes. Where his best friend got this shit in such large quantities, he didn't know either. Probably a military supply store. This was Maine after all.

The tranquilizer gun had made a reappearance, as well.

They had tools and heart and little else.

But that was why they were all here. The sirens had come up with a game plan, one they had pieced together amongst themselves after Lorelei told them about "sleeping shots." There was nothing the humans could do beneath the waves, but even if they could, this was the merfolk's fight now.

Their fight for salvation.

CHAPTER
THIRTY-THREE

NIREED

FOR DAYS, NIREED AND HER SIREN SISTERS—AERSILA, Undine, Melusina, and Delphine—had watched their targets from a distance, a pod of eight, led by a shimmering, bronze-scaled male and a golden one.

That was a big grouping for mermen. Any larger and they would have torn themselves apart, too many territorial, sickness-addled creatures in one place. They couldn't live in communities like Nireed and the rest of her siren siblings did.

If it weren't for the sickness, all would be ripe for mating with. But that's why they were here learning the male pod's patterns, waiting for the right moment to strike. Shorewalker and Cure Creator may have saved her sisters, but now it was up to them to save the rest of their people. No matter how long it took, Nireed would fight to reunite them, one male pod at a time.

A little one darted from behind the golden male, startling a gasp from Aersila.

Make that a pod of nine.

The boy, no bigger than a seal pup, couldn't be much more than two years old. Aersila trembled beside her, a choked sob swallowed for fear of making sound. Nireed slipped her hand into her sister's and squeezed, stomach flipping.

Her pod couldn't keep most of their boy babies.

Nature was often cruel, but what this sickness did to her people was the worst kind of cruelty, forcing them to betray their instincts, their community, each other. And the grim, unthinkable reality of the past three generations, and the illness that took so many of their boys, had forced them to give up the afflicted to protect the rest of their children.

In meetings with the humans to discuss reunification, Cure Creator explained that Nireed's siren siblings all shared the same sickness, just experienced different symptoms. A "sex influenced trait," she'd called it. It was why it mostly only affected the boys, but sometimes, although rarely, took other children, too.

Bile rose in the back of Nireed's throat, followed by a burning in her eyes. Being buried underneath a sea rock avalanche would be more pleasant than remembering. But what her pod mates had to do to survive would never be far from her mind.

They left the afflicted as close as they dared to the male pod settlements, hoping that they would be found and adopted like this one had been and raised as their own, because their grand foremothers learned the hard way that even at such a young age, the afflicted were ruthless, finding horrendous bite and claw marks on the other children. Some died, their wounds too grievous to overcome, their little hearts giving out.

Even with the sickness lowering inhibitions, and hardening what was left of their instincts, it hadn't dulled their maternal ones, no matter how much some pretended otherwise. The terrible task of giving up children had never been bearable. Nireed saw over and over the grief it caused. How low it reduced her fierce warrior sister, curled up on herself in a patch of seafloor muck, the softest bed their world had to offer, unable to move, unable to eat.

Aersila had only ever given birth to boys.

It was a cruel twist of fate for all she risked in attempts to get pregnant and grow their pod. Nireed nurtured Aersila through grief more times than she dared to count. Nature had never been kind to their people.

With a slight shake of her head, she tamped down the aching feeling rising in her chest. She had to be strong for her sister. For this mission. Focusing on the water passing through her gills helped, easing the heaviness that settled over her.

The little tyke was hundreds of feet away, trailing after the golden merman, but there was no mistaking his Emera coloring, even at this distance. Silver scales, fins slashed with orange. Like mother, like son.

Aersila watched the child and the pod with sharp focus, nursing her grief in silence.

Longings to cradle and nurture and protect a child of her own pressed in, hitting her suddenly and forcefully, a crushing sensation that forced the air from her lungs, like diving too fast in deep water. Her body trembled with feverish desire, nature's way of making her interested, despite the dangers, and she understood why Aersila had been so desperate.

Scooping a handful of muck from the sea floor, she slathered it over her scent glands. Now was not the time to attract male attention, but soon, if they succeeded, it would be welcome.

Together, they tailed the male pod. Hiding. Observing. No more. No less.

Even when the males began stalking a whale, one of the wise ones of the sea, they did not interfere. It pained and disgusted them to watch the males hunt, tire, and kill the noble creature, but too much was at stake to risk a premature altercation.

They waited for the large meal to put the males into a sleepy stupor.

The male-pod cavorted and feasted on whale meat for days. The more they ate, the slower, more sluggish they moved, until they drifted into a pit in the seafloor, full and happy from abundant rich food, and fell asleep at its base.

The whale's death would not be in vain. Nor would years of her siren siblings' pain.

CHAPTER

THIRTY-FOUR

UNDINE

Shorewalker's Two-Legger friend, Cure Creator, strapped what they called a "recording device" to Undine's upper arm. It would allow them to see and hear what the siren hunting party did from the boat. She couldn't fathom how. They'd showed her the other machine, a boxy thing with a glowing face and an uncanny ability to reflect part of her vision.

A fascinating gadget, but it wouldn't do the Two-Leggers much good hundreds of feet down, where they wouldn't be able to see anything in the dark. Not until the hunting party was right upon their targets, illuminated by their deep-sea glow.

"Use this to cover up your light," Lorelei said, holding out a stick of black rock. "It's a kohl-based paint. It will keep the mermen from being able to see you."

Undine took the stick and dragged it across her arm, where it left a black streak. She used it on her arms, her tail, and her face, covering up every luminescent node. The only thing she left uncovered were her hands for communication. Plenty of creatures glowed in the deep. The small amount of light her hands produced would not be alarming to the male pod. She helped the others do the same, taking care of places they could not reach, before asking for reciprocation.

From a woven basket, they pulled out potent strips of shark hide, and wrapped their bodies with it to mask their scents. They might still smell like prey, but with full bellies, the males wouldn't stir for shark. Then they strapped pouches with "sleeping darts" inside to their waists.

Preparations complete, Undine touched her forehead to each of her warriors', lingering a moment at each, imparting her respect, her gratitude, and a blessing of strength.

They followed her over the side of the boat and began their descent.

They didn't have far to swim. The Two-Leggers had brought them as close as they possibility could. There was nowhere else to go but down.

At the edge of the pit, each picked up a sizable chunk of sea rock, letting its weight carry them down into the black abyss. Silent, undetectable by sound or touch. Minimal movement meant reduced vibrations, and when sight or scent failed, this was how their kind sensed other creatures.

Down and down they sank.

1,200 feet. A depth the sirens hadn't seen since their foremothers fled. It was quieter down here, this far from the surface. Silence was a gift, but for the purposes of their mission, it was even more imperative that they take care not to make sound or disturb the water.

As they neared the pit floor, they could make out the light-lit silhouettes of their targets, each laying on a bed of seaweed, fins twitching just enough to keep water movement flowing along their gills. Their bioluminescence glowed soft, flashing in all sorts of patterns while they slept.

None stirred at their approach.

Undine touched down first, signaling to her unit that she reached bottom with a subtle flash from her hands. She was soon followed by the others, who signaled back. They placed the sea rock in their arms gently down into the muck, careful not to make a single sound. With the barest twitches of their fins, they drifted into position. One siren at the head, another at the tail of each male.

Communicating with more subtle flashes of their hands, to ensure their movements stayed in unison, they withdrew the sleeping darts from their pouches and lined up their points.

Undine gave the signal. Three short bursts of dim light.

They jabbed down, needle meeting flesh.

The males awoke, thrashing and hissing, breaking that blessed silence. But Undine and her warriors held them down, waiting for the sleeping medicine to carry them back into a deep slumber. They succumbed quickly.

Save for the little one, whom Aersila gathered into her arms, her siren warrior pairs took a male each, towing them to the surface where the Two-Leggers waited.

Undine followed at a distance, watching her people gradually ascend toward the light.

She smiled.

CHAPTER
THIRTY-FIVE

AERSILA

HER LITTLE BOY WAS WARY OF HER. CRUEL NATURE HAD given him a good reason to be, and for as much as she was proud of his strong instincts—it hurt to see him flinch and hide behind Aquilus, the gold-scaled merman who raised him.

Though he was too small, just a babe, to have memories of the day she gave him up, of the day when she left him near the male pod's territory swaddled in seaweed, hoping they would adopt and raise him, he would've been taught to swim clear of the non-male merfolk.

"You're safe, Ryn," Aquilus signed, a soothing quality to his hands' gentle movement. "No one's going to hurt you. Your mother, her pod, they were very sick, just like we were very sick, but we're all healthy again and can be one pod now. A family." He paused to rest a hand on top the boy's mess of dark curls, and something yanked in Aersila's chest to see Ryn gaze up at him with such trust and love.

There was nothing she wouldn't give to receive that same look one day. "We can talk from afar," she suggested, even though she yearned to scoop him up into her arms and hold him tight. She would earn her son's trust and patience in time.

"That sounds reasonable," Aquilus replied, looking to her boy. "What do you say?"

Ryn nodded, creeping out from behind him.

Though he didn't stray far from Aquilus's side, Aersila could now see most of his sleek, silvery form and amber luminescence as he signed, "Father tells me you're a great trident-wielder."

She smiled—for herself, for her son, for the merman who saved his life.

While Aquilus wasn't Ryn's blood father—the one who was hadn't survived the sickness that ravaged their species—the gold-scaled merman not only had assumed the role, it appeared he'd also earned the title.

"Are you the best?" Ryn edged closer, curiosity overcoming fear.

There was none better. Not even Undine could best her in trident fighting. "No one's beaten me yet," she answered. "It is a heavy weapon, but I am very strong and fast. Have you used one, Ryn?"

He shook his head, glancing to his father when he said, "No. Father says he is terrible at it and would only teach me bad habits."

Aquilus only chuckled. Must be true.

"I could teach you how if you'd like. Your father, too. It could be a group lesson."

Grasping his father's arm, Ryn looked up, pleading. No words needed to be signed to understand the question there or the excitement sparkling in his eyes. Seeing her boy's eagerness made hope soar in her heart.

She didn't know what was supposed to come next or what the right things to do or say were, but this seemed like a good beginning. Commonalities. Filling a need.

Ruffling the boy's hair, Aquilus cast Aersila a warm smile before tipping his head forward in agreement.

CHAPTER
THIRTY-SIX

LORELEI

Love was in the air. Or the water to be strictly accurate.

Just two months following "the cure," and so many of Undine's pod were pregnant, including the siren leader herself, spurred by some biological drive to save their species.

Caught up in the wave, Lorelei's own hormones went haywire.

"I don't know how I can tell," Killian murmured, nuzzling her neck. Barely in the door from his last offshore run, he'd backed her up against the nearest wall. His hands roved the length of her body until they found the hem of her sweater dress. "You don't smell any different, but I'm hard all the time. Just ready to go."

He hiked up the skirt, the thick fabric bunching around her waist and swore. His fingers brushed the bare skin at the tops of her stockings, between her thighs. Pleasure raced up her spine, her back arching at the lightest touch, ready to come undone.

"Where's your underwear, Lorelei?" His breath was hot against the shell of her ear.

She mewled as his fingers dipped into her wet heat, one knuckle rubbing circles around her sensitive bud. No underwear. No point. The last time this happened they ripped her favorite pair. "Forgot to put them on, Captain."

He growled, whisking her off her feet.

He carried her upstairs and dumped her on the bed.

It was honestly a miracle he bothered. Lately he'd taken to having her whenever and wherever the urge struck. Not that she minded. At any given moment, she was rearing to go. If Killian wasn't home, she could spend whole afternoons with her vibrator.

This "mating" frenzy business was absolutely nuts. She had no idea a person could be so turned on all the time.

Lorelei shrugged out of her dress, too stifling to keep on, and watched Killian yank off his shirt, pull open his belt, and unzip his fly. She licked her lips, riveted by the bulge, and while it was familiar, she'd been thinking about it all day.

After shedding his pants, he held up a foil packet. "Condom or no condom?" His tone was light, but the heat in his gaze was anything but.

She gulped, harpooned by the bigger underlying question.

They had gotten in the habit of using two kinds of contraceptive simultaneously to ride out the siren baby fever. And in that time, he hadn't asked this. She was on the pill, but there was always the chance of failure, especially now with her "mating-addled" brain, which made her rather forgetful about taking it. Last week, she forgot three nights in a row. Her phone alarm would go off, but then she'd get distracted by something else and next thing she knew three days had gone by.

She would have forgotten a fourth night, if Killian hadn't pressed the pill packet into her hand and told her that she'd been missing doses.

Now he stroked his dick idly, precum beading at the tip like an offering, patiently awaiting her answer.

Shit. Shit. Shit. They hadn't exactly talked about this. They were getting married, yes, but it never came up. "I'm not sure I want kids," she forced out. It hung bluntly in the air between them. She wanted to smack herself.

He nodded once, tearing open the foil packet. She searched his face, trying to determine whether he was disappointed, but a small smile played at his lips as he rolled the condom down his length. "I'm happy to follow your lead," he said, yanking her to the edge of the bed by the backs of her stockinged knees. She yelped in surprise.

Gripping her hip, he tipped his dick to her entrance and pushed, gliding right in on natural lubricant. Usually there was a little resistance, but not today. He squeezed. "Shit, that feels so good."

He rocked into her with long, languid strokes, a thumb at her clit sending shockwaves throughout her body. "If you want them, I'll give them to you," he said, thrusting more forcefully to emphasize the point. Her inner walls clamped around him, causing him to curse. Dammit, she hadn't been even slightly interested in babies before, but this dirty talk was so, so hot.

She lay splayed out across the mattress, arms thrown back behind her head, tangling with the mess of her hair, skin too hot and tingly, her brain feverish with desire. How easy it would be to give in, caught up in this moment between them, to take off the condom, to stop taking the pill. To let Killian knock her up.

"But if not, that's all right, too," he continued. "Just happy to have you."

Her body screamed, *yes, take me bare!* while her heart basked in his words, and her mind whispered a quiet, uncertain no.

"Killian…" she breathed, chest heaving. "I want…but I don't. I'm so confused."

In his eyes, she saw nothing but certainty. "Then we keep the condom on," he said.

The heat didn't ebb away, but the pressure building in her chest around the decision did. Killian rubbed soothing circles across her hip, and there it was again, a smile tugging at the corners of his mouth.

"What's that look for?"

"I'd thought maybe you'd been skipping on purpose. Just in case I said yes."

She took his hand, imploring him with her eyes. "Killian, I would never do that behind your back. I…"

"Shh." He smoothed a line up her torso, pressing his palm between her breasts, keeping her flat on her back. With a sensual roll of his hips, he buried himself in deep, drawing a moan from her lips. "I know. That's not what I meant. You're the one who suggested we start using condoms again. Just thought maybe you were weighing your options, working up the courage to ask. You missed six days last week."

"What?" Lorelei sputtered. Six days? No, she took the pill when he handed her the packet…

He smirked, rolling his hips again, a slow drag of his pelvis against her oversensitive clit. She shivered, back arching off the mattress. "You took one midweek when I gave it to you. Then missed the next three days."

She flung her arm across her eyes and groaned. How could she be so careless?

Killian gathered her up in his arms, the mattress dipping with his weight as he joined her, settling them closer to the headboard. "Thought maybe you wanted a baby." His voice was dark and low, near her ear. He nipped at the soft lobe. "Was startled at first, but the more I thought about it, the more I could envision it. There's nothing I wouldn't give you, Lorelei, but only when you're truly ready. If that day comes, all you need to do is ask, but no matter what you decide, I'm all in."

She slid her arm away, called to the depths of his stormy blues. She sought his lips, eyes pricking at how much she loved and trusted this man. A bruising kiss followed in its wake, as slow and languid as his thrusts, tongues caressing, lips sucked plump. There was a pattern to the movement of his hips, too. He'd roll them, grinding sensuous circles around her core, rock once and then thrust. It was utterly new. Measured. Ripe with meaning.

"Is this how you'd take me if you were trying to knock me up, Captain?" Her voice was low and breathy.

He pressed his forehead to hers, burning her insides to a crisp with his molten stare. "Yes, but after that comment, I don't have any more patience for going slow." He pushed up onto his knees, spreading her legs as far as they would go. He thrust once, hard and fast. Then again and again, the breaks between each rapidly shrinking.

Hands braced against her hips, he set a brutal, punishing pace. The whole bed creaked and groaned beneath them, but that only seemed to encourage him to go faster. Lorelei clung to his sweat-slicked thighs for dear life, losing herself to the intoxicating crescendo of one climax after the other.

"Don't break the condom," she gasped, a sliver of sanity pushing through the pleasurable fog. The irrational, and unfortunately dominant, part of her siren brain would undoubtedly like it if it did.

"Won't." His pace didn't even stutter. Muscles taut, and eyes blazing, Killian drove into her fiercely, a storm unleashed. "But I'll feel it if I do."

Lorelei tipped her head back, putting all thought and worry from her mind, losing herself to sensation. Everything tingled, even her tongue, building to one more exploding point. She plunged over the edge again before he did, blunted nails digging into his thighs, crashing hard upon the rocks of oblivion.

Bucking forward, his lips parted as he came, utter bliss written across his face.

He didn't move or speak for a long time. Neither of them did.

Coherent thought returned in bits and pieces. They'd had great sex before, but that was something else.

"You okay?" She chuckled, nudging his hips with her thighs.

He groaned; his eyes squeezed shut. "That was next level."

She grinned. They agreed there, but she wanted to hear what he had to say about it. "How so?"

He didn't answer right away, but when he opened his heavy-lidded eyes, he looked absolutely dazed. Ravished. "The way you kept clenching around me...it was like your body was trying to wring me dry. Fuck, it felt so good."

This kind of dirty talk was a new frontier for them, and it reached her on an unexpected level. Had they discovered a mutual kink? Or was this just a product of her siren biology? The idea that he could get her pregnant was hotter than the reality, so probably the former. As long as it wasn't real, she'd take more of it.

But her forgetfulness? That was nature conspiring against her.

When she explained that to Killian, he pushed back a damp strand of hair from her forehead and kissed her. "I'll help you remember."

CHAPTER

THIRTY-SEVEN

LORELEI

WINTER CAME AND WENT, AND YET, PEOPLE HADN'T STOPPED whispering about her.

It was the height of spring, when Maine's stubborn snows finally thawed, and the trees began to bud with new life. Why couldn't this time for fresh starts and new beginnings apply to her own life? Winter isolation had done nothing to dilute the gossip.

So much for "out of sight, out of mind."

The door to the human world was shutting Lorelei out, her only ties to it the small knit family she made in Haven Cove, Maine, and even that had shrunk.

Walt. Marci.

Standing at the water's edge, toes buried in the sand as she looked out over her small, private cove, her heart ached for reconciliation.

It had been months. Far too long not to speak to people she loved and adored.

She pulled her phone from her back pocket and stared at the screen, weighing, debating the consequences of giving the Walshes a call. Reaching out surely wouldn't push them further away, right?

But maybe a group text would be a better, softer start. It would give them time to process and consider their response. She began to type: *Thinking of you. Maybe we could talk soon?*

Before she could send the text, her phone vibrated in her hand, the screen lighting up with an incoming call. Tears sprung to her eyes. It was the Walshes' home phone landline. Maybe they had been thinking the same.

Wrapping an arm around her middle, fingers bunching in her shirt, Lorelei answered, "I was just about to text you."

"We miss you," Walt said, and she could hear it in his voice. The tears, a longing akin to homesickness.

"Would it be all right if we brought over lunch and talked?" That was Marci.

"I would love that."

When they hung up, Lorelei went inside to straighten and freshen up. It would just be her and the Walshes. Killian was at the gym this morning with Will, and they had afternoon video game plans, which was likely to turn into a bros' sleepover, judging by the new horde of snacks featured in a picture Lila sent of their pantry.

Maybe after the Walshes' visit, she'd invite Lila over for wine, dessert, and charcuterie. It would be good to decompress after the heartfelt emotional labor that was to come.

An hour later, Lorelei heard a car roll up the driveway and park, followed by the thud of two closing doors. There was a light knock at the door a moment later.

She opened it to find Walt on her stoop holding a bouquet of flowers, a bottle of Prosecco, and Marci with a wrapped tray of assorted tea sandwiches—chicken salad and smoked salmon and dill. Just seeing them standing there, smiling warmly but just a little bit uncertain, brought tears to her eyes again.

"What's all this?"

"We wanted to apologize as well as celebrate," Marci said. "Can we hug you?"

Nodding, she launched herself into their arms, and they hugged her tight around the things they carried. "I'm so, so sorry for scaring you," she said. "I didn't want that. Please know that I would never ever hurt either of you or Lila or Will or Killian. You're family."

"And you're a second daughter to us," Walt sniffed over her shoulder, squeezing. "We were scared, and shocked, but," he pulled away, wiping his eyes on his shirt sleeves, careful not to smack anyone with the flowers or the bubbly, "you saw what could have been a bad situation and deescalated it."

"We're sorry for not reaching out sooner," Marci added, continuing the hug. "We should have. What happened with Carrie, how you handled the situation, might not be how we would have done things, but she needed a little scaring."

Did Marci really mean that? Lorelei pulled away, watching them both.

The couple shared a look. "We've known Carrie since she was a little girl," Walt began, choosing his words slowly and carefully. "A childhood friend of the kids. We tried to be welcoming and supportive for Will's sake, because through him she's family, but sometimes, that's not enough. Some family members aren't safe to be around. Some family members aren't good people."

"We needed time to process," Marci cradled the sandwich tray close to her chest. "Parse out our feelings. Carrie's not been a good person, but you have, and we failed to show you that."

Fresh tears sprung to Lorelei's eyes. She pressed her hands to her cheeks, overwhelmed and yet so relieved. "I was afraid I'd lost your love."

"You never lost our love."

They came together again for another group hug.

After, Lorelei ushered them inside, found a vase for the flowers, and set the table with plates and champagne flutes.

"We went and saw your museum," Walt said, pulling out an old flip phone. Sitting beside him, Lorelei watched as he scrolled through all the grainy photos he snapped with it. "Was hoping maybe you could give us a virtual tour?" He'd certainly took enough photos for it.

She smiled wistfully, both touched by the gesture and heartbroken. "It's not my museum anymore."

"Not if we have anything to say about it." Marci placed an arm around her shoulders, giving her a comforting squeeze. "We filed nepotism complaints on your behalf and had a conversation with Jackie. She's working on a piece about your wrongful termination. Whatever it takes, we'll get you reinstated."

Dry eyes just weren't in the cards today. "You didn't have to do that," Lorelei whispered, too choked up to give the words any volume.

"You sacrificed your dreams and your privacy so that Lila could keep hers. Of course, we did. And you're a daughter to us, too, remember? We'll fight for you."

"Lila has fought for me every day since I told her what I am, and she has done so much for my kin. I owe everything to her."

"That's our Lila. Fiercely loyal," Marci said proudly. "She told us that you got to see where the merfolk live. How was that?"

"Wonderful," Lorelei breathed. "They were so welcoming."

As they filled glasses of champagne and tucked into the tea sandwiches, she told them all about it.

CHAPTER
THIRTY-EIGHT

LORELEI

THE SKY DARKENED AND RAIN BEGAN TO FALL, SCOURING away the days of joy her reconciliation with the Walshes had given her. Lorelei's breathing remained even but worry gnawed at her insides. It had taken her a year after *The Osprey* not to seize in a panic every time the weather took a turn while Killian was out at sea.

There'd been red skies that morning, harbinger of a coming storm.

Red sky at night, sailors' delight.

Red sky at morning, sailors take warning.

Storms didn't have to be devastating. Killian and his crew navigated them all the time. They sometimes got tossed around a bit, yes, but they always came home.

But as the wind picked up and the steady rain shower battering her windows turned into a torrential downpour, a severe weather warning alert blared from her kitchen radio, chilling her to the bone.

Killian, please. Come home to me.

Her lights flickered, then cut out.

CANDLES SAT ON EVERY AVAILABLE FLAT SURFACE, CASTING everything in a dull orange glow. Overkill for someone with her photic senses, but the shadows of the room closed in, and she did not want to be swathed in darkness.

Wind howled outside, whipping about the cove at ferocious speeds, buffeting the seaside cottage so much it rattled. The trees creaked and groaned, some bending at startling angles. Fragile branches snapped, falling with heavy crashes. The smaller ones pelted her home. Clattering. Scratching. Just so much noise.

Rain beat against the windowpanes too heavy to see more than silhouettes and flashes of lightening, but Lorelei could feel the tempestuous ocean waves, roiling, churning, and hungry. This was the side of ocean that took and did not return.

A terrible, dangerous beauty.

She wasn't alone. Lila and Marci had come over shortly after the severe weather radio broadcast, their hair pulled up and covered by silk scarves, just before the heavy winds hit. This wasn't a night to endure alone if one had the choice, not with loved ones in the clutches of a pitiless sea.

They sat on the hardwood floor in front of the couch, no question of logic, some innate, mutual agreement that sitting on it seemed unbearable. A kind of antsiness that needed the ground's firm support, not cushion.

They checked NOAA's weather app once and set it aside. Seeing all that red swirling across the map made them queasy with fear.

Ashen, Marci said under her breath, "This storm's a ship sinker." Lila didn't seem to catch it, but Lorelei did. Siren hearing was sometimes a cursed thing.

Knots twisted over and over in her stomach, waterlogged, and pulled tight. The weather was just as bad out at sea where their men fished, or worse. Killian, Will, and Walt were at the mercy of a ruthless ocean, tossed about in a vulnerable hunk of metal.

At some point, Marci made them all hot tea. A distraction. Something to busy the hands when the mind was in turmoil. Though a simple, soothing comfort in times of stress, their cups went cold, untouched.

Lorelei similarly preoccupied herself with a stray hoodie string she found under the couch. All the various kinds of knots she learned during her sailing days, she tied in miniature one after the other. She'd fly through one, unravel it, and start again with another. Cleat hitch. Bowline. Butterfly loop. Square knot.

Even knowing what she was, a creature the ocean could not drown, Lorelei huddled next to Marci and Lila, trembling. A monstrous wave rose before her, the ocean's gaping maw widening before slamming down and devouring all in its path. The screams of crewmen pounded in her ears, and the stench of fear and blood and death burned her nose.

It was only memory, mixed with present fear, but it squeezed her throat shut and dried out her mouth. She blinked to clear her blurring vision. Why was the room spinning? She discarded the string in her hands. While she could tie knots with her eyes shut, nausea crept in, heavy and cloying.

Oh God, she needed to get up and go find a trash can.

With tingling, shaking hands she wiped sweat from her eyes. Her leg muscles twitched, brain and body in disagreement about what to do. It wasn't even significant enough to qualify as a half-assed effort to stand.

Please leave the Dawn Chaser *be. You took my friends. Don't you dare take my family.*

"Honey, listen to me." Marci's rich, soothing voice cut through the surging storm. Lorelei latched onto it like a lifeline. "Put your head between your knees."

Lorelei complied.

"Good. Now breathe in. Then out." The short, simple sentences were easy to follow, mercifully distracting. "That's it, just concentrate on my voice. Breathe in. Deep breath. Now out. Good, good. Stay in the present. Keep focusing on your breath. Breathe in. Breathe out."

Memory and fear receded to repetition until there was nothing but Marci's voice and the steady rise and fall her chest.

"Thank you," Lorelei exhaled.

Marci didn't say anything, just threaded their fingers together and her daughter's. She held all three of their hands in her lap, eyes closed, and head tipped forward. Her lips moved, but no words came.

Prayer.

They sat together like that for a long time.

There was nothing worse than waiting for bad news. Greta Roth had taught her that in the most heartbreaking way possible.

Thunder boomed, and all three of them shot up five inches at the deafening crash that reverberated to the bone. A sharp series of knocks on the front door followed, and they all jolted again. It was almost more startling than the thunder.

Who the hell would be out and about in this weather?

"Shorewalker!"

Lorelei shot to her feet. *Nireed?*

It was hard to distinguish the voice in all the surrounding noise, but it was definitely one of her siren sisters. No one else called her Shorewalker. But what could have driven her here in this wicked storm? Not exactly an easy swim on even on a fair-weather day.

Couldn't be anything good, but she didn't dare make assumptions. Contemplating any of the grim possibilities might break her.

When she opened the door, blustering wind and rain rushed in, soaking her front in seconds. Down on the stoop, Nireed crouched low to the ground, protecting her head with her arms. Small, bleeding cuts from wind-blown debris marred her skin. Taking the siren by the elbow, Lorelei pulled her inside and slammed the door shut.

They both dripped puddles onto the floor.

Marci hustled into the kitchen, possibly for towels.

The siren panted heavily, bent forward with her hands propped against her knees. "I swam here as fast as I could. When we learned..." She sucked in rasping lungfuls of breath.

Dread sapped the warmth from her limbs. "Learned what, Nireed?"

She straightened, raising her arms above her head. "Was out on a hunt with Aersila, Melusina, and many others, but stopped for a bit of storm play. Pods of the Still Sick came. Twenty strong. They attacked your mate's boat."

Somewhere off in the corner of her eye, Marci dropped the stack of towels she was holding, and a wailing cry rose, soul-deep in anguish. Lorelei braced herself against the wall to keep herself upright. *No. No. No. No. No.*

"They are alive," Nireed added quickly, placing a hand on Lorelei's shoulder. "We fought off the Still Sick, but the boat is sinking, and the Two-Leggers will not let us bring them to safety, no matter what your mate says to try to convince them. They do not trust us, and told us to get out, that they would patch the boat enough to stay afloat and summon the Coast Warriors. Your mate disagreed, it's not enough, but he will not leave them behind. Cure Creator's mate and sire won't leave any one behind either. The other Two-Leggers will drown before they let us help. You need to come Lorelei. They know and trust you. If you speak, they will listen."

Lorelei gave one firm nod and dashed upstairs for her shark armor and harpoon.

When she returned wearing her custom wet suit, and other gear, Lila waited for her at the bottom of the stairs. She grabbed Lorelei's hands, squeezing them hard. A wild desperate look blazed in her eyes, dark-brown cheeks streaked with tears. "I can't lose them, Lorelei. That's half my family."

"I know." It was half her family, too. Marci was on the phone with somebody, possibly the Coast Guard. Lorelei hugged Lila once, quick and fast, then pulled away, slinging her harpoon across her back.

She followed Nireed into the storm.

CHAPTER
THIRTY-NINE

KILLIAN

THEY SHOULD HAVE LEFT WITH THE HEALTHY MERFOLK WHEN they had the chance.

Killian and his crew came down here to get equipment to patch the hull when Will raced down from mid-deck waving frantically and pressing his fingers to lips. Everyone got the message quick. Hands stilling, mouths shut tight.

"Merman," Will mouthed.

As the crew all piled into the engine room, quiet as could be, Killian propped open the door to the freezer hold. Maybe the overbearing smell of fish and refrigerant would distract him, throw him off their scent. Killian filed in after his crew, where they all hunkered down on the floor, and locked and blocked the door.

"Rub grease on your skin," he whispered as loud as he dared. "Mask your scent."

They complied.

Claws scraped metal in a long discordant screech, dragging along walls from the flooded end of the hull. It must be him, the virus-ravaged merman, lurking in the hallway, just on the other side of the door. Sniffing. Hunting.

And now they were stuck inside this waterlogged death trap, pinched between two unsavory options. Stay here and meet the sailor's gradual, then sudden demise. Or go up against a creature who could rip them all to shreds in seconds with its supernatural strength.

It didn't matter that they outnumbered it seven to one. They had no weapons, save for some patching tools and a water pump too heavy to swing. The collateral damage it would take to overpower the feral merman was unconscionable, but they might not have a choice.

Staying put meant certain death. Drowning.

Where was Will's fucking tranquilizer gun when they needed it? Pilothouse, that's where, and no good to them here.

Killian swiped a greasy hand across his face, then around his neck, rubbing the stuff into his skin.

Those creatures hit the bow hard and fast, clawing their way in. One climbed up the side and tore through the pilothouse, McAdams barely making it out with his life. He was saved only by *siren ex machina*, the wave of healthy merfolk that spilled over the side to fend off their attackers, driving them back into the deep.

Thank Christ they did, or he and his crew would all be chum.

McAdams and too many of the others didn't know the difference between the groups of merfolk. Killian saw a rescue. They saw murderous, territorial sea creatures fighting over prey, and flat out refused their rescuers' help when the fighting stopped, even knowing the boat was slowly sinking, and that a patch may or may not hold them together long enough for the Coast Guard to arrive.

If the radios weren't too damaged to call for help.

Killian leaned over and whispered the question in Will's ear, "Radios?"

Will frowned, shaking his head. He'd gone up to check, which was why he was initially separated from the group. "Saw merman," he whispered back, too afraid of making sound to use full sentences. "Snuck away to warn." He gestured to the group.

It was uncharitable—they didn't know what he knew about the merfolk—but fuck those guys. Not a goddamn one of them listened to a word he or Will or Walt had to say. So much for being the fucking captain of this boat. They held a goddamn vote like this was a fucking Democracy.

And his stupid, moral ass wouldn't leave his hardheaded crew to die.

Killian leaned into his anger, letting it take the reins, because if he wasn't pissed, he would be scared shitless about dying and weepy that he wouldn't get to marry the love of his life.

CHAPTER
FORTY

LORELEI

SHE FOUND *DAWN CHASER* THIRTY MILES OUT, SUBMERGED BOW
pointed west; the crew had been heading home when the storm hit. It
had passed now, ravaging the coast and inland towns instead.

With the engines cut, the boat sat eerily quiet and dark, dead in the
water. Aft tilted above the surface by a water-laden fore, revealed a
glimpse of the barnacle-encrusted underside, its propellors silent, still,
and dripping seawater. The pilothouse was flooded, not completely
underwater just yet, but all the electronics and radios would've been
destroyed. She had no idea if the crew had gotten out the S.O.S. as
intended, but Marci had called the Coast Guard.

No matter what, help would be coming.

But in time?

Dozens of gouges and slash marks scarred the bow. The mermen had
torn into the boat, prying apart steel to create a gaping hole in a feat of
alarming supernatural strength.

Nireed signed, "Get them out," and dove down to join their kin.

Beneath the surface, Lorelei saw familiar faces—Undine, Aersila,
Delphine, Melusina, Aquilus—and many, many others, all pushing up on

the boat's hulking, water-laden mass. Judging by the sheer numbers, most of the healthy merfolk community had come, straining against the weight, trying to keep her man and his crew alive.

They were only thing keeping *Dawn Chaser* afloat. And they would tire fast.

She zipped through the water toward the gash in the hull. She had to get Killian and the others out now. It didn't appear that they did much patching, which should have been their number one priority. The fact that they didn't probably meant something had gone terribly wrong. Like they got flooded out and trapped.

Or a section of the boat's interior collapsed...

Whatever the problem was she would have to face it alone. None of her kin below could be spared to come along. She maneuvered through the opening, careful not to scrape skin or scale against the rough, jagged edges.

That's when she smelled it.

Something sick and feral and distinctly male. What she didn't smell was blood. Thank God for that. Blood meant she was too late, a thought she banished quickly. The situation was too dire to fall down a rabbit hole and waste time contemplating what-ifs. She dimmed her bioluminescent light and forced her nerves under control, slowing her heartrate. Fear and panic were beacons to a predator.

She would know, after all.

There wasn't anything she could do about her natural scent, no muck or shark hide to mask it, but she pressed on, head on swivel with a harpoon gripped tightly in her hands. She drifted through the sunken, narrow hallway of the bottommost deck toward the half-submerged stairwell, barely twitching a muscle to propel herself forward. The way was lit by the faint yellow glow of egress light strips running parallel to the walls.

When she reached the stairs, which led to Killian's cabin and the crew's quarters, she slowly shifted into her human form, readjusting her customized wet suit and shark armor to cover her lower half. Showing up half naked to a rescue wouldn't exactly inspire trust in a group of people she'd only interacted with a few times.

She ascended with feather light steps to mid-deck. Bracing herself against the narrow walls, she crept up the slant of the hallway. She silently checked Killian's cabin, the crew's quarters, the head. The galley. Nothing.

They must have been on the level she'd just come from, but in the aft section of the boat not yet underwater. Where the merman stalked. Shit. She had hoped to avoid him.

Taking the aft set of stairs, she descended once more.

Judging by the loud crash coming from the freezer hold—splintered crate and spilled ice—the merman was preoccupying himself with the fish there, which explained why he hadn't scented or heard her yet. And why Killian and his crew, if somewhere nearby, were overlooked. The frigid temperatures, stench of dead fish, and the constant hum of the industrial refrigeration unit, kept running by an auxiliary generator, would dull his senses, overpowering anything beyond that enclosed space. If this asshole hadn't ripped the door half off its hinges, she would've shut him in and been done with it. But nothing was ever that easy.

She slinked down the stairs, leaning against the railing to maintain balance in the boat's tipped state, and at the bottom, pressed her ear to the engine room door, listening.

Please be in here.

A quiet cough. Some murmuring and rustling.

To free up both her hands, she strapped her harpoon to her back, careful not to smack it off anything.

It was a long shot, but she slowly twisted the door handle. Barely budged. Locked from the inside. She eased it back up quietly, not even a soft click. How was she going to get them to open the door without alerting the merman? If there was a larger gap between door and floor, she could have gotten writing implements from Killian's cabin and shoved a message to them underneath.

She drummed her fingers against her lips. She could quietly sing. And she could match the hum of the refrigeration unit, so the sound didn't seem all that out of place. It would be a risk, but maybe her song didn't even need to register in the human ear, something mystical and inexplicable at work that drew Killian to her.

Two years of hindsight and theorizing dredged a revelation she knew to be true deep in her soul. On that dreary, early morning they met, cast adrift upon the open ocean, Lorelei had summoned Killian to her with her frightened, terrible singing. No one should have been able to find her so quickly. But Killian did. He always did.

It was dangerous, but she had to try. If she didn't, the whole crew would drown.

If the merman came for her, so be it. She would fight him off tooth and claw until her last breath.

Lorelei leaned against the door, hands and cheek pressed up against the wood. Low and soft she hummed for Killian, more feeling than words or sound. A language shared just between the two of them, one only Killian had ever been able to understand.

Come to me, love. Let me save you.

Muffled whispering kicked up at once, different voices all jumbled together.

"You hear that buzzing?"

"Think it's coming from one of them?"

"Lorelei." Killian. Oh, thank God.

"Wait, what's he doing?"

"Get off my leg, Ian."

"If they've come back for us, I'm going with Cap. Leaving your idiot asses behind."

"Will, you high or something? They'll eat us!"

"'K, well. Bye."

There was more shuffling. Then another round of whisper yelling.

"It's a trap!" Ian. Another, too. Maybe the helmsman?

"Don't be an Odysseus, man!" Lorelei rolled her eyes. *Great.* One of them was a scholar.

"Quiet, all of you. Your fear is going to get you killed." That last one was Walt. *"Let go of the captain."*

The whispering stopped.

Heart twinging, she sensed Killian's presence on the opposite side of the door. No smell, no sound, just soul-deep certainty. He was so close. Only a thin slab of wood between them.

There was a soft snick as he unlocked the door and opened it. A cloud of engine grease wafted out, only the barest hint of human flesh beneath. He filled the doorway, skin and clothes streaked from head to toe in the oily substance. She wrinkled her nose, burning under the olfactory overload.

That had been smart thinking.

She brightened her bioluminescence just a fraction, only enough to be seen by him and the crew. God, she wanted to hug the shit out of him, but there was no time.

"Quiet," she signed. "Merman in the freezer hold. Go upstairs to top deck, then out." Killian nodded, retreating into the room to quietly translate. Save for Will and Walt, the crew was cowering in a corner on the floor. When Killian returned, the whispering rose again.

"That you, Lorelei?"

"How the…"

"Oh shit, girl, you're a mermaid?"

They weren't loud, and the merman was still making a noisy mess in the freezer hold, but it was better if they didn't speak at all. She overemphasized tapping the side of her index finger to her lips to explain this—the widely understood sign for 'shh.' They quieted.

"Go now," she signed to Killian.

He sent Will and one of the deckies out first. Will squeezed Lorelei's shoulder as he passed by, mouthing the words, "Thank you."

The helmsman stumbled out next, clumsy on the sloped, rocking surface. She shot forward to steady the man before he hip-checked the staircase railing, preventing a sharp *cling!*

That was far too close for comfort.

Another deckie followed. Then Ian.

Killian was helping Walt up from his sitting position on the floor when Ian tripped halfway up the stairs and smacked bodily into the grated metal steps.

Cling!

Everyone froze.

A moment of terrified silence fell amongst them.

The merman came crashing out with a hiss, slamming into the wall opposite the freezer hold. Ian screeched and stumbled the rest of the way up the steps, but Killian and Walt were still down here with her.

"Run!" she yelled, snatching the harpoon from behind her back.

To the last breath.

She swung at the approaching merman. The steel tip grazed his chest, leaving a red slash. He was mostly shifted into human form, which made him clumsy. That worked in Lorelei's favor. She also had the high ground.

But he was the more practiced killer.

She went to jab, but the merman dodged out of the way and lunged, tackling her to the ground. He grabbed her face by both sides and slammed her head down. Splintering pain cracked through her skull. She saw red first. Then stars.

It had all happened so fast.

Shouting and a scuffle ensued around her. She had no bearings on what was happening. But the weight of the merman lifted off her and she rolled over onto her stomach, wiping something warm and wet and sticky from her face. Her blood or his?

With an agonized groan, she pushed off the ground and rose to a crouched position, fumbling for the bottom step beside her for balance. Fuzzy colored spots dotted her vision, her sight slowly returning. She pressed the heel of her hand to her head.

Everything was spinning and the floor had gotten more slanted.

Some of that might've been the concussion, but she didn't think so for the last bit. The boat shuddered and groaned all around her.

"My girl, you need to get out of here." Walt sat on the ground in front of her, half in the engine room, half out in the hallway, clutching a bleeding shin with shaking fingers. The toe of his steel-toed boot was covered in merman blood.

A horrible, guttural scream ripped her heart asunder.

Killian.

She whirled around, ignoring the woozy pounding of her skull.

Killian twitched on the floor, head lulled to the side, pinned beneath the merman. Its nose was bloody and smashed in, but otherwise relatively unscathed. The same could not be said for her love. It had raked its claws deep into his chest and ravaged his shoulder. It was so brutal a wound, he'd passed out from the pain of it.

A primal shriek exploded from her lips as she hurtled herself at the merman, knocking him flat, slicing and tearing out chunks in a feverish frenzy, wherever teeth and claws met flesh. Foul kindred blood oozed down her chin, her chest, her hands, but she did not stop until it threw her off.

Twisting as quick as an eel, the merman slammed her into the ground once more. Clawed hands found her neck, squeezing, choking. She felt herself edge backward, a slow slide down the deck toward the sunken bow. He climbed on top of her, straddling her hips, which stopped the slide, but also trapped her lower body so she could do nothing more with her legs than kick them uselessly at nothing.

But her hands were free.

She dug her claws into his thighs and raked down, shredding through hard muscle. She swiped at his belly next. His groin. Anything she could reach. He howled, seizing her wrists, the only weapon left to her save her teeth, but anything vulnerable was out of reach.

He stared down at her, lips curled back in a snarl. Such ferocious hatred in those glowing yellow eyes. After the damage she'd done, he was going to kill her, she knew it. She'd be torn apart just like the freezer hold door and *Dawn Chaser's* bow.

She turned her head away, meeting Killian's eyes briefly as his consciousness slowly returned. Then Walt's. The old man struggled to get up, reaching for her. Though it was futile in the creature's iron-tight hold, she still writhed and yanked, trying to free herself, to the last breath.

Clang. Clang. Clang. Clang.

Through the space gap between the merman's torso and right arm, she saw Will come pounding down the steps, a rifle in hand. He braced one boot against the railing for balance against recoil—also, when had the boat slanted enough for him to do that?

He pointed and fired.

The merman twisted and hissed above her, a red-tipped dart jutting out of his shoulder. She threw all her weight to the opposite side, using the distraction and altered balance to hurl him off herself. She scrambled to her feet, tugging Killian along by the scruff of his shirt.

The merman shakily returned to his feet.

Will fired again.

This time the dart lodged in the merman's chest. He stumbled backward, wobbly from wounds and sedation. Tripping over his own feet, he tumbled backward, head over heels down the slope of the sinking boat. He disappeared into the dark tunnel of the hallway.

Splash.

The whole boat groaned, then shifted, sliding downwards.

"Come on!" Will shouted, slinging the tranquilizer gun over his shoulder. "Gotta get outta here." As he helped Walt to his feet, Nireed and Undine appeared at the top of the stairs and rushed to help. "We could not hold it any longer."

Walt hobbled up the stairs as fast as his limp would allow. The rest of them awkwardly followed, carrying Killian up the narrow stairway.

They dragged and climbed their way toward the stern, now pointed toward the dark, cloudy night sky as *Dawn Chaser* began its plunge, water rushing up from below. Lorelei and the others lowered Killian over the side into the awaiting arms of the nearest group of merfolk. They cradled his head, keeping him afloat, and shot away from the boat.

Will and Lorelei helped Walt over the gunwale, then they, too, jumped in.

The merfolk each took a hold of a crew member and sped away, putting distance between them in the boat. Being sucked under by a sinking ship might be fine and well for a creature of the deep, but the fishermen would drown.

When they'd reached a safe distance, they all bobbed together in the water, seven human crew members buoyed by a community of merfolk, watching silently.

Dawn Chaser let out its final surface-side groan, one great bellowing death knell, and sunk beneath the waves.

Lost at sea.

CHAPTER

FORTY-ONE

LORELEI

A NEW RACE HAD BEGUN. A RACE AGAINST TIME AND THE limitations of the human body. Even at the height of summer, Maine waters rarely reached fifty-five degrees. If they didn't get the already hypothermic crew to shore fast, they would die of exposure.

Once wounds had been wrapped in seaweed, the merfolk strapped the crew to gurneys like the one brought for Nireed's return home last September. Anyone not pulling swam circles beneath, driving off sharks and other sea creatures attracted to the blood.

As they sped for shore, towing the humans through frigid water, an orange and white helicopter soared overhead, blades beating loud in the sky, racing toward *Dawn Chaser's* last known location. It must have come up from Cape Cod; Haven Cove had a Coast Guard station but not a helicopter unit.

They pushed on. Thirty miles of hard, weighted swimming.

When the merfolk finally dragged the fishermen onto shore—in the little cove that nestled Killian and Lorelei's seaside home—they were exhausted, rasping for breath as they crawled hand and fin up the sand.

Shouting rang out from the cottage.

The front door banged open as Marci and Lila dashed down the sandy slope.

Supplies. Warmth. Get the crew warm.

Adrenaline coursed through Lorelei's veins. Hours of fighting for survival overrode frazzled, panicked brain, and she yelled, "Get us some blankets now!" They skidded to a halt at her firm, authoritative tone. "In the house. Any you can get your hands on, bring them, and hurry!"

Lila hesitated, tears streaking down her dark brown cheeks, but Marci yanked her along. "Honey, this is how we help them." They disappeared into the cottage, and moments later, ran out with comforters ripped off the beds, blankets and towels pulled from the closets.

"Wrap them up, but don't rub their extremities," Lorelei rattled off, taking one of the blankets for Killian. "Chest and shoulders are fine. Prop up their feet if you can. No food. No hot liquids." When Killian treated her for hypothermia two years ago, on the day they'd met, she'd paid attention.

Undine signed a translation and several merfolk jumped to help, because more hands were needed to tend to seven men. Shivering bodies were wrapped, sand was pushed up under feet. For whatever differences they may have had in the past, her kind really knew how to respond to an emergency.

Lila held a phone to her ear, crying as she gave the person on the other end their address. Emergency services.

Lorelei quickly assessed the crew.

They all shivered, lips purple or blue. But still lucid. Ian was groaning. Will cracked some off-color joke she barely registered. They were all moving and talking to some degree.

All except Killian, his eyes were shut.

She crawled over to him, blanket dragging behind her through the sand, panic seizing at last. She felt his skin. He was cold. So, so cold. Like ice. And his breath was so shallow she could barely hear it, even with her heightened senses. Still alive, but just barely.

Choking on a sob, she gathered him up into her arms, pulling the blanket over top of him, tucking it in. *Please, not like this. Not here, not now.* She cradled his head to her chest, brushing sea-soaked fringe away from his eyes and thumbing a streak of blood-mixed grease off his cheek. "Stay with me, Killian. Help's coming."

We have years ahead of us, long, long happy years.

He was still, too still. Not even a hint of recognition that he'd heard her.

"It's not your time."

Tears soaked her cheeks, a wail climbing in her chest, but she swallowed it, hugging him close. She was losing him, but he wasn't lost yet. And maybe...

Song leapt to her lips, an old sailor's tune learned from the mother who raised her, made soft, gentle, and melodic like a lullaby. She poured her soul into it, the love she had for Killian, every cherished moment of joy, beckoning him back from the brink of death. If there was one impossible task her voice could surmount, let it be this.

But if she failed, and God please let it not come to that, but if it did, let her beloved know peace as she sang. Let the sound of her voice soothe his passage into eternal sleep.

> *I love a jolly sailor that ploughs the raging sea,*
> *And firmly pray, arrive the day, he returns to me.*
> *My heart is pierced by Cupid, I disdain all glittering gold,*
> *There is nothing can console me but my jolly sailor bold.*
> *His hair it hangs in ringlets, his eyes as black as sloe,*
> *May happiness attend him wherever he may go.*
> *For when he goes, I fear, he'll ne'er return again.*

Sirens wailed in the distance, emergency vehicles quickly growing louder.

When the ambulances arrived, the EMTs filing out were startled by all the merfolk on the beach, but true to their professions, shock was suppressed, and they got to work, bringing stretchers and first aid equipment down to the shoreline.

She continued singing, waiting for her love's return, tenderly stroking his face.

There is nothing can console me, but my jolly sailor bold.

With a deep, rasping breath, his eyes fluttered open, the color of a summer's storm. "Lorelei."

CHAPTER

FORTY-TWO

LORELEI

Summer came to Haven Cove, and with it, the tides of change.

Without a boat, *Dawn Chaser's* crew picked up odd jobs around town, whatever they could get to make ends meet. Killian remained at home, recovering from his injuries.

Phil and most of the board were ousted, replaced with interim leadership. The merfolk stayed in the deep, the pregnant members of their community having just given birth, but they swam up to Lila's HCMRC research vessel anytime it entered their territory to show off their newborns. The marine biologist said that the babies were pretty darn cute, although a little feral and bite happy.

As soon as the seas were calm enough, Lila and trusted members of her team would treat the little ones with the latest batch of virophage. She was also working on getting merfolk territory declared a marine sanctuary, as well as running regular educational trainings for the new leadership, so the bullshit that happened during Nireed's time in captivity didn't happen again.

And while Killian healed at home, Lorelei returned to the museum she built. She'd been surprised to get her old job back, and even more surprised to learn that Carrie had spoken to HCMRC's new management on her behalf, one of many voices to do so, and resigned. When Lorelei asked family about it, she was met with more surprise. No one had put her up to it.

A lot had changed at the museum in Lorelei's absence, but it was for the better.

Most notably, more staff had been hired, so her workload was much more manageable. And work stayed at work, especially with a new Assistant Museum Director there to help her run things.

Wandering through the exhibits, Lorelei made small talk with a few of the patrons.

And that's when she saw her.

She almost dropped her tea.

A woman in her early fifties stood in front of a new display detailing merfolk culture and their reuniting pods, something temporary until they could plan out and construct a new wing. The woman had dark auburn hair streaked with white at the temples. Freckles bridged her nose, dotting white skin, and her eyes were a vibrant green. Not quite the color of sea glass, but close. Subtle age-lines creased her mouth— now pursed in concentration—and flanked the corners of her eyes.

She dressed casually, but smartly, in dark wash jeans, and a collared, sleeveless blouse. Over her arm draped a leather tote, and a cream, cashmere sweater, no doubt brought to ward against frigid museum air conditioning.

Lorelei's hands trembled so badly she had to set down her cup on top of a nearby case—a huge no, no, but this was her museum dammit. If anyone showed her a glimpse of what she might look like in twenty years, it was this woman.

Brushing clammy palms down the sides of her slacks, she took a deep breath, making the decision to approach. One, she was introducing herself to the other patrons, so it would be rude if she ignored her. And two, she might not ever get the chance again. *Act like a normal human being. Act like a normal human being. Just talk museum stuff. This doesn't have to be weird.*

As her shadow fell over the display, the woman looked up and jumped, placing a hand over her chest. She blinked several times like something had gotten in them. "Oh gosh. You startled me."

Taking several steadying breaths, Lorelei fought an overwhelming urge to cry.

Why did this woman sound so much like the woman who raised her —Marquette County Justice Greta Roth? A blend of German and Yooper accents. There was something about the square-set of her jawline, too, that was familiar.

The woman cleared her throat and thrust out her hand. "Annaliese Kruetz."

That name also sounded familiar.

Speechless, Lorelei shook her hand. It was just as clammy as her own, which saved her from mild embarrassment. After a firm, brief squeeze, Annaliese pulled back, folding her hands behind her back. She fidgeted under Lorelei's relentless stare, struggling to find the right words to say. "Beautiful museum," was what she settled on.

Snapping back into director mode, Lorelei straightened. "Thank you and welcome. Where're you coming from?"

"Ann Arbor, Michigan. Saw a syndicated article about this place in the local paper. Published in January, I think? There were a few others before that, all talking about mermaids. Wild stuff. Had to come see for myself where all the work was done."

Lorelei nodded along. Jackie's latest articles were about the virophage, and its use on merfolk populations to reduce species-destructive behaviors. "Well, the real work was done in the research center next door by a good friend of mine, but this museum has greatly benefited from her findings. Have you had a chance to take a tour of the facility?"

Annaliese shook her head. "I wanted to stop by here first. The reviews I read were glowing, and there was a nice write-up of you in my old hometown paper. I messaged you on LinkedIn a little while back actually—I don't know if you remember that. You're originally from the Upper Peninsula, right?"

"Oh yes! I thought your name sounded familiar. And yes, I'm from Marquette County."

Annaliese averted her eyes, swiping a finger across the lacquered words of the information panel in front of her. "And you really built this place from the ground up?"

"I did. And not a day goes by that I don't wonder how I managed to pull it all off. Poured a lot of love and a lot of tears into this place."

"It's phenomenal." She smiled wistfully. "Well, anyway, I'm sure you're extremely busy, so I won't take up too much more of your time. But if it's not a bother, I was hoping you could maybe recommend a few restaurants or coffee shops to check out while I'm here? I was in my early twenties the last time I visited Haven Cove."

When she met Lorelei's eyes once more, there was pain there, but fierce determination, too. "A lot has changed since then."

FORTY-THREE

LORELEI

A TEXT MESSAGE NOTIFICATION LIT UP LORELEI'S PHONE screen with a number she didn't recognize, but it had one of Michigan's area codes, so she read it.

It's Annaliese Kruetz. We met at the museum yesterday—you gave me your business card. I know this might be weird, but I was wondering if you might like to get coffee with me this morning? I wasn't completely honest with you about who I was when we met yesterday, and I know that sounds ominous, but I knew Greta Roth, and I was hoping we could talk in person. You can most certainly decline. No hard feelings if you do.

She knew Greta. She wanted to talk.

Adrenaline raced through Lorelei's veins. With shaky fingers, she accepted the invitation and suggested a time and place to meet. In her heart, she knew the truth. And that truth was exactly the reason why Annaliese reached out—first online, then in person, and now again.

Her biological mother wanted to reunite.

THEY FOUND AN EMPTY TABLE AT THE BACK OF A COFFEE shop in town and sat down with their tea. It was busy, tourist season being in full swing, but there was privacy in the constant buzz of conversation all around them.

"Thank you for meeting with me," Annaliese began, nervously picking at the cardboard sleeve around her cup. "I know that was such a weird text message to receive, but I promise I'll explain everything."

I'm listening, go ahead, explain away—nothing she could think of to say seemed encouraging enough, so Lorelei just nodded, her heart thundering wildly in her chest.

Annaliese took a deep breath. "I knew Greta Roth, and I loved and trusted her more than anyone else in the world. Not a day goes by that I don't miss her, and wow, there's no easy way to say this. You see, I'm your..." She faltered, face burning.

There was a story Greta had told Lorelei many times.

About how she came to be adopted.

A baby was left crying on her doorstep with a brief note pinned to the blanket, and on it a name was written. *Lorelei*. It sounded like fantasy, a whimsical fairytale, Lorelei knew that, but she'd never dug into it. Instead, she accepted the protection of fiction for the gift that it was from the mother who had raised her.

"It's okay. I know."

Surprise lit the woman's face. "You do?" she asked shakily.

Lorelei held out her hand, palm facing up. "You're my mother, aren't you?"

Though Annaliese trembled like a leaf, she clasped her hand, gripping it firmly, never looking away even when tears began to streak her cheeks. It was a wordless affirmation.

Lorelei started to cry, too.

"How long did you know? I didn't think she told you."

"She didn't, but when you came to the museum, I had a gut feeling. The resemblance is hard to miss."

"I'm sorry it's taken me this long, but I was so scared..."

Remembering their brief online conversation, and that Annaliese had asked if the coastline was safe, Lorelei said, "You don't have to explain if you don't want to." She wanted to spare her mother in whatever way she could. Shorewalkers like herself were conceived by violence. Undine had told her that once. "I know the merfolk did terrible things."

"I was scared of you, too," Annaliese admitted quietly. "I didn't know what was nature, what was nurture, and with everything that happened, it was too much. I couldn't cope."

"I understand." And she meant that. There was no resentment in her heart for that choice, even though it made her sad. "I had a great childhood, a great life. You placed me in very capable hands."

"You're very sweet to say so, Lorelei. Thank you. She was a remarkable woman, wasn't she?"

The best she'd ever known. "How did you know Greta?"

"She was my mother. Your grandmother. Kruetz is my married name."

It was Lorelei's turn to be surprised. "W-what?"

There was a resemblance, yes, and for that the thought had crossed her mind yesterday at the museum, but it also seemed so improbable. Greta had been adamant that she'd no interest in romantic or recreational relationships. Never had and never would. It had come up when Lorelei began dating and asked for advice.

"Artificial insemination," Annaliese explained, perhaps noting her confusion. "Anonymous donor. She never wanted a partner, which maybe you know, but she loved kids and wanted one of her own. First there was me. And then you, when I couldn't raise you myself."

"Did she know what I was?"

"I told her, but she never believed that part of the story, trauma affecting memories and all. Years went by, and when you never showed signs of being anything other than a normal kid, I began to think that maybe I was mistaken." She spun her cup around. "My mother sent pictures and updates of you whenever I asked for them. We'd meet up sometimes when you were over a friend's house for a weekend sleepover. More so when you were in college. Sometimes she asked if I wanted to meet you, but I wasn't ready. And then she got sick, and I was still afraid. The closest I ever got to you after you were born was her funeral."

Lorelei's heart broke. She understood, but it hurt to hear that her mother had been so close, and yet so far. So afraid.

Pausing, Annaliese took tissues from her purse, handing one to her and keeping one for herself, tears flowing from them both. "I sat at the very back of the church. It was hard, grieving her from afar, but I couldn't tell you who I was then. It wasn't the right time or place for either of us, but a year passed, and I still never worked up the courage to reach out. Then I saw you in the news, first surviving that ship sinking, and not long after, in the mermaid articles that followed. As relieved and grateful as I was to read you were alive, all my old fears returned."

Dabbing her eyes, Lorelei said, "I did struggle for a time, but I had a lot of help. What changed for you? With reaching out to me, I mean."

"Reading about the research and your museum work helped me understand you in ways I couldn't grasp before, but the virophage treatment was what put my mind at ease the most. I needed to know I would be safe, and once I had that assurance, I realized I'd regret it forever if I didn't ever once try talking to you."

"I'm glad you reached out," Lorelei said, squeezing Annaliese's hand lightly for emphasis. "And I look forward to getting to know you."

They talked for hours.

CHAPTER
FORTY-FOUR

LORELEI

Siren married sea captain one foggy August afternoon on the sands of their private cove.

Lorelei spent the morning with Lila, Nireed, and Katrina, leisurely getting ready for the ceremony. They had the whole cottage to themselves; Killian was getting ready at the Walshes's.

The air buzzed with a staticky nervous excitement. They laughed and giggled themselves silly on too many mimosas, swaying to instrumental music—something not offensive to Nireed's ears—and plucked finger foods from trays brought by Marci, while also giving into her admonishments to drink more water.

Her longest, oldest friend braided her thick auburn hair into a loose fishtail braid, tied off at the end with white ribbon, then draped over her shoulder. The siren who taught her to embrace her oceanic origins, and who saved her loved ones, wove in pearls and small sprigs of Mystic Spires Blue, a type of sage that brought tiny pops of cool color to her hair. And the woman who faced innumerable uncharted waters with her, who protected her, and gave her and her kind the gift of dignity and control, applied a clear lacquer to her nails.

As they primped and preened, Nireed regaled stories of how sirens of old used to claim their lifelong mates in elaborate wooing rituals that were starting to return. Lila talked about her own wedding, and how nervous Will had been.

Lorelei's dress was made of ivory tulle, delicately embellished with flowered appliqué that started at her sheer shoulder straps and trailed down the plunge of her bodice to flowing skirt. Standing before a floor-length mirror, she smoothed down the front with shaking hands, drunk on joy, and maybe a little tipsy from all the mimosas.

Now for the final touches.

She picked up a worn, red velvet box from her dresser, opening it to reveal two polished pearl earrings on age-yellowed satin that had once belonged to Greta Roth. Her grandmother had worn them to her swearing in and every court case that followed. Tears filled her eyes as she donned them, followed by a simple silver ring band borrowed from Marci, the mother-in-law of her heart.

What might Annaliese Kruetz be doing now? Had she returned to Michigan? Lorelei had considered inviting her; but that was a lot of emotionally charged pressure for them both on a day such as this. There would be other opportunities for them to continue working on a relationship, and there was no need to rush it.

As her bridesmaids readied themselves, in dresses of different shades of blue, chosen based on what flattered them best, Lorelei sat down at her desk and wrote a letter to Killian. Part reflection on their time together, part vows that she'd give to him tonight. Or tomorrow morning before brunch, depending on how much downtime for reading they gave each other after the reception.

Pictures came next. Then time for the ceremony.

As guests got situated outside, Lorelei waited in the living room, nervously picking at her wildflower bouquet, waiting for Walt to come get her. She nearly jumped out of her skin when he slipped in through the front door, dapper in his black tux and bow tie.

"My girl, you look beautiful." His eyes watered as he held out his hand for her to take. "You ready?"

She let out a ragged breath, placing her hand in his. "I'm ready. Don't let me fall."

"Never."

He opened the door.

She gasped, tears springing to her eyes.

Merfolk dotted the cove—Undine, Aersila, and the others who had been a part of the *Dawn Chaser* crew's rescue—each holding vigil with candle lanterns floating between their hands, glimmering in the fog that rolled off the water. A chorus of siren song began as a low melody, then rose in tempo as Lorelei stepped down onto the cottage stoop, hand threaded through the crook of Walt's elbow.

They sang a song that Lorelei loved. That they learned human music for her... She sniffed, happy tears rolling down her cheeks, touched by the thoughtfulness and foresight. Lila and Katrina must have helped coordinate it.

Walt covered her fingers with his, squeezing them gently, and held her steady as they descended the sandy slope to the water's edge.

Their small gathering of human guests stood in two short rows on the sand. Marci. Killian's crew. Jackie Gaten. Ed Knudsen from Portland. Susan Lennard from Marquette. And, of course, the photographer.

But she wouldn't have it any other way. While she longed for the mother who raised her, and the one who might one day become a regular part of her life, this was as close to a perfect wedding day as she could ever hope to have. These people were the family of her heart, and they were plenty.

She locked eyes with Killian.

Her anchor. Her lifeline. Her beacon in the fog. Her soul's other half.

Heart in her throat, she choked back a sob, trying not to ugly cry on her wedding day.

Misty-eyed and grinning from ear-to-ear, he was so handsome in his slate grey tux, hands clasped behind his back, dark brown hair tousled by sea breeze. Along his jaw he sported the thin layer of scruff she liked. White shirt. Black tie. And pinned to his lapel was a boutonniere made from Mystic Spires Blue, just like the ones in her hair.

Their closest friends flanked him to either side. Will and Lila to the right. Katrina and Nireed to the left.

Walt brought her to her soon-to-be husband, kissing her cheek before rounding to the other side of them to also serve as their officiant. Lila had helped him maneuver an online course, so that he could marry them.

Giving her bouquet to Katrina, Lorelei turned to Killian, scarcely able to draw breath. This was it. Face to face with her husband to be. He beamed down at her with a watery smile and tears in his eyes, one good blink away from escape. As he threaded his fingers through hers, ever seeking her touch, her nerves settled, and she breathed.

This man was her comfort, her joy, her safe harbor. No one could predict what the future may hold, life as changing and unpredictable as the seas, and they'd weather together whatever storms came, but this moment was certain, a gift.

When Walt placed a hand on each of their shoulders, a wide smile pushing up his round dark brown cheeks, they gave him their attention. "I am so proud and happy for the both of you. Two people couldn't be more meant for each other. You ready to do this?"

"Yes," they said, wearing matching beaming smiles.

The sirens' song fell to a low, melodic hum.

Pulling out a little black notebook from his pocket, Walt read out loud a passage about love, transcribed from a shared favorite book of theirs. When he finished, Lila joined her father, hooking her arm through his, and read a poem about family and courage.

It was a short, sweet little ceremony—just how they wanted it.

Walt finished by binding their hands together with braided rope, from which hung an antique compass. A hand fasting of sorts that they adapted to suit them. "Land or sea. Storm or bright sunny day. Wherever you both go, however the weather may fair, may you always be able to find your way to each other, and may you ever know the coordinates of your beloved's heart."

"I love you," Killian mouthed.

She squeezed his hands. "I love you."

"By the power invested in me, thanks to my daughter, the internet, and my special computer glasses, I now pronounce you husband and wife."

Careful not to press against his chest, heavily bandaged beneath his shirt, Lorelei stood on her toes and kissed her husband.

CHAPTER

FORTY-FIVE

KILLIAN

WHITE LACE POOLED BETWEEN THEM, AND KILLIAN WAS grateful for having the foresight to get the inside of his truck detailed, the floor mats scrubbed and scrubbed again. Muck and fish guts had no business occupying the same space as his bride and her wedding dress.

Driving along the quiet, wooded road, he snuck glances to where Lorelei sat in the passenger seat, her hands folded neatly in her lap. And not for the first or last time, she stole his breath away. She looked out the window with a serene, thoughtful expression. The rings he slid onto her finger sparkled in the waning summer evening light, as she absently played with them, spinning them round and round. And whenever there were breaks in the forest, opening to one of Maine's great sun-dappled ponds, her hair captured the setting sun, reclaiming it's fiery, golden glow as if it was always meant to be there.

They'd driven this road too many times to count, and yet, she never seemed to tire of the landscape, the miles upon miles of trees and hills. That for all its familiarity, it was still a sight to behold in awe and love.

Lorelei's ties to the ocean deep, and it's ceaseless, unfathomable wonders, were strong, but Haven Cove had also become her home. And so had he. This ethereal creature as beautiful and dangerous as the sea had chosen him.

"So where are we going?" She looked away from the window then, to him, her unnaturally green eyes sparkling as she smiled, almost giddy. It had been ridiculously hard to keep their honeymoon plans from her, but he wanted it to be a surprise, and she trusted him to choose well—something that suited them both. He'd made all the arrangements, instructed her to pack layers and variations of casual and formal wear, then loaded their luggage into the back seat.

"The docks. I bought a new boat and thought we might 'break it in' it."

She snorted, laughter not far away. "It's not a mattress, Killian."

"When has that ever stopped us?"

She rolled her eyes but gave him an indulging grin. "Good point."

"Was also thinking we might take it out for a tour along the East Coast," he said, one hand on the steering wheel, the other rubbing the back of his neck. "For our honeymoon, I mean. Stop port to port, try the food, see the sights, and anchor out at sea whenever you want to stretch your fins." A furious blush heated his cheeks. God, he hoped this didn't sound lame. "I also hired a scuba instructor down in Key West who's discreet and will give me a crash course so I can swim with you. If you'd be okay with that, of course. But if not, that's okay. I mean…"

He was babbling now. The wedding was over, but why did the thought of disappointing his wife make him even more nervous?

Ah, damn. His wife. He grinned like an idiot.

She placed a hand on his arm, her eyes twinkling. "Relax, Captain. That sounds like the perfect honeymoon."

He exhaled. "It does?"

Lorelei nodded eagerly, an arresting smile stealing across her face. "Our maiden voyage as husband and wife."

His stomach did a wicked fluttery somersault.

"I don't know why I hadn't thought of it before." She touched her fingers to her lips, giddiness creeping in. "But I freakin' love the idea of us swimming together."

He parked at the pier and helped Lorelei out of his truck, taking her hand and holding her train as she slid out. "Next part's a surprise, too," he said, loosening his dress tie. A brief spike of pain shot up his neck, but he suppressed a wince. He didn't want Lorelei to worry; the bite wound hurt was healing fine. "Is it all right if I blindfold you?"

She arched one perfectly sculpted eyebrow, her bright smile transforming into a wicked grin. "Tie me up, Captain."

Seductress.

Stepping behind her, he reached around to gently lay the satin tie across her eyes, his fingertips caressing her skin as he pulled the ends around to the back of her head. He tied off his makeshift blindfold. "How's that? Too loose? Too tight?"

"A nice amount of snug."

"Good." And because he was forty and a sap, he whisked her off her feet without warning, and she squealed with delight. If anyone could get away with the good ol' threshold carry, he hoped it was him. He carried her across the docks to where his new boat was tied off, whispering in her ear all the naughty things he was going to do to her once they got on board. She told him to walk faster.

As eager as he was to make good on his filthy promises, there was something he needed to do first. Setting her down on her feet, he positioned her so that she faced the stern. "Ready?"

"Ready."

He tugged the tie free.

Her hands flew to her mouth, eyes wide and shining. "Killian," she breathed. "You didn't have to do that."

She was the woman who saved his life, his crew's. She was his greatest love. Of course, he had to commemorate her in this way.

On the stern, sprayed in washable paint, were the words "Just Married."

And beneath them was the name of Killian's new boat.

The Lovely Lorelei.

Thank you for reading! Did you enjoy? Please add your review because nothing helps an author more and encourages readers to take a chance on a book than a review.

Find more from Desirée M. Niccoli at www.dmniccoli.com

And read MY SONG'S CURSE, by City Owl Author, Poppy Minnix. Turn the page for a sneak peek!

Also be sure to sign up for the City Owl Press newsletter to receive notice of all book releases!

SNEAK PEEK OF MY SONG'S CURSE

BY POPPY MINNIX

Being a siren sucks.

Every customer stares at me in attentive silence as I sit at the least conspicuous table in the back corner of this mom-and-pop Italian restaurant.

Well, excuse me for clearing my throat.

Going out in public wasn't the best idea, but this afternoon, I held a heated conversation with the actors on my television. They apologized to each other with caresses and phrases of sweetness, but I ended up on the floor, hugging a pillow in the empty silence. When a show becomes my reality, it's time to leave the house.

Now, as usual, I've enthralled the humans. *Whoops*. They study me as if the next thing I do will make their lives complete. The attention is normal, but I'm the last being they should covet because there's much more to my species than being a lust magnet. A few more words from my hypnotic voice and they'd lick my shoes if I asked them to. Not that I would.

So now, it's time to return home. I push my chair back, but a shadow obscures the dim glow of overhead lights.

A man looms over me, dark and decadent, oozing charm with his confident smile. Well, hello, handsome. Other diners stand to follow him toward me.

"Stop," I tell them. "Return to your seats. If you work here, continue your duties." I bring my gaze to his. "You stay."

Even though our conversation will be as fake as the actors I argued with earlier today, my heart thumps an excited beat. It's been months since I've sat with someone.

I slide the empty chair out from under the table with my foot. "Sit." I keep my voice quiet and controlled, but it's a deep purr of promise.

He does what he's told, waiting with a familiar expression of hope mixed with dedication plus a dash of "do" me. Poor humans are so easy to captivate.

I let my fork drop against my bowl of pasta primavera, creating a loud clang that shatters through the room. "Name?"

"Jordan Oltier."

"Okay, Jordan." I draw circles on the checkered tablecloth with my fingertips. "Tell me three things about yourself."

He concentrates, lips pursed, and eyes to the ceiling. "I play basketball, own a dog named Maizy, and I'm a nurse at Grison General in the pediatrics department."

Wow. Mr. Oltier sounds perfect. I dig deeper just for giggles. "Do you have a wife, fiancée, or girlfriend?"

"No."

"Boyfriend?" I ask, taking another bite of pasta.

Unlike most humans, his focused pucker relaxes into a grin. "No."

His big hands rest against the cream-colored tablecloth. They'd unzip my dress and splay across my back, hot fingers digging into neglected skin. Eagerness flares in his eyes.

I haven't invited someone in for a long while. Each move we'd make would play out in a script with me as the director. Except I'd force my leading man to do whatever I wanted, unsure if he enjoyed himself or what he'd do if he had free will. After, he'd return to the humans, used for a night with fuzzy memories of me that would fade by the hour, while I'd hold on to every fake touch because it's the closest thing I have to a life in an empty room of endless time. I don't want that for either of us.

Still, what's the harm in talking about it?

I prop my elbow on the table, cupping my jaw. "What were your thoughts when you saw me? Before I spoke?"

"You were the most beautiful woman I'd ever seen. Confident and brave. Maybe a screamer." He lights up like the thought delights him.

He wouldn't enjoy my screams, but his comment makes me grin. I ask him my favorite question. "What do you wish to do with me?"

"Kiss you, then tie you up."

Yum. I didn't peg him as the type.

He shifts forward, his stare hard and unwavering. "And run a knife down your sternum thirty times, cutting deeper each time until I could touch your bones and play with your heart, the slickness of your blood—"

"Stop."

I hate it when this happens.

Chilled silence reigns in the restaurant, not because of creepy confessions but because my voice is a beacon to every creature that isn't a siren. They stare, not at this serial killer but at me. They should rage, call the police, or run for it. Instead, they wait for my attention, hanging on each sound. I wish they wouldn't.

"How many have you killed?" I ask.

"None," he replies.

Relief replaces the tight hold of terror in my chest. "Do you want to kill someone?"

"Yes."

His enthusiasm still simmers, but I don't appreciate this brand of passion. People tell me odd and honest things, but his confession is one of the more disturbing ones.

I lock onto his dark eyes, and my voice shifts into a deep and deliberate tone. "You will never kill. Think of how to help others instead of harming them. Pay for your dinner and leave."

Wannabe-serial-killer Jordan walks to an empty table near the front of the room, places bills down, and glances at me over his shoulder. He nods before exiting.

Odd. They rarely look back after I order them to go.

The room is so quiet, chills raise on my arms. I'm tempted to break a plate or turn over a chair to make a racket. Even the prep workers stare, frozen in the kitchen doorway.

A man and woman walk in, stopping short in confusion. The couple follows as each person's gaze is drawn to me. The man gives a low whistle, earning a smack on the chest from his companion. With a chuckle, he presses his lips to hers.

I want to sigh or say aw, but I bite my lip and keep quiet. I won't ruin meaningful kisses for those able to enjoy them.

His hand sneaks around her waist, and she melts into his embrace as the world shushes, leaving them alone to savor each other. He chooses her above others, even a siren, and his body language is a gift of insight into his mind.

Lucky humans.

Eyes follow my every move as I pin money under my plate and make my way to the exit.

Squeezing past the couple, I snatch a few buttermints from a dish on the hostess stand and call over my shoulder, "I was never here."

As I step into the warm night air, the chatter inside resumes. The customers and staff won't recall that I took over their dining experience, and those who see me around town will remember me, but I'll be nondescript. Forgettable. I'd love to understand why I'm this way, but even my most knowledgeable sisters tell me, "Just because, Lu." It's like they don't care to find out our history and where the three original siren mothers went.

Nonetheless, my ability is as frustrating as it is a comfort. I may not have friends besides my sisters, but I've altered wannabe-serial-killer Jordan's brain to a normal human mode...or he may go insane. He won't kill anyone, though. Win? I shrug to myself.

Not ready to return to my empty house, the endless downtown sidewalks beckon me. Couples file out of bars and head home or to the beds of others. They talk in loud laughing phrases about human world things—friends, politics, and pop culture until they notice me. Staring replaces the conversation. The urge to speak up is unmanageable; *I enjoyed that movie too. Yeah, the new governor is a douche, except he has good educational policies. Your girlfriend has princess syndrome.*

A hush falls over the city this time of night, leaving me to meander in relative peace. The rhythmic clack of my heels echoing off brick and concrete soothe me and send my thoughts wandering to the human culture I've experienced this evening.

My phone buzzes in my purse and I drag it out as I check if anyone is within earshot. Few people walk the streets. Smiling at Amah's name, I answer in a whisper. "Hello, Ma."

"You sound happy. Why are you whispering?"

I wince. I nicknamed my oldest siren sister 'Ma' for a reason, not just because it fits her real name or because she's the closest thing I have to a mother. Amah makes sure we take care of ourselves and behave. I'm one for two. "I'm walking downtown."

The tap of her nail clicks against metal. "Tell me about tonight's outfit," she says, toneless.

I glance at the sheath dress that clings to my every curve like a warm hug. "Sweats."

"Liar."

"Fine. My favorite green dress. I went to dinner, had primavera, stopped potential crime." Ma won't appreciate that. She takes a natural approach to the mortals. Farm what you need from them, then set them free.

"Oh, Lula. Only you. Let's see it's...my goodness, eleven where you are? Darklings and otherworldlings may be out. Please go home soon."

The memory of my first darkling encounter makes my steps slow. Lena's death was more than a century ago. It's over. I shove away sad thoughts. It's my night out on the town, my time to pretend I belong somewhere. I'll save heartbreak for when I'm alone again.

"The otherworldlings fit in with the humans," I say, clacking along the sidewalks. "They won't make a scene, and I can control them if they do. Plus, the streets are empty." Eerily so, even for the late hour on a weekday.

"I know. I just worry. Have you spoken to Gerty or Venora lately?"

"I spoke to Gerty last month, but Ven and I chatted two weeks ago."

"Gerty isn't returning calls. Ven's in love, again, and has been hard to catch. She tells me he's intense."

"Intense?" Venora's the romantic out of my seven sisters. I'm happy for her if she's found another to keep her warm and off the phone, but she holds onto her sweet, doting men and women a little too long before setting them free. "Not her typical choice of companion."

"No, he's not. He withstands her thrall well, but she claims he's human."

"You think he's an otherworldling?" The non-human species resist our ability better than humans, but they eventually succumb.

The chipped sidewalk catches my heel, and I stumble before a boarded-up building. I've wandered into an area of town that would terrify most people.

"I should go," I whisper.

"Let me know if you hear from them."

"I will. Love you, Ma."

"Love you, too." We hang up, and I pivot, put my phone away, and walk the direction I came.

"Mm, now there's a fine piece." A droning voice close behind me grabs my attention.

I spin and get a glimpse of green spiked hair before a fist rams into my midsection, and the air rushes from me in a harsh 'whoosh.'

Crumpling, I open my mouth to inhale, but can't get a breath.

Two pairs of scuffed boots and three sets of colorful kicks step closer. Straightening up shoots a pang through my gut. The five men circle—sharks scenting fresh blood. Each is menacing, with piercings, scars, and bared teeth. The same devil face tattoo marks their necks. Their sick laughter promises hate and pain, and I need to speak right now. A couple puff up, jerk toward me with aggressive movements, closing in to block my exit as I gasp to find my missing air. Nothing happens but a wheeze. Not good.

"On the corner tonight, sweetheart?" One harsh voice says. "I could use a good workout." As if I needed clarification, he steps closer to brush his hardness against my side. I move to hip check his crotch, but he hurries back, barking a laugh.

"Got a little fighter here," he says. "Fun, fun."

Balling my fists, I struggle to growl, but nothing comes out. I'd command them if I could only get a breath. These are the type of beings that need to be enthralled for good.

Someone jerks me upright as the man with hair like spring grass steps close, inches from my face, and shows off a cracked incisor. "What's a high-class bitch like you doing on our turf?"

His voice is a low growl. Demon? He'd be a runt if he were. My nose tingles with a lack of oxygen as I gulp at the night air that can't find room in my lungs yet.

"This is our street, Mama. Ain't nobody gonna save ya. Ready for me? Hmm?"

A man jogs out of the shadows. "Let her go." He strides forward into the dim light, his jaw clenched tight. He's wearing a plain gray tee, no tattoos cover his neck, and the ferocious scowl he wears tells me he doesn't belong to this group.

The man next to me gives a dark chuckle, reaching into his pocket for what I'm sure is a weapon. Finally, I inhale enough air to speak. "Step...back."

The three that haven't yet spoken walk backward in sync. My thrall and I have a rocky relationship. This is a proud, appreciative moment.

The one holding onto me releases my arm, but Grass-head in front of me only twitches. It's as if his body wants to move, but his mind fights it.

Coughing forces more air in, then out of my burning lungs. "Go home."

This time, four turn and walk away without another word. The stubborn fifth remains. Some humans have more resistance than others, and since otherworldling species hold out long enough to harm those around them, I always work fast.

I hum, though it's shaky. Three seconds of my note and he drops his proud stance. He swallows and blinks several times, then he raises his smitten gaze.

Placing my hands on my hips, I straighten so I'm as tall as he is. "Are you listening now?"

"Yes." He nods, a tapped bobble-head doll, and relief loosens the tension in my back. At least until I notice the onlooker still stands ten feet from us. My ability should have seeped through, even if he were deaf.

Witnesses are an issue, but sometimes life throws you gang

members and you have to make community servants. Or liquified bad guys. It can't come to that, though. Not here.

I'll handle the other man in a moment, but first, my focus falls on the enthralled asshole. I should make him jump in the sewers and let the wildlife deal with him. My sore stomach aches under my hand. "Treat women with respect. No punching, name-calling, and no grinding against unwilling participants, got it? That's just gross."

Past his shoulder, spray paint and neglect touch everything, but between two boarded-up buildings lies a big dirt lot under a streetlight. There's potential to give someone the purpose they need.

I point. "Start a community garden. Get your people involved and donate extra food. Go make plans."

He scurries away, leaving me with the stranger.

The streetlight illuminates him, a spotlight on a golden-haired movie star. Tonight must be tall and handsome night. This guy better be less psychotic than wannabe-serial-killer Jordan.

I ball my fists and shove my resurfacing libido aside. My body is so desperate, it has already forgotten the punch. "Did you not hear me? Go home."

He ambles toward me. Stubble lines his sculpted jaw. It's been far too long since I've experienced stubble burn. He halts a foot from me and stares with rare golden eyes. The color is inhuman. My hands fall from my hips, power stance forgotten.

"I heard you fine, Firecracker." His voice soothes, even though his powerful frame and towering height tempt me to step back. "Are you okay? I can't believe they punched you. That shouldn't have happened."

My eyes widen. No one resists my power except my species. There are no male sirens, right? I play over every detail of siren history. The three mothers exiled from Olympus only gave birth to females then disappeared. I'm the fourth generation from the line of Agalope, second youngest of eight sirens, so I'm aware that I don't know everything about our species like Amah does. I'm soulbound to my species though, I'd connect to this being, wouldn't I? I've learned much in my hundred and eighty-two years, but a resistant male is new. He appears concerned for me. Maybe he's slightly enthralled?

"I'm fine. Leave."

His furrowed brow smooths to an amused angle. "Care to explain how you turned a gang of felons into future gardeners?"

What? Wait. How? *Words, Lula, you can do this.* "Why aren't you headed home right now?"

"Because I'd rather be here, making sure you're safe. Are you okay?"

I should run. I have no weapons beyond my voice. Amah has warned me time and again that my curiosity will get me killed, but I have to figure him out. "What's your name?" He doesn't look like a Grizaldak the Torturer.

"Call me Alex."

That name works for him. I deepen my timbre, letting my vocal cords relax into each word. "Leave, Alex."

He tilts his head and perfect lips purse. "I'm not sold that you want me to."

This isn't right. I review my list of otherworldlings with the ability to disguise themselves as human and dismiss each species that doesn't match—no fangs, no fur, no tail. Tall, but not giant height. Two stunning gold eyes. I narrow the possibilities to a few choices. Shapeshifter, Nephilim, or incubus. Bad, worse, or worst.

I can't deal with this tonight. If I sing my siren song, even the saintliest among beings would murder for me, but after a verse, they become sleepy and unaware that their organs are dissolving. If I hit the chorus, there's not enough of them left to order around anymore. But releasing my power hurts even if the creature's evil. They scream in agony, and I have guilt-laced nightmares for months.

No, thank you.

This one tried to help me though and doesn't appear to be a danger to humans. I pivot, and the sidewalk leads me from the friendly enough bad guy.

"Hey, hold up," Alex calls.

"Go away." I break into a tiptoe run.

"Hey, wait." A hand snatches my forearm within a second, and Alex spins me. I slap at him, but he snags my wrist in mid-air and plants my hand against his chest, ducking his head, face level with mine. "I won't harm you."

"That's what incubi say before they suck out someone's life force."

The ancient song etched in my DNA spills from my lips in a rush of power. It's a cadence from celestial tongues, except the heavenly notes bring death.

Alex's eyes widen. Under my palm, his heart thuds a peaceful rhythm.

My voice carries with more strength, pulling deep from my soul. Releasing it makes my body hum, but my thoughts seize up as I wait for the disaster to come. When I get to the chorus, he bites his smiling lip, and the song dies in my throat.

"Beautiful. You're a siren."

He knows what I am. And he's still standing. How in the hell is he still standing? His face isn't showing pain. He's grinning like the guy at the restaurant did at his companion.

Oh, shit. Not good.

Fear sends tendrils of tightness to every muscle in my body. Black spots threaten my vision as my overwhelmed mind merry-go-rounds and the ground sways. Alex moves in, supporting me with a strong arm. "Hey, it's okay. I won't hurt you."

He must have calming pheromones because the heat of his skin calls to mine and I sink into his hold, breathing in his sweet citrus scent. Focus, Lula. Incubi are masters of seduction, but even an incubus wouldn't smile at my song. They wouldn't hold me as if I belonged in their arms, because they'd be busy on the ground, having their insides liquefied.

"What are you?" I ask.

Alex's amused expression falters, sending tightness through me again. I try to jerk away, but he clings and blurts out, "A demigod."

No way. A deity on earth? There's the slightest glow to him, a confident golden hue that draws me to him, telling me he's here to help. No otherworldling has that.

My palm lies over the heart of a god.

I've never met a deity. Amah says they abandoned the Earth long before I was born.

He—Alex—observes me, squinting. In the old days, people worshipped the gods that visited Earth in preposterous ways, right up to tossing themselves off cliffs to gain the divine's favor. Three decades ago, a nymph told me she came across two and tried to please them, but they wouldn't accept anything from her, only wanted to talk about humans and otherworldlings. Maybe this deity has questions too.

I breathe slowly, attempting to tame my speeding heart. "What's your real name?"

He leans forward, millimeters from my cheek, warm breath brushing my ear. "Alexiares."

I shudder, letting that information settle. I've studied him—the demigod who wards off wars. The son of Hercules and grandson of Zeus, the king of Olympus. Damn.

My eyes wander his features, searching for any clue to the phenomenon that is this deity. "I don't affect you?"

"Oh, you affect me."

Unable to keep the sarcasm at bay, I groan and step back from him. "My ability, I mean. Siren, remember?"

"Did you just eye-roll at a deity?"

I grin instead of performing the thousand apologies I'm sure he's expecting. My power doesn't work on him. I'm still wavering between belief and impossibility. It's a flaw, a dream, a crazy oasis mirage envisioned in a desert when I need it the most, except I'm not thirsty for water. I've never had an honest conversation with a male.

His full grin is disarming. "No, your ability doesn't affect me. You could ask me to kiss you and it would have no impact on me."

Intrigued, I eye his lips. "Really? Kiss me."

With a step forward, he cups the back of my head, fingers threading through my hair, and peruses my features with intent I've only seen in romance movies.

I'd contemplate that look, but he inches forward. Chills rise in response to the electricity shifting between us. I didn't believe he'd kiss me.

He's a deity.

He's also a stranger, and I should pull away.

"No impact, huh?" I whisper.

"Just a taste. Tell me to stop." His eyes search mine.

He radiates warmth, smells like my best dreams, and for one moment, I want someone to kiss me because they want to.

I relax into the hand cupping my head, tilt my chin up...

And wait.

Don't stop now. Keep reading with your copy of MY SONG'S CURSE, by City Owl Author, Poppy Minnix!

And sign up for the latest news, giveaways, and more at www.dmniccoli.com

Find more from Desirée M. Niccoli at www.dmniccoli.com

And discover MY SONG'S CURSE, by City Owl Author, Poppy Minnix!

Ultimate control has its downside, especially when it comes to romance. But will it be enough to keep them together?

As a siren Lula Aglaope can bend anyone to her will with the smallest whisper, but she'd give up her power for one meaningful, honest conversation.

She wants a normal life, like the open, true connections the humans seem to pull off with such little effort.

When she meets Alexiares, God of Warding off Wars, all thoughts of normalcy fly out the window. The beautiful demigod cannot be controlled! He's frustrating, irresistible...and utterly off-limits.

Alex has watched Olympus slowly fall apart. The old gods continue their archaic control of the Universe, denying the progress of humans and other deities. But Alex has plans to repair the damage, and Lula is a major player.

She just doesn't know it yet.

Falling for her is the worst idea. And just when things move in the right direction, danger arises that no one expects, plunging the sirens into the deadly Olympian spotlight.

With Lula's sisters missing, and a pile of broken laws surrounding them, will Alex and Lula change the Universe for the better or destroy it?

Please sign up for the City Owl Press newsletter for chances to win special subscriber-only contests and giveaways as well as receiving information on upcoming releases and special excerpts.

All reviews are **welcome** and **appreciated**. Please consider leaving one on your favorite social media and book buying sites.

For books in the world of romance and speculative fiction that embody Innovation, Creativity, and Affordability, check out City Owl Press at www.cityowlpress.com.

ACKNOWLEDGMENTS

In *Called to the Deep*'s acknowledgements, I shouted out Dr. Sean Todd, marine biologist, and professor at the College of the Atlantic in Bar Harbor, Maine. And I will again here. He answered an integral worldbuilding question that had stumped me from the outset: what does the Gulf of Maine look like? It's not tropical. The water's murky, cold, and there aren't any coral reefs. Setting descriptions give me enough trouble as it is, and no one should "White Room" the ocean's rich ecosystem, but Dr. Todd helped me visualize my setting's topographical terrain and sea floor in a way I couldn't on my own. During our speculative conversation about mermaid physiology and cetacean morbillivirus, he also detailed significant human events in history that the ocean's creatures would've felt viscerally, events the merfolk community in *Song of Lorelei* would've known and passed down in their stories.

Credit for the idea to use virophages goes to my brainstorming buddy Devin, who has a background in epidemiology. Many artistic liberties were taken, of course, especially with the timeline of developing a treatment for a viral disease, but we snuck some real science in there. I also want to thank another brainstorming buddy, Reese, for explaining "sex influenced traits" to me and basic genetics, keeping me, a casual science lover, from thoroughly embarrassing myself.

Next, I want to thank Tee Tate, my editor at City Owl Press, for helping me conclude the last half of Lorelei and Killian's story, and my agent Kaitlyn Katsoupis of Belcastro Literary Agency, who continues to be the best champion for this bonkers, people-eating mermaid romance series.

Agatha Andrews is a true Hype-Queen, and I'm so grateful to her and fellow authors Charish Reid, Paulette Kennedy, Kate Prior, Megan Van Dyke, Nisha J. Tuli, and Katherine Quinn for their early praise and support of *Called to the Deep*.

Huge thanks to my beta readers Katie Erin, Morgan T. Jackson, and my husband Kyle for every editorial suggestion, excited exclamation, and reassurance, as well as Katie Rose and Dani Frank for continuing to flood my DMs with spicy book talk; and all my friends and family for their steadfast love and support.

Special shout outs to my mom Darlene for getting my book into our hometown library, Morgan W. and the found family I gained while living in Maine for hosting my very first book signing, and my mother-in-law Deirdre for throwing a killer book launch party and for trying to get Reese Witherspoon to add sexy mermaids to her book club reads.

To the book community, and the monster lovers, thank you so, so much for all your boosting and support! I appreciate you all.

xoxo,

Desirée

ABOUT THE AUTHOR

By night, Desirée M. Niccoli writes adult romance featuring vicious monsters, villains, and the supernatural, often served with a side of eco-horror and paired with (mostly) emotionally intelligent characters and heart. By day, she is a public relations professional living the nomadic military life with her husband and two cats Pawdry Hepburn and Puma Thurman. Although born and raised in Pittsburgh, Desirée has since lived in coastal Maine (where her spooky heart truly lies) and Maryland.

Want to be the first to get a look at covers, sneak peeks, and more? Sign up for her newsletter and find more at www.dmniccoli.com.

facebook.com/dmniccoli
x.com/dmniccoli
instagram.com/author_dmniccoli

ABOUT THE PUBLISHER

City Owl Press is a cutting edge indie publishing company, bringing the world of romance and speculative fiction to discerning readers.

Escape Your World. Get Lost in Ours!

www.cityowlpress.com

f facebook.com/YourCityOwlPress

X x.com/cityowlpress

instagram.com/cityowlbooks

pinterest.com/cityowlpress

www.ingramcontent.com/pod-product-compliance
Lightning Source LLC
Chambersburg PA
CBHW060611030726
47498CB00005B/1631